The Scottish Bitch

by Jameson Tabard

Published 2016 by Beating Windward Press LLC

For contact information, please visit:
BeatingWindward.com

First Edition
ISBN: 978-1-940761-21-3

For my Kevin.

Chapter 1

Tuckage. That was all Latrine could feel. Her package was tucked and pulled so tight she believed she had a vagina. It was the drag queen version of method acting, and she proudly was the Meryl Streep of the drag world at that moment. She had to accept it as truth to quell the anticipation and the uncertainty of the evening. By morning, not only would she have made her debut stateside, but she'd also be named the newest Countess of Central Florida.

Her anxiety was not helped by her husband's tardiness. They needed to get to the club. Latrine understood selling tickets at the basketball arena could be keeping him a little longer, but punctuality wasn't his strongest quality anyway. If he dared to present a pair of courtside seats as redemption, they'd be ripped up on the spot. There were more important matters to attend to, and no ticket to a game with bouncing balls not biologically attached to a human body was going to relieve her frustration. She was only half-made up and half-coiffed—nowhere near the enchanting goddess necessary to thrill the crowd and the judges. Each second of time that passed felt like a sequin falling from her gown.

Latrine stood as close to the main road as possible so Peyton wouldn't have to waste time pulling into the parking lot outside their flat. The chorus of crickets and critters native to the balmy Florida landscape forced Latrine to stand squarely on the asphalt, even if it meant having to dodge oncoming traffic. A diva simply did not wait beside the road in the uncut grass for fear of venomous snakes or long-tailed lizards or rabid raccoons. Her shiny red-pleather platform heels seemed to glow, their iridescence increasing in intensity.

Two twinkling beacons of hope set against a dark, moonlit sky headed in her direction. It was Peyton's van, careening around the bend in the road. He leaned forward over the steering wheel as if to add a few extra pounds of inertia to impel it forward.

The van's brakes screamed and shrieked.

"What took you so long?"

Peyton rolled down his window. "For fuck's sake. Get in."

"Yes, sir," said Latrine with an edge of facetiousness. She climbed into the back of the van and planted herself in front of her vanity. Peyton slammed on the accelerator, throwing her off the back of her stool, legs thrust up overhead. Fortunately, her makeup was tucked away in a proper bin, or it'd be strewn about from Peyton's recklessness.

"Love, can you be careful driving? I have to be precise here." Latrine climbed back onto her stool and tried to focus.

"We're running late," he shouted from the front of the van.

"I know we are."

"You should be mostly dressed."

"I am, but these finishing touches require precision."

Latrine looked at herself in the mirror at her vanity, soft lights illuminating her face. A clothing rack with an unimpressive few outfits hung pathetically in the background. The hangers slid back and forth across the stainless steel bar as Peyton drove. Her nerves simmered just below the surface of her concealer. Peyton had been telling her all week she had the capacity to win. She had the right dress, the right wig, the right song, and on top of it all, the right heels. She rifled through her makeup kit as it trembled from Peyton's tense driving. For a moment, she couldn't be sure if the shaking was all in her mind—her vision obscured by her own anxiety. She applied her eyeliner, casting sideways glances at Peyton as he drove.

She had to let go of their tardiness and give him all her trust. He was her rock. Someone she could look up to, despite his height. Peyton was a pygmy Teddy Graham in a jar of gingerbread men. He was a shriveled chick pea in a crate of organic brown eggs.

He was a mini-whisky bottle on a shelf of wholesale bulk carafes. She would never tell him that though. He was known to bite.

They met in Glasgow at an underground club. He wasn't put off that she was from Edinburgh, even with there being the presumption that people from the capital always thought themselves better than everyone else. Latrine accepted his being a Weegee—a Glaswegian—and didn't hold it against him. They were compatible in other ways. He was a great top, especially after he'd been drinking. Their liquor cabinet was always stocked and ready to go.

Latrine smiled to herself as she applied her mascara, just as the van dipped into a pothole. A frantic glance in the mirror revealed a smear angling out of one eyelid like Elizabeth Taylor in *Cleopatra*. She wiped the cake of makeup from her face with a gentle cloth, reapplying with a more ginger touch and compensating for any sudden dips in the road. She looked down at her rainbow of lip colors and decided on red. Bright red. Eye-catching red.

With a more lingering look in the mirror, her cheeks were sculpted into sharp crags perched high above a glen. Her coiffed red wig was nestled upon her head, wavy tresses hugging her shoulders like a warm blanket. But no wig, no rouge, no drag queen would be perfect without applying the pièce de résistance.

Glitter.

Latrine loved glitter. Every gay she knew loved glitter. What gay didn't?

"Are you throwing that glitter shit again?" Peyton asked.

"Just a wee bit."

"That's right. Just a wee bit only."

"Are we almost there?" She said to deflect his attention, tossing some extra sprinkles across her upper chest.

"Almost."

When Peyton stopped at a traffic light, he peered into the rear view mirror. Latrine stared back at them. His eyes were as blue as Loch Lomond on a clear summer day. Isolated in the rectangular frame, they caught Latrine's attention like in a Salvador Dalí painting. The skin on the back of his neck—rare fine porcelain on which to serve a sugary scone. His hair—a golden mane of barley cropped above his ears.

"You look beautiful," he said.

Latrine's heart blushed. She could feel his appreciation of the time and effort it took to get to that level of beauty, rising from the dull depths of the ordinary Scotsman he married and metamorphosing into a dramatic drag queen.

"You really think so?"

"You're going to rip the place a new arsehole."

Before Latrine could thank him for the compliment, he slammed on the gas, forcing her to brace herself. She grabbed her wig, glancing in the mirror to see if it was crooked. A slight adjustment and it was ready to go. As the van rounded a corner, she peered out the front windshield. The colored neon ofthe Parliament House cast rainbow hues into the van. Her stomach dropped, and the well of gastric juices boiled in her gut. Her body trembled so hard her press-on nails chirped like an orchestra of crickets.

The van passed a bunch of parked cars outside what looked like motel rooms. They rounded a corner, and a lakeside beach was visible. Peyton slammed on the brakes. Latrine nearly vomited.

"We're here." Like a gentleman, Peyton hurried to the rear of the van to open the door. The multicolored lights heralded the arrival of Latrine, front-lighting her like she was a top model during Fashion Week. He held out his arm like he was Leo and Latrine was that bitch Kate descending an opulent staircase on the *HMS Titanic.* That was how she felt. She didn't care that the ship sank. With Peyton by her side, she was the Unsinkable Latrine. Confidence coursed through her veins, neutralizing the gastric magma chamber in her gut. The calming presence and reassurance of Peyton was a lighthouse forever guiding her to shore.

"Will you hurry the fuck up already?" When she stepped off the van, Peyton yanked her by the arm so hard she almost ate the pavement. Latrine compensated with a large step forward on her ten-centimeter stiletto heels, trying to keep upright for fear of falling. One slip, and the queens would impale her with snickers and gossip in a massacre worse than Glencoe. Her career would be over before it even started.

Parliament House was a gay resort—the tacky offspring of a motel fucking a club. Peyton led her toward the motel portion, which was on the unfortunate path to the club area. The pulsing sound of dance music shook the ground, filling their anticipatory silence with distracting rhythms. Latrine's insides warred with each wobbly step. Her body didn't know whether to be nervous or excited. Confidence versus chaos. She knew that once she hit that stage, she would be performing before an American crowd for the very first time. If she did well, she could win the competition. If she won, she would get to move on to Duchess Regionals. Then maybe Nationals. She could be the next Grand Dame.

They reached the outdoor courtyard of the motel. Thunderous music shot them in the ears. They stopped and looked out at the throngs of gay men clad in minimal attire. Peyton glanced up at Latrine.

"Are you ready to push through?"

She swallowed and took a deep breath. "I'm ready. Get me to that stage."

• • •

Peyton hadn't really gotten the chance to take her in. Her efforts paid off. His pride beamed as she strutted in her stilettos, one step at a time. It actually looked like she was concentrating with each step, like she was trying to keep from falling over in her insanely high heels. He knew she'd shock the judges—not from her outfit—but because of her beauty. Her hazel eyes popped when she wore that eyeliner. She was tall and slender, just the right proportions to be a winning queen.

Parliament House was a madhouse. Gays everywhere. Gays on the dance floor. Gays in the bathroom. Gays at the bar. You need a drink? There's a gay for that. You need your cigarette lit?

There's a gay for that. You need your arse wiped? There's a gay for that. Fucking. Gays. Everywhere. Peyton knew Latrine was going to win and reign over all of them. They'd be her subjects. Queen Latrine. *All hail the Queen.*

They entered a gated area with a swimming pool, packed with shirtless gays busy sipping their vodkas in Red Bull in their designer swimming apparel. They entered another building and walked through a tacky bar with pec-tacular bartenders trying to keep the thirsty packs intoxicated, yet hydrated. The entire club seemed to be laced with the same scent wafting through the air—a smell that was a foul mix of sauerkraut, body odor, and forgotten dreams. Some gays stared them down as they passed. Peyton couldn't tell if they were giving them the stink eye or checking them out. American gays seemed different, tougher to read.

They passed through a hall with ceiling-to-floor mirrors on both sides, and a few twinks compared the size of their ribcages, all in a competition, it seemed, to determine who looked the most anorexic. A sign pointed them to the famous Footlight Theatre. Peyton thought a queue had formed before the theatre's entrance, but it was just a mob of gays loitering outside the doors. Fortunately, they made like an overeager bottom's ass crack and parted at the obvious royalty coming through. After dodging many inebriated men down the side aisle of the theatre, they finally reached the backstage area.

The curtains were a glittery tinsel, the fecal droppings of a disco ball on stage. Peyton was repulsed. He saw Latrine was enamored by the shimmering lights being reflected, her head looking in all directions like they were in the gay Sistine Chapel. His attention was diverted by the booming baritone of the emcee talking to the audience. They approached the wings to take a look, but a hand reached out to stop them. Peyton locked eyes with a black woman, a real woman—or at least, he thought she was a real woman.

"Who's this?" Miss Black Woman asked.

"I'm Latrine Dion. I'm competing tonight," said Latrine.

"And you?" Miss Black Woman looked at Peyton. She had her hair pulled back in a simple ponytail, far too simple for even the local contest of the Grand Dame Competition. She wore a black t-shirt that said *Security*. Why she couldn't at least cut up the t-shirt into a crop top? He hated her but masked his distaste.

"I'm her husband and manager, Peyton Dingwall."

"She missed her place, Dingwall."

"I'm sorry. What's your name?" asked Peyton.

"Duffy MacDuff. You Irish?"

"Scottish," the both of them replied.

"Fucking Irish," said Peyton under his breath. "Why does everyone think we're Irish?" Being stereotyped made him want to spit nails.

"Competition started thirty minutes ago. She missed her place." Duffy turned and watched the stage, her arms folded.

"You have to do something," Latrine said to Peyton.

"You're always the damsel in fucking distress." Peyton tapped on Duffy's shoulder. "Let me talk to the boss."

"You'll have to wait." She pointed to a giant black queen on stage. Peyton stared at her. He finally matched the commanding voice with that of the thing dancing on stage. Twatla Tharp wasn't a man—at that moment. She was wearing a form-fitting tweety-bird yellow evening gown that accentuated a very big pair of fake titties. Her hair was a shitheap of curls pouring out of a tiara so big it looked like her head would collapse from the pressure. She had yellow nails like lemonade ice-picks and was adorned with costume jewelry that made the Crown Jewels look unimpressive.

Peyton looked at Latrine as she stared at the stage in awe. As he followed her gaze back to Twatla, he finally honed in on what she was saying to the crowd.

"Give it up, ya'll. Give it up for Miss Ina Godda the Diva."

Twatla sashayed off stage. Peyton saw his chance. He could run over and chat her up while the next queen performed. But just as he was about to make a mad dash for her, the music started, and he froze. He couldn't believe his eyes. He looked at Latrine. She was dumbfounded. Ina Godda the Diva was so fierce, so daring, so fabulous, you couldn't keep your eyes off of her.

Standing at what looked like six feet tall in heels, she wore a sheer navy blue kimono with a faint pattern embroidered over the boob area, resembling a bonsai tree. Her jet black wig was pulled up into a large bun, impaled by a pair of chrome chopsticks and a strange black rod.

Within the first few bars of music, Peyton could tell what it was. Ina Godda the Diva flailed her body around to the bass of Cyndi Lauper's "She Bop." With each beat, she contorted her body into moves resembling a Kabuki show. To say the audience loved it would be an understatement. The gays jumped up and down like it was a free concert in Hyde Park. Within a minute of the song, Ina Godda the Diva ripped open her kimono to reveal a pair of silicon-enhanced breasts. Her nipples were obscured by a pair of mirrored pasties, miniature disco balls that refracted the light like lasers shooting from her boobs.

Latrine gasped—a sound she likely couldn't control.

Whenever Cyndi squealed the title of the song in her chorus, Ina Godda spread her legs and covered her mouth as if she were a geisha Minnie Mouse. With a slight Japanese bow, she reached into her wig, threw the chopsticks off stage and grabbed the black rod, collapsing her wig into flowing black tresses that whipped around her. The black rod, it turned out, was a fan, which she unfurled and incorporated into the routine. She fanned herself, twirling it in intricate moves, weaving it under and over her body. Peyton wished she would just shove a cork between her legs and end the song already. The craning of his neck to see if Twatla was on the other side of the stage caused a dull pain.

It was obvious to Peyton that Latrine enjoyed watching Ina Godda the Diva the way the Scottish Rugby League would enjoy *Braveheart* after they'd drunk twelve pints each. He knew he needed to snap some sense into her. "You okay?"

"I'm fine. Just nervous."

"You should be," Duffy added.

Peyton turned away from her and rolled his eyes. *Shut the fuck up, Duffy.* As the music ended, Twatla assumed her position on stage.

"Give it up for Miss Ina Godda the Diva, ya'll!" she said.

The crowd roared, and dollar bills flew at the stage.

Fuck yes, Peyton thought. *They throw money at you?*

Ina Godda bent down to pick up her tips. Peyton noticed a couple of gays down front swipe a dollar bill off the stage, out of the eyeline of Ina Godda. With that, Duffy darted out from backstage, leaping into the audience and grabbing the two bastards by the collar. He could hear her demand for them to put it back. One of the gays held up the stolen dollar up to Ina Godda. She made a show of opening the fan, closing it, and smacking him on the head with it.

"That's my girl, Duffy. Give it up for my wife Duffy, ya'll. Keeping everything all lawful and shit up in here," Twatla said.

The crowd threw an enthusiastic cheer Twatla's way, but her voice sliced right through it.

"Judges, can we see the score for Miss Ina Godda the Diva?"

The judges held up a 9.5, 9.5, 9.6, 9.7, and 9.6. Peyton looked at Latrine, and she took a deep breath with a dour look on her face. He grabbed her hand.

"I will get you on that stage. You're getting all perfect tens, okay?"

She managed a smile as Twatla's voice let out another thunderous roar.

"And now, queens, ladies, bears, daddies, twinks, et cetera, et cetera, et cetera. We have for you a sexy bitch. This bitch is so sexy we didn't even want her near this stage because she'd burn it down, ya'll. But she made us an offer we couldn't refuse, so give it up for Miss Cunny Corleone!"

Twatla exited left to the other side of the stage again. Peyton considered just running across the stage to talk to her before the next performer started, but he was too late. Cunny Corleone strolled out on stage in a skin-tight leather jumpsuit and corset, holding her fake boobs in place like a vice. He couldn't believe she had actual real fake titties. And her heels. They had spurs on the backs of them, like she was ready to sheer off the hands of the poor bugger that got to bag her for the night whenever he grabbed her legs in the spread eagle position. Zippers and chrome chains that would make even a dominatrix cower covered the leather jumpsuit. Her blonde extensions were tied up into a high pony-tail, flinging around her head like yellow mistletoe flapping in the wind. She kind of looked like if "Blonde Ambition" Madonna fucked "Human Nature" Madonna. Not surprisingly, her song was "Ray of Light." Peyton wanted to smack her and tell her to get her Madonna decades right. That song was after she had Lourdes. Every gay knew that.

Latrine looked on, folding her arms. Cunny tossed her hair back and forth and around again like a leather-clad maypole. She performed what looked like Olympic-level figure skating with simply her ponytail. Her hair took off for a triple lutz, swung behind her and threw in a triple toe loop for good measure. It was some serious haireography. How she didn't topple over from dizziness in those heels was a silver-medal feat—silver because Latrine would take the gold.

Peyton turned away from the athletic carousel of hair to see Twatla stroll by. Seeing his chance, he crept over to her as she picked up a clipboard.

"Twatla?"

No answer. She didn't look up either.

"Ms. Tharp?"

"I'm listening."

"Latrine is here."

"Oh how nice," she said with attitude.

"We know she missed her place."

"Damn straight, she did. If she was still performing, she'd be docked five points."

Peyton leaned into her. She backed up slightly, like she might catch a bad case of the Scots. He whispered, "You know, I put aside some season tickets at the arena for you. It's going to be quite the season. Wouldn't you like to see every game? They've got your name all over them."

She looked at him for a moment, causing his knees to quiver with anticipation.

"One for Duffy too?"

Peyton hated the name Duffy. It was daffy. "One for Duffy too."

"Courtside?"

"Courtside."

"She can go last, but remember, I'm the encore."

"And she gets to keep the five points?"

"Fine. Whatever." Twatla stormed away as Cunny's rays of light dimmed. Thoughts about how Twatla never once said there'd be a penalty for showing up late rushed through his head, but he wouldn't question her. Not when Latrine was back in the game. He strolled over to Latrine who looked frozen with fear. He flashed a smile at her, hoping to thaw her out.

"Love? You're in."

"I'm in?"

"Last one before the encore." Peyton could see the color returning to Latrine's face, her nerves kicked off the field like an old deflated football. He could see the spirit revive in her. He was proud. She was ready to take the stage and make it her own.

"You think I can take Countess?"

"Tomorrow we'll pick out your gown for Duchess Regionals."

• • •

Latrine looked out at the judges holding up Cunny's score. She got a 9.4, 9.5, 9.4, 9.4, and a 9.3. Cunny didn't quite stick the landing, apparently. A smile crept across Latrine's face.

Peyton gave her a nudge. "You're on. Show them what the Scottish can do."

Latrine waited for Twatla's introduction. She couldn't tell exactly what she was saying. It was all a muffled blur. But when she finished, Latrine strutted out onto the stage and struck her opening pose.

• • •

As Twatla passed Latrine walking out on to the stage, she could tell her knees were about ready to buckle. She knew Latrine was new to it all. Her years of experience had given her a sense of smell for bitches like her. Latrine had barely mastered the art of walking in heels, but compared to the other queens competing, she was an amateur. Amateurs just didn't make Countess. They didn't deserve it, and furthermore, they'd be an embarrassment at Duchess Regionals. Sure, she let her perform, but she was staunch in her belief that Latrine wouldn't be winning. She could make that happen too. The judges were on her side. They didn't know about Latrine's thinking she was hot shit and how she couldn't be bothered to show up on time to her first competition. But they would if it were necessary.

Twatla hated all the pretty little white queens who thought they ruled the world. She hated how they sauntered about, thinking they were all creative and shit, and then they'd go ahead and turn in a mediocre performance to a mediocre song in a mediocre dress. She was sick of how they all thought they didn't have to work hard because they naturally looked feminine in drag. They all got to take their makeup off, revealing their gleaming baby faces like the Karate Kid. Then they walked around the club looking to land a sugar daddy for the night. Latrine was just another one of them. An entitled bitch.

Twatla looked at Duffy when she got back to the wings, their eyes smiling at each other, knowing Latrine looked terrible. From behind, they could see just a mass of sheer red-tulle bustle and a mop of teased ginger hair like you'd see in a Glamour Shot in Texas, circa 1991. The girl looked tragic.

"You were nice when you announced her," Duffy whispered.

"She didn't deserve it," said Twatla. "By the way, we have courtside seats for the season at the Pillsbury Scones Arena."

"How did you…?"

Twatla didn't respond. She just looked at the stage and nodded. That was all Duffy needed. She smiled, tossing a glance back. Only she didn't lock eyes with Twatla again. Her eye caught someone else.

Twatla turned around to see who the distraction was. It was Detective Ross, Duffy's cop partner.

"You made it," she said.

Ross was almost stark naked save for a pair of square-cut Aussie Bum trunks. You'd think with a body like his, he'd walk more like he was on a runway, but he didn't. He walked like his ass was having an allergic reaction to them, completely out of his suit-and-tie element. He stood before Duffy, kind of hunched over, his arms crossed over his chest. It was clear he wanted to crawl into a ditch and curl up in the fetal position.

"I knew you had abs under that uniform, Ross," Duffy said with a hint of lust. Twatla wasn't happy. She could see Duffy's eyes dropping to his sculpted stomach with sideways glances at the peaks of his biceps. Twatla looked around to see if anyone else saw the display of her wife ogling another man, but every queen backstage seemed to be glancing at his arms too.

Duffy reached out her hand, and, in slow motion, counted the number of abs rippling across his stomach. Twatla grabbed her arm and relocated it to her chest.

"Are my tits straight?"

Ross looked up. "Wow. I didn't even recognize you. You look great."

"This old thing?" Twatla softened a bit, content in his acknowledgement of her beauty.

The crowd's cheers crescendoed. They all turned around to see Latrine Dion, flailing about onstage to Celine's rendition of "I Drove All Night." She was driving the crowd nuts. Twatla scoffed at the song choice, thinking to herself that Cyndi Lauper did it better. The dress looked ridiculous from the back, but the front was actually impressive with its sequin patterns in the form of some Celtic dragon. It flew up like Marilyn on a subway grate when she started pirouetting across the stage. Her hair whipped around her as a protective shield from the tornadic winds generated from the centrifugal force. Her bracelets dangled and clanked to the beat. The smile on her face grunted with Scottish pride, as if she had just inked a deal to grant their independence and she was sticking it to the English. For a moment, an ever-so-brief moment, Twatla was slightly intimidated.

As the song grinded to its final bars, Latrine threw her hands up into a final pose and bowed. Money flew onto the stage as those queens welcomed a new brand of scotch to the US of A. Twatla hated scotch.

Just as Latrine bowed and started picking up her tips, her boy Peyton dashed out onto the stage to help. Twatla grabbed Ross's arm and nodded toward the stage. Ross darted out to grab Peyton, seeming to pick him up by the collar. It was like watching a mangy cat dangling an unruly kitten from its mouth. Latrine took her final bow. And then another. And then another.

Until Twatla marched out onto the stage. "Can we have the scores for Miss Latrine Dion?"

• • •

The judges held up a 9.5, 9.6, and three 9.7s. Latrine knew that was enough to top Ina Godda the Diva and Cunny Corleone, and she shrieked internally. Assuming they scored higher than the queens who performed earlier, Latrine had it in the bag. She blew kisses to the judges and waved to the crowd.

"Beat it bitch. It's my turn." Twatla had the mic down by her side as she nudged Latrine to the side.

Latrine scurried off stage and threw her arms around Peyton. She had come to America with a dream, one she was making come true.

• • •

Duffy glanced over at her as she was hugging her runt of a husband. She towered over him as they kissed, and she wanted to give her a swift kick to the knees to knock her down to his level. She shook her head to snap out of it, realizing Twatla was on.

Duffy loved watching Twatla perform. It was why she married her. She was a stud in the bedroom and a diva on the stage. Not many girls got to try on dresses with their wife, stop at the makeup counter for a makeover with their wife, and then make it home in time for the Bucs game—with their husband. They even got victory mani-pedis after each win. It was the best of both worlds.

Twatla struck her opening pose on stage, and the music started: Whitney Houston's "Million Dollar Bill." A few gay squeals of delight over the opening chords assured Duffy that Twatla had them in the palm of her bedazzled hand. Yellow was definitely her color. She worked that parakeet-yellow dress like it was a Chinese finger trap, slinking and stretching her taut frame into place. The color popped against her milk-chocolate skin. She was a Mr. Goodbar waiting to be unwrapped.

The music pulsed. Some of the gays in the audience thrust one hand in the air, as Ms. Houston commanded. Duffy watched as her girl worked it. She involuntarily tossed her hands into the air too, shaking her hips to the beat, taken by the grooves cut deep into the echoing chambers of Whitney's voice. Twatla made *her* feel like a million dollar bill. Duffy looked around backstage as the queens all danced along to it. Duffy grooved on over to Ross and grabbed his hand, forcing him to move his hips. A small smile flashed over his stern face. She wanted him to let go for once. They weren't cops at that moment. The seriousness should be left at work.

"He's really good," he said.

"She," said Duffy. "She's my wife."

"She."

On stage, Twatla waved her arms in the air like the best R & B divas did, painting the notes with her hands. The song even told her what to do with her hands, and Twatla knew how to listen when Ms. Houston told her what to do. And those notes. Those powerful belting notes delineated by her precise interpretive choreography. If Whitney's voice was the closest thing to God on Earth, then Twatla ensured everyone she was really the second coming, sashaying and twerking in her glamorous gown. Twatla was the only queen who could sing about a million dollar bill but look more like a billion while doing it.

The music reached its breathtaking final bars. Duffy anticipated the adulation, the undying adulation of their gays. She never tired of seeing the way they showered Twatla with cheers and with praise. As Whitney belted her last note, she struck her final pose. But to Duffy's surprise, only a polite clap of gratitude replaced the normal thunderous applause. Twatla was their comfort food—their den mother. Without her, that club and community were nothing. Duffy couldn't figure out what was wrong with her gays. That performance was fierce. She could tell the subtle applause left Twatla uneasy.

Twatla took her bow unfazed and then walked offstage and down to the judges' table in the front row. Duffy could see her whispering to them in an ad hoc meeting. She always knew when Twatla was being serious because she'd clenched her fists when she talked. There, down by her sides, were her fists, gripping tightly. The judges smiled at her, scribbling some notes as she spoke.

Duffy cast a glance over at Latrine and Peyton. Latrine smiled a big toothy grin, which was surprisingly not as fucked up looking as the rest of her peoples' when they opened their mouths. To the satisfaction of those two Scottish expatriates, Twatla headed back on stage to lead the program into its finale: The awarding of the title of Countess.

"Thank you, Ladies and Ladies," Twatla said. She was always so generous to her subjects. They needed to appreciate her more.

"Thank you," she continued, "That was fun. I know what you're all waiting for. Ya'll's waiting to hear who wins the title of Duchess for our region, aren't ya'll?" The crowd went wild. She definitely knew how to bring the crowd back to her. "Well, wait no further. Can we have all ten contestants to the stage, please?"

Peyton grabbed Latrine's hand. She looked down at him. He smiled at her and stood on his tip toes to kiss her. It was kind of a cute gesture coming from a garden gnome. Latrine glided over to the stage in her heels, trying to hide the strain of being an amateur queen in four-inch stilettos. She took her place in the lineup, and it was complete. Duffy lamented how similar the queens were. Not one of them stood out as unique. They all kind of looked the same: Big hair, big dresses, big egos. Couldn't one of them wear a freaking understated pantsuit? She longed for a queen to emulate Barbara Walters.

Duffy pointed Detective Ross over to the flowers and sashes since he was the objectified male for the night. When Twatla announced the runners up, he was responsible for draping the sashes and handing them flowers. It was supposed to be a fun job, but it was clear he wasn't too comfortable. It took a bribe of Starbucks for a month to get him to agree to do it.

"It has been a fabulous night," said Twatla. "And each and every one of these ten ladies has performed their hearts out, and no matter what happens, we have a lovely gift basket for each of you backstage. Tonight, you're all winners. But I know you all have your eyes on the big prize, so let's not wait any further and get right down to business, shall we? Now, I'm going to announce our two runners up and then the judge's choice for our local Countess. Remember that our Countess *and* the first runner-up get to move on to the Duchess Regional Finals in Tampa. The top five Duchesses move on to the National Grand Dame Competition. So, our second runner up, who will also serve as an alternate choice if anything should happen to our Countess or our first runner up is…"

Ross strolled onstage and handed her an envelope. She smiled at him.

"Thank you, Detective Rossie," she announced. "This is Rossie, everybody. Strike a pose, Rossie-poo."

Ross stared daggers at her.

"Isn't Ross cute, ya'll? I think he just needs a little encouragement."

A few catcalls erupted from the audience. Ross's glare softened as he walked off stage. As the catcalls faded, Twatla ripped open the envelope.

"Our second runner up is… Miss Latrine Dion!"

A polite applause. Perhaps a little confusion. Latrine looked completely shocked. Ross regaled her with a sash and pink roses as she tried to feign a smile. Duffy wished she could smack some manners into her. Peyton spouted off more "fucks" than a dude with Tourettes. Twatla smirked at Latrine before taking a deep cleansing breath.

"Thank you, Rossie. Can we get a little booty shake?"

"No."

"Aww, Rossie ain't playing nice, ya'll."

Shouts of "boo" from the audience forced Ross to hurry off the stage.

"I should just get my own Starbucks this month," he told Duffy after he returned to the wings.

"Just take it in stride. It's a compliment. If the gays like you, you're hot. If they don't, then that's when you need to be worried."

He crossed his arms over his chest. "I don't want to feel violated, that's all."

"Oh no. You're onstage. They'll worship you while you're on stage. You only get violated if you go on the dance floor dressed like that."

"Oh."

Twatla opened the envelope. "And our first runner up, the lady who will be joining our Countess to represent us in the Duchess Regionals Competition in Tampa is… Miss Cunny Corleone!"

Cunny shrieked in genuine excitement, her ponytail wagging with glee. Ross placed a sash on her and handed her a bouquet of yellow roses. Cunny was super-gracious. Ross headed offstage and picked up the next envelope.

"And now, the moment you've all been waiting for. Rossie, the envelope,"

Ross handed Twatla the envelope before facing the audience and making his pecs dance.

"Oh, okay," Twatla said, surprised. "Work it, boy."

The crowd squealed with delight before he exited. Twatla opened the envelope and looked up at all ten of the contestants. Latrine's face wore a nonplussed scowl.

"The honor and title of Countess, who will join our first runner up in representing our region as they compete for the title of Duchess and the winner of $5,000 to spend on gowns and glitter and whatever the hell else us queens need to get all glammed up is…"

The pause seemed to go on for an eternity.

"Miss Ina Godda the Diva!"

The crowd gave a mixed reaction. Definitely some confusion, but Duffy knew the right person had won. Latrine missed her spot. It was only fair. And Ina Godda was better and would put the money to good use anyway. Latrine could try again the next year, so she could wipe that sour look off her face. Peyton needed to shut up and take a Xanax.

Onstage, Ross placed the sash over Ina Godda and the crown on her head. He handed her a dozen red roses. Ina Godda curtsied before her subjects. The applause got warmer.

• • •

Ina Godda the Diva ran her dainty hands along Detective Ross's abdominal muscles as he handed her a bouquet of crimson-colored roses, not at all surprised she'd won. She was steadfast in her belief that no queen in that room had ever done what she had done on that stage. She had transformed Cyndi Lauper's "She-bop" into a legendary routine that sat on the shelf alongside her other winning performances.

As Ina Godda the Diva sauntered down the runway with her tiara, her sash, and her bouquet, she was reminded of just how powerful she had become in Orlando. The veneration of her fans. The appreciation from the judges. The reverence from her fellow contestants of whom she was reciprocally grateful. They were healthy competition to keep her on point, but in the end, she wasn't going to feel guilty about winning again. The strongest and most creative queen to represent the community at the Duchess Regionals had won again. There, she'd compete alongside queens who were actually at her caliber and could provide her with the challenge she deserved: a challenge she would meet and overcome.

• • •

Latrine leaned down to give him a hug, but he didn't seem to be in the hugging mood. He fumed. All the queens congratulated Ina Godda, kissing her arse since she was the new reigning Countess and they were her vassals. Someone even curtsied.

"Bloody unfair." Peyton was ready to spit nails. "I heard how they cheered for you. I saw your scores. They were way better than hers. Did you see the look on the judges' faces?"

Latrine heard what Peyton was saying, but her attention had been diverted over to Twatla, who whispered something to Duffy. Whatever it was piqued Duffy's interest. She released a laugh, covering her mouth and casting a sideways glance over at Latrine. As Twatla and Duffy slapped hands, Latrine felt her heart sinking, confident the gesture reflected the extent to which she'd been screwed.

"Those buggers." Latrine noticed Peyton had his eye on them too.

"Fucking wankers, the both of them."

Latrine just couldn't understand why she lost. Perhaps it was jealousy. Maybe they were mad she got the biggest applause. Maybe it was because the judges definitely liked her better than anyone else in the competition, including the terrible performance Twatla gave at the end. Maybe they were mad because she had the bollocks to perform to Celine—the world's greatest diva.

"I can't believe this. We need to smack down the fucking cunts." His voice was throaty and tense.

"Keep your head, Peyton."

"I am keeping my bloody head. You know you want to bash their fucking skulls in for doing whatever they did." Beads of sweat formed on his brow.

"I guess I'll have to wait until next year."

"They stole that title from you. Ina Godda and Twatla. It was all a conspiracy. I know it."

"This has taken a lot of energy. I'm done in." She figured a warm bath at home would help.

"I'm *not* done in. I want to give them what they deserve."

"Can't we talk about this some other time?"

"How about we go get your gift basket and fuck with them a wee bit first."

The gift basket. She'd forgotten about that. Latrine took solace she at least got something. Since cash was out of the question, a lovely basket of spa gift certificates, bath oils, and the like would be an adequate booby prize—if indeed those were actually in it. Peyton took her by the hand and led her over to a cramped dressing room with unflattering fluorescent lighting. Some of the other contestants transformed themselves from their magical stage personas to streetwalker-goddess apparel for the predictable purpose of clubbing into the wee hours. Ina Godda, clad in a pink satin bathrobe and a wigcap, removed her false eyelashes in one corner. The lighting did nothing to hide her many facial imperfections. The makeup didn't do much to help her either. Latrine made eye contact with her in the mirror and issued a phony smile.

"You know, Latrine, you're lucky you didn't hurt yourself. That kind of twirling is dangerous for a neophyte." Ina Godda's fangs were in full view as she wiped her face with a cloth.

"I thought I did great. The judges thought so too." Latrine raised her stinger for a counterattack.

"You keep living in *Mayberry,* or whatever your people's version is. *McMayberry.*"

Peyton leaned over to Latrine and whispered in her ear, Latrine still keeping her eyes on Ina Godda to make it obvious he was talking about her.

"I don't know what that means, but it's bitchy, and she's a bitch. This queen stole your prize money, your chance to go to Regionals, and your Countess title. She's completely unworthy the honor of Countess. Plus, the audience liked you better. They cheered louder. They hollered louder. They clapped louder. You were robbed, and she knows it. Now, you need to be rough with these bitches, got it?"

Peyton's voice had reached a whispering scream, and the whole room watched him turning beet red. Latrine noticed Ina Godda gawking at him like she was about to unplug her curling iron and shove it down his throat. Cunny, wearing a cute navy blue robe and nearly completely out of makeup, rose from her dressing table in the corner and hurried over to the center table.

"Let's check out the gift baskets." Cunny began rifling through some of the novelty items in hers. Each basket bore a label with a contestant's name.

Latrine spotted hers and rummaged through it. Peyton stood by her side. She figured he was trying to calculate its total monetary value. There was a bottle of lube, a few gift certificates, various lotions, and what looked to be a butt-plug training kit: a variety of sizes from pygmy to python.

Peyton moved on to inspecting Ina Godda's basket, presumably to see if she got anything better. He held up a thick dildo, maybe about twenty centimeters in circumference. Cunny reached out and tried to grab it from him, but his grip was firm.

Peyton yanked it away from Cunny. "Look at the size of this thing. Goldilocks would think this was too big, but not you, Ina Godda. This big bear one is juuuust right for your gaping hole."

Latrine laughed to herself. Ina Godda glared at him in her mirror. Cunny took it from him and placed it neatly back in Ina Godda's basket.

"Cunny, dear. Why don't you take that one? I already have the best at home." Ina Godda's glare had softened as she continued to remove her makeup.

"You do?" Cunny asked.

"I have frequent trysts with none other than Mr. Marco Polo." Ina Godda wiped the lipstick off her mouth, casting proud, animated glances at Cunny.

"The porn star?" Cunny seemed to genuinely believe her.

"Of course. I met him at a meet and greet in San Francisco when the dildo molded from his own loins was cast into my needy hands. I will never forget the moment he handed it to me. We had a connection."

Latrine saw the girl was nutters. Peyton seized the moment to fill Latrine's basket with some of the gift certificates pilfered from Ina Godda's as she continued to descend deeper into the thick, complex tapestry of her own delusion. Nobody else in the room seemed to notice his thievery.

Ina Godda's eyes closed as her head moved side-to-side in romanticized, theatrical gestures. "I gazed into Marco's turquoise blue eyes as he bid me 'hello.' He handed me the box, biceps rippling, with a huge smile on his face. I asked him if I could touch his body, and he responded by grabbing my hand and placing it on his firm chest. He gently guided my hand over his resplendent pectorals and his erect nipples before winking at me. That beautiful specimen of a man wanted me. And now I get to make love to him every night."

"I didn't think Marco Polo would go for a plus-sized queen," said Peyton.

Ina Godda the Diva let out a high-pitched gasp. "I am not plus-sized, you hobbit."

The tension was broken when Twatla walked into the dressing room accompanied by a middle-aged woman dressed in what looked to be a cross between hippie chic and gypsy-street fair. Since the announcement of Countess, every time Peyton laid eyes on Twatla, his fists clenched. Latrine glared at her too, prompting Twatla to roll her eyes. Latrine didn't take offense to it though. She saw it as an unspoken admission of guilt.

"Ladies," said Twatla, "I just wanted to introduce you all to my friend Rhiannon. Included in your baskets is a gift certificate for a reading with her. She's a fabulous clairvoyant, and ya'll are going to love her."

Rhiannon waved at them with her liver-spotted hands, chunky

bracelets clanking back and forth. Her dull and brittle brown-gray hair was the product of too many perms over her lifetime. Bright red was painted over the spot where once there were thin lips. Latrine tried not to stare too long.

"Why don't ya'll discuss when you'd want to have your reading?" Twatla added.

Twatla whispered something about 'keeping the bitching to a minimum' to Rhiannon as she walked out. Latrine glanced at Peyton, whose red face and beads of sweat looked like he was hovering over the loo and passing Hadrian's Wall out of his arse.

"Why don't we all go tomorrow?" Latrine asked. She knew she probably shouldn't have volunteered, but circumventing any gossip about being a sore loser by sounding enthusiastic felt like the right thing to do.

"Tomorrow works." Rhiannon looked at Cunny.

Cunny gasped slightly. "I'd love to do it tomorrow. Ina Godda? You free?"

Latrine hadn't intended to extend the invitation to everyone in the room but tried to avoid showing her displeasure.

"Marco and I have a date tomorrow." Ina Godda placed a new wig on her head and was adjusting it in the mirror.

"So you need to get your Polo on." A big smile was plastered on Cunny's face.

"She needs to get *on* her Polo," Peyton muttered.

"You know, as much as I'd love to join you queens, I fear I'll contract a debilitating migraine if I continue to inhale the stench of failure." Ina Godda's eyes darted back and forth between Latrine and Peyton in the mirror.

"You're the one who's going to be spending the day bouncing up and down on—"

"I'll be spending the day in absolute bliss, not in absolute piss with the likes of you. Now if you'll excuse me, I have a lot to do to prepare." Ina Godda got up and stuffed her wares in her bag.

"A lot of douching to shit out the stick in your arse." Peyton didn't even deign to muffle his voice.

Ina Godda grabbed her bag and strutted over to the table in the center to retrieve her basket. The room waited in silent anticipation for her reply. Instead, she shot him an unctuous smile before turning to leave. "Have a blessed day."

• • •

Cunny always hated when things escalated to bitchfest level. Watching queens fight made her nervous. Her stomach felt like it was still being cinched by a corset when she'd long since taken it off. She noticed Peyton seemed mad at Ina Godda. She found that cute—when a man defended his girl.

"I really would like to go home now," said Latrine.

"We cannot go home now," Peyton spit back. "I want to confront the fucking cunt."

Cunny wasn't sure which 'fucking cunt' he was talking about. There were a lot of 'fucking cunts' in that building. She thought Ina Godda could be kind of a fucking cunt at times, but most of the time she was just a cunt. She knew that everyone could have their own cunty moments—including her. That's where she got her name from. Her friend Blanche BuDois, a fierce queen from Atlanta, dubbed her Cunny in honor of the goddess of all Mafia films after Cunny once brought her a dozen cannoli. She admired Blanche and hoped she won her local competition. That would mean they'd get to go to Regionals together. They could be frenemies—in a good way.

"We don't need to confront anyone, Peyton," said Latrine.

"Who do you want to confront?" Cunny asked.

"That's none of your fucking business." Peyton spit a little. Cunny felt a drop land on her face.

"Leave off her. We want to chat with Twatla and Duffy is all."

Cunny was grateful she could at least understand what Latrine said. Peyton was so pissed he sounded like he swallowed a bag of marbles, which prevented his tongue from hitting his teeth when he said any word that had a "T" in it. Cunny noticed he spit because of his accent, not completely understanding why foreign guys did that. She assumed he was British. Or maybe he was from that other country over there—with the Lucky Charms. Irish. She thought he was a spitting Irishman. Like a kilted camel. She knew Latrine and he were from the same country, so she was mystified that one of them could be so indecipherable when angry. To Cunny, it was like Latrine was Neiman Marcus Irish and Peyton was Walmart Irish.

"Oh, well why didn't you say so?" Cunny felt bad for Latrine because she was really good. Queens who felt bad after a performance needed cheering up. They should feel on top of the world. She wanted to make that happen, make her feel good. Helping Latrine would make her feel welcome in America. "I can go get them."

"We can go get them too, you dafty."

Cunny immediately jumped to the conclusion that Peyton hadn't had his Lucky Charms. She assumed not having Lucky Charms was like how Irish women got their periods—they got bitchy.

"She's not a dafty," said Latrine.

Cunny nodded in agreement. She wasn't a dafty, even though she had no idea what that meant. "Why don't I come with you all then? I can be there for support."

"Support for what?" Peyton was all riled up.

"I just want to help you." Cunny threw him a bone to stop him from foaming at the mouth. Bones always tamed rabid dogs.

Latrine grabbed Peyton by the arm to talk some sense into him. "She just wants to help. It's bloody nice of her. She's not an eej."

"She is an eej."

"I is what I is." Cunny was sure her smile could calm Peyton down. She wanted to pat him on his head too. The definition of *eej* escaped her.

"Okay, let's go then. That's really nice of you to offer to help us find them, Cunny." Latrine had a genuine smile on her face. It warmed Cunny's heart.

With that, they joined hands and skipped out to the stage

area to see Twatla—or at least that's how it felt in Cunny's head. They were actually walking. Cunny loved to skip, so much so she thought about putting it into one of her routines. Like Judy Garland in The Wizard of Oz. She was desperate to do a Dorothy routine, but the songs weren't flashy enough. Cunny was sex on a stick. Bondage. Chrome. Rubber. "Somewhere Over the Rainbow" just didn't work in a dominatrix outfit.

They approached Twatla and Duffy, and Cunny guessed they saw them coming because Twatla rolled her eyes again.

"Excuse me, Twatla?" Peyton was actually being tame.

"Yes?" Twatla sounded like she was on edge. Like she was talking down to him.

"We noticed a problem with the addition of the scores," he said. "Latrine had a higher score than Ina Godda."

"But you're forgetting the deduction for being late, honey," she said to him, kind of smiling through it.

"I thought you said there would be no penalty."

"I never said that." Twatla's eyes darted over to Duffy.

"And after all I was going to do for you." Peyton's voice was getting a little louder.

"Like what?"

"You know."

"I don't know anything." She looked down at him as she shrugged her shoulders.

Peyton stared right back at her. Cunny could see his blood boiling through his skin. She figured a trait of all pale Irish men was that when they got mad, you could see the blood pumping through their veins. That was happening.

"We just think it's an honest mistake," Latrine said, trying to keep the situation cool.

"Yeah, totally a mistake." Cunny didn't know for sure. She just didn't want to see Latrine ruin her chances for the future.

"I don't know what you're implying here, Peyton, but you should be happy with what Latrine has gotten," Duffy said. "She got a nice gift basket and she had a great experience by being here in the first place. Do you really want us to redo the math?"

It sounded like a threat to Cunny. She wanted to muzzle Peyton before he attacked.

"I think we're good with it. We just wanted to voice our concerns," Latrine said, smiling a little.

"Thank you for sharing." Twatla motioned to Duffy to leave, and they walked away.

Peyton's head looked like a pressure cooker. Steam shot from his ears. He made a high humming noise, like someone needed to run cold tap water over him. "We should've made her eat fucking crow."

"No. Think about it. If I try next year, they could hold a grudge and find some other arbitrary excuse to shit on me again. If we keep trying to get them to change it, they're just going to get mad."

"Who cares if they get fucking mad? What they did was wrong." Peyton said it loud enough for them to overhear in case they were still nearby.

"Well, Ina Godda the Diva is Countess now, so you guys are going to have to just accept it," said Cunny. They looked at her weirdly. "I mean, there's no use crying over spilled milk."

"Nobody spilled any fucking milk, spastic." Peyton said. "They spilled a bottle of whisky, and an expensive one at that, so you can leave off."

Cunny looked back and forth between them, a blank stare on her face.

"Let's just go home and get some sleep. I'm bloody tired," said Latrine.

"Yeah, you need to get some sleep for tomorrow," she reminded Latrine.

"Tomorrow?"

"The reading."

"Right," Latrine said. "Text me directions to your place, and I'll pick you up."

She handed Latrine her phone to her to input her number.

When she finished, Peyton grabbed Latrine by the hand, pulling her away, muttering something Cunny couldn't understand. She smiled and waved as Latrine tossed a glance over her shoulder, smiling back.

Chapter 2

Peyton felt an overwhelming desire to knee Twatla in her bollocks and punch Duffy in the vagina the whole night. Scratch that. He wanted to use her vagina as a punching bag and bruise it up worse than it probably looked when Twatla was done screwing her. He had to lie and tell his boss those tickets were for him and Latrine. Latrine didn't even know anything about basketball, and he could give two fucks about it. After all that, they had the bollocks to cheat? He was so agitated he could feel his hands getting sore from gripping the steering wheel too tight. Latrine was to be his satisfaction that night. It was her duty—being his own personal Julia Roberts in *Pretty Woman*. He tapped on her leg to wake her.

"Are we home?" Latrine lifted her head and opened her eyes.

"Almost."

She yawned, closing her eyes again. He grabbed her arm.

"What?"

"Don't go to sleep."

"Peyton, I'm pure done in."

"I'm not tired. I'm really not tired." His voice dropped an octave with the innuendo.

"Not tonight, Love."

"You look so sexy tonight." Peyton's unspoken mantra was always *feed the ego; feed the penis*.

"I do?" Latrine seemed genuinely stunned.

He pulled into the car park and put the van in park. Latrine unbuckled her seat belt.

"Wait!" Peyton's anger management was whisky and fucking, and he was willing to play up the romance to get his way. He got out and ran over to her door. As he opened it, he held out his arm to escort her to their flat. She put her arm through his like she was Scarlet O'Hara and he was that horny bugger Rhett Butler ready to pounce like a fucking lion. Her coy smile told Peyton it worked. She was ready and willing to give it up.

As soon as they walked into their flat, Peyton ripped off his shirt. He guided her by the hand to the bedroom. He threw her down on the bed, and unzipped her dress, tearing it off her body. To Peyton's horror, her Spanx undershirt hugged her upper body. He hated those fucking Spanx. He wanted to spank those fucking Spanx. She grabbed the edges and worked it over her torso. Peyton never considered her obese by any means, but trying to rip off those Spanx when all he wanted was a good fuck was like dangling a carrot over a crippled rabbit and telling it to jump. He kept tugging at the Spanx, lost in the futility of his efforts. She whimpered a wee bit. He made her sit up and lean forward so he could get a better grip on it. Big Ben was near collapse, so he knew he had to act fast. He gave one big tug to the Spanx and fell backwards, squarely on his arse.

"You okay?"

"Barely." Peyton got right back up and pulled his pants down with one tug, taking his usual place on all fours over her.

They kissed. During foreplay and before the rough stuff, Peyton liked to think they were like that scene on the beach in Hawaii in *From Here to Eternity*. He would pretend he was Burt Lancaster. She'd be Deborah Kerr. The waves crashed over them as they made passionate love. It was their romantic moment. *From Queer to Eternity*. The present was the queer. Later, he would fuck her into eternity.

Peyton unbuttoned her pants and pulled them down.

"Fuck!"

Latrine laughed. More fucking Spanx. Disrobing a drag queen post-performance was a bit like trying to find the treat under a series of those Russian dolls where you lift one and then there's another. And another. And another.

"You couldn't take off your tuckage?" he asked.

"I was pure done in. I just wanted to go to sleep."

"How do you sleep in your tuckage? Here. Let me get it off you."

He started pulling her Spanx down, which at that point was akin to ripping a sausage casing off a bratwürste. She ground her teeth together as he tried rolling them down. Ripping off a pair of tight pantyhouse was about as sexy as giving birth. *Fucking perfect.* Peyton just wanted to fuck his mate, and their own little scene from *From Here to Eternity* was becoming more like *From Here to Maternity.* Thoughts about a woman having a baby invaded his mind. The winds abated. He could feel his mast, which was formerly at full sail, start to sag. He desperately needed Latrine to blow hard to fluff it back up.

"What happened?" she said.

What happened? WHAT HAPPENED?

"Fucking Spanx is what happened."

Peyton grabbed her head, and she sucked away like her life depended on it. Not before long, he was back up. He turned her over and shoved it in. The pounding made the bed quake like a magnitude 8.5. Undeterred by the force, she moaned with pleasure. Peyton kept nailing her, throwing his hands in the air with each thrust, like he had a Scottish flag in his hand, waving it at the World Cup. He imagined the crowd going wild as he scored, applauding each thrust as if cheering on an entire nation. He felt the Scottish pride beaming down at him. All the important men in Scottish history smacked him on the arse and told him he was doing a good job. One thrust was for Rob Roy. One thrust was for Sean Connery. Another was for Ewan MacGregor. Another for Robert the Bruce. One for James McAvoy, and another for William Wallace. He wasn't just fucking her for himself. He was fucking her for Scotland.

Peyton finished and threw his arms up into the air, completely proud of his victory. He plopped down beside her. She smiled at him, cuddling up beside him and putting her hand on his chest. It felt right. The moment felt right to pounce. The anger management sex was just stalking the prey. He could go in for the kill, and she'd surrender with no problem.

"You know what?" Peyton tried to catch his breath.

"What?"

"Ina Godda's a complete no-talent bitch."

Latrine kissed him on the neck and snuggled beside him.

Peyton put his arm around her. "I know you're new to this, but if that no-talent wanker wins Duchess and gets to move on, there's no justice. Look how far you've made it, and it was your first one."

"I know. All I need to do is hire a choreographer and practice more for next year."

Peyton gave her a sweet kiss on the forehead. It was a condescending kiss. He wasn't giving up his pursuit of justice any time soon.

"I can help you and teach you to dance. You don't need to hire a choreographer." Peyton stood up on the bed and danced like he was in a Monty Python revue. Latrine laughed.

"Sweet pea, that's nice of you, but I really need a professional. You can come watch my rehearsals though."

Peyton smiled to himself. There was no way he could teach her to dance or design her routine, but he needed her to think he had faith in her. And she did. She planted a friendly kiss on his cheek, which told him she felt somewhat bad about crushing his dreams of being her choreographer. He never wanted to be a fucking choreographer. Choreographers were bloody prancercisers. He threw a sideways glance at her. Taking a deep breath, he looked up at the ceiling, attempting to be lost in thought. He could feel Latrine watching him, concerned.

"What's the matter?"

"I really want to fucking burn Twatla and Duffy's house to the ground or something."

"We get revenge by winning next year."

"Next year? Fuck that," said Peyton. Latrine looked at him, confused. Peyton turned and looked her in the eye, rubbing her cheek with his thumb. "I know you don't want to mess with

Twatla and Duffy, but I wonder what would happen if we moved Cuntess Ina Godda out of the way."

"Out of the way?" A gap opened between them as Latrine rolled over onto her back.

"Aye. Out of the way. I mean, we could always move that bitch Cunny. Do something to her."

"Cunny didn't do anything to us." It seemed out of the question to Latrine.

Peyton could agree with that, despite his annoyance with her. "So then it's pretty clear it's Ina Godda. She's the other one going from our region, so we need to move the bitch."

"But how would I move her out of the way?"

"You sabotage her routines."

"Like how?"

Peyton paused, searching for the right proposal. "Who was the ice skater that got hit in the knee?"

"Nancy Kerrigan. But I'm no cricket player. I can't knock her knee out of whack. I don't see what the harm is in waiting until next year?"

"Okay, fine. You don't go and she wins. And you don't even get your chance. No Duchess. No $25,000 prize money. No moving on to Grand Dame. No chance at $100,000. No buying a house. We keep biding in this flat." Peyton looked away purposely, having planted the seed.

"What's wrong with this flat? It's bigger than the one in Glasgow you bided in."

Peyton leaped out of bed and made a show of his pacing. Latrine sat up. The crossing of her arms over her bare chest hinted at her discomfort.

"That's a fact, Peyton."

"Aye. That's a fact. That's a fucking fact. I hate these cramped flats. I want to bide in a house. I want my own land. I don't want to bide in a flat anymore." It was true. He did want to move. But the house was a great, tangible reward for a well-plotted revenge scheme.

"Sweet pea, it took you a few months to get your work visa. You have a job now and we can save up money." Latrine had remained calm and rational to that point. It was pissing Peyton off.

"I don't make enough. We'd have to wait years for a down payment."

"Then we wait years. We'll do it. I can get a real job as soon as my own visa comes through. It shouldn't be long. And if I win next year, that brings it even closer faster."

"You know, you can always ask your parents back home for some cash." It was a genuine risk to go there, but Peyton had to try it.

Latrine sank into the bed. "Peyton, that's not an option. You know they don't like my doing drag. They stopped paying for everything when I told them."

She took the bait. Peyton sat on the edge of the bed. "Well, tell them you stopped. They won't know."

"They won't, but then they'll ask if I'm seeing anyone new. And unless you want to be my Asian beard named Pei-Lin, that's not going to work." Her hands drew up to her face so she could massage her temples.

Peyton smacked the bed. The impact echoed through the internal forest of coiled springs. "They don't have to know! Just lie and say we broke up, you've hung up your heels for good, and you're now dating a lovely lady named Kate Middleton."

"And then they come to visit and I have to find a Kate who's willing to put up with that. Besides, it took Wills years to find the right Kate. I'd also need to somehow convince the Kate I'm straight." The look on Latrine's face signaled the entire conversation was floundering. All attempts to goad her into his plot had tumbled off a cliff and were treading water in the ocean before getting sucked into the undertow.

"Fine. You don't even want to try. You don't want to move our relationship forward and get our own fucking house. You don't want me to be the king of my own castle. We'll wait."

Peyton plopped down on the bed and turned away from her. He could feel her breathing. It was the kind of breathing where she was deep in thought, thinking about the possibilities, thinking about what she could do. He had thrown a lifeline to his sinking plot, hoping she'd have a change of heart and save it. Her silence suggested she would. The longer the silence, the more time she'd had to contemplate the idea. Her energy was changing. He could feel it.

"So I need to win this money this year."

He turned and looked at her, nodding his head up and down.

"How can I guarantee I even get to go?" she asked. "There's no guarantee Twatla will even let me go if something happens to Ina Godda.

"Leave Twatla to me. I can find an even bigger bribe if I need to. First, you need to move the bitch out of the way."

"But *how* is the big question? How am I going to make her so incapacitated she can't compete? Dunt her head?" Latrine got up and walked to the bathroom. Peyton could hear her turn on the tap and drink water from her cupped hands.

"We'll think of something."

Peyton really meant *she'd* think of something. He really needed her to think about it, believing if she came up with the idea, she'd own it. She'd take responsibility for it. She would get the job done. If he thought of it, then it'd be his plan, and she'd only be doing it to make him happy.

Latrine climbed into bed as he rolled over to his side, facing away from her. He clapped his hands, and the lights went out. He could tell Latrine was still sitting up, still thinking, still pondering the ways. He got her wheels turning. The task was clear, but she was still weary, probably nervous about the possibility of getting caught and the possibility of getting in trouble. He knew Latrine. His efforts proved a success. She was considering it.

•   •   •

Latrine couldn't get out of bed. Peyton snored away beside her, the kind of snoring after a night of brilliant fuckery. She hadn't slept much despite how tired she was. Peyton had gotten her thinking about what would happen if she did take out Ina Godda. The hypotheticals. She'd get to go to Regionals, but what if she didn't win? What if her routine wasn't strong enough to beat Cunny? What if there were another Countess from another area they didn't know about who was poised and ready to take the title? It might not even be Cunny they had to worry about. But the thought of twenty-five thousand USD kept popping into her mind. They definitely could use the cash, and she was starting to feel guilty about not contributing to Peyton's dream of owning his own home. The guilt grew exponentially since she sent in her paperwork late to get her work visa—a secret she kept hidden since he was always nagging about her getting a job. They'd had money problems since landing in the US. She knew where all the anger came from. After a lifetime of privation in Glasgow, Peyton was growing impatient.

As she glanced over at him sleeping, she could see the history of his struggles in the fine lines around his eyes. They depicted his being the youngest lad in a family of football players—a gayboy in a family of hyper-hetero tough arses. The creases developing around his mouth were laugh lines masking the name-calling from the lads on the streets. The faint wrinkles his forehead represented how his brothers would gang up on him and push him around, once even sending him to hospital for a few weeks because of multiple fractures. But the glimmer in his eyes when he smiled showed how he learned to fight back. They were his sly tools for negotiating. He always said it was like the time spent in hospital ignited a blaze within him, and he vowed never to be called a fannybawbag again. It took him a bit to make them start to take him seriously, but he became a brash and mercurial one. That's why so many people took him for having a Napoleon complex. He'd had to weasel his way out of some slick situations with bullies, crafting stories about how one bloke was talking shit about another. Then the neighborhood would form factions and fight each other, completely forgetting about the lad they'd previously tried to squash like a midge.

Latrine understood she was different. She came from a different lifestyle and had a different upbringing. She had it easier—at first—and she resented how Peyton would blame her for it all, feeling like he shouldn't expect her to deliver on things that just weren't a possibility. He shouldn't have been surprised when she told him her parents would say no to any request for money. It was because of him she seldom visited her family in Edinburgh anyway. He of all people should've understood that nobody can control where they come from or who their parents are. It wasn't her fault her family had money and his family was poor. She shouldn't be blamed for growing up in New Town in a big Georgian-era home while he grew up in a two bedroom flat on the edges of Glasgow. And he shouldn't hold a grudge against her because she got to attend the best schools and graduate from the University of Edinburgh while he gave up on his education.

He never had an issue with coming out because he'd been picked on for so long and everyone kind of knew he was gay anyhow. He didn't understand how the moment Latrine came out changed her life forever. Latrine got to be honest and open with her parents, but they were clear they didn't want her dating men. When she told them she wanted to do drag, they threatened to renege on any promises they'd made for her financial security if she went through with it. Peyton didn't understand what it was like to be promised something by the two people a young adult had trusted most of her life and then have that promise dangling over a precipice.

It was crushing. He wasn't there during that transition period. He never got to see her actually try to live on her parents' terms— trying to live a life that went against who she was. For the longest time, Latrine avoided her passion. She wanted to shop for the most fabulous dresses and be on stage, but doing it would mean giving up any hope she had for financial stability. Peyton met her after that, when she'd started making trips to Glasgow to get her fix of gay pubs. And when they started dating in secret, he made Latrine believe he could support her. He gave her the courage to confront them about the truth of who she was.

Peyton eavesdropped occasionally on her phone calls with her parents. He was aware of how tense it'd gotten. There just wasn't much for them to say to each other. Latrine had accepted that since they weren't supporting her in any way, it was okay not to have a compulsion to call. It was actually Peyton who wanted a place in America, far from their pasts and far from anyone who wanted to shit on their love. It was probably the best idea he ever proposed. She was eternally grateful for that. The possibility entered her mind that she had the power to make his dream of being an American homeowner a reality—if she got to go to Duchess Regionals. If she figured out a plan. If she even won the title.

Latrine leapt out of bed with renewed ammunition. She gave credence to the belief the fortuneteller-gypsy lady would give her the insight she needed to hear. She became a wee bit glad she was going to do it—with Cunny, a girl she could trust. And going with another competitive queen meant she had to start thinking about what to wear.

When she opened her closet, her meager wardrobe laughed at her. She was sure Ina Godda's wardrobe was a rainbow of fruit flavors, but hers was a monochromatic mass of various shades of Scottish flag blue, with the occasional flash of red peeking through. One thing was for sure: If she got to go to Regionals, she needed to shop. What she had just wouldn't do, but she'd never tell any other queens that her dress collection could fit in the back seat of a mini. And with that thought, she suddenly could sympathize with Peyton a wee bit more—growing up in Glasgow with only a few outfits with which to live his life on the streets.

Latrine threw together an outfit for the day as Peyton's snores provided a rhythmic backdrop to the morning. She donned a navy blue pencil skirt, baby blue sweater, royal blue scarf—all to match her Scottish flag brooch. She positioned her brunette wig on, carefully parting the hair to one side with a little flip at the bottom, like Mary Tyler Moore. She was a cross between a 1960s American secretary and a stewardess. After applying her makeup with the precision of a laser, she took one last look in the mirror and smiled at herself.

"You look fabulous," said Peyton with a yawn.

"You're up."

"Just give me five minutes to change." Peyton took the sheet off, revealing his pale chest.

Latrine turned around to face him as she put in an earring. "Oh sweet pea, I think it's just going to be Cunny and me today."

Peyton looked like he just kicked his football up on a ledge, forcing him to go beg his older brother to get it down. He flopped back down in the bed and crossed his arms in full tantrum mode.

"That bitch Cunny doesn't want me there."

"No, Love. It's not that. It's that this is just for the girls. It was in the gift basket for all competitors," she told him. His lip looked like it started to pout. "Don't be scunnered."

"I'm not scunnered."

"You're totally scunnered." She walked over to him and kissed him on the forehead, not only to appease him, but also to blot her lipstick. "I promise to tell you all about it when I get back."

And with that, she grabbed her purse and scurried out the door, hopping into Peyton's van to embark on her journey to Cunny's flat. She sped along the short drive, Celine Dion's "I Drove All Night" filling the space. She hit the brakes in front of Cunny's apartment but paused to let the song finish. Cutting off Celine Dion while she was on a roll was sacrilege. Once she hit her final note, Cunny emerged from her flat.

Latrine wanted to roar with laughter. Cunny was clad in a floor-length black satin gown with a leather-and-lace corset cinching her at the waist, making her tits look like two fluffy marshmallows on a bed of licorice. Her black wig was pulled back off her face in a barrette with a few stray ringlets draping her face. A black leather handbag dangled from her wrist. As a matter of fact, the only color on her entire person was her blood red fingernail polish catching the sun. She looked like she had emerged from a coffin hidden deep in the recesses of a Transylvanian castle.

She opened the passenger door and sat beside Latrine, embracing her and kissing both cheeks.

"How are you, girl?" Cunny asked.

"Aren't you hot?"

"Not like temperature-wise. But yeah, I'm hot otherwise." Cunny buckled her seatbelt, although her corset was probably stiff enough to restrain her in the event of an accident.

Latrine drove off and cranked up Celine's "I'm Alive," and to her delight, Cunny started singing along. Latrine started to get a little giddy and slapped her leg.

"You're a Celine fan?"

"I like me some Celine every now and then. Sometimes I even listen to her French stuff. I have no idea what she's saying, but it sounds pretty and all." Cunny lowered the visor over the passenger seat and examined herself in the mirror. "Wait! OMG! Is that where you got your name? Latrine Dion?"

Her own reflection had apparently led her to that epiphany.

"Yes! Yes, of course," said Latrine, without a hint of sarcasm. She started to agree with Peyton that Cunny was a wee bit of a dafty, but liking Celine was an indication of a natural aptitude for good taste.

"I like everyone really. Mariah. Whitney. Dolly. Shania. Kylie. Madonna. Cher. So many."

Latrine smiled as her eyes were drawn to Cunny's unavoidable cleavage. "By the way, your titties look bloody brilliant."

"Thanks! OMG that's like so nice of you to say. I had them done last year. They changed my life."

Latrine continued to steal glances at them as she drove. "I thought they were illegal on the contest circuit."

"Nope. They overturned that rule. As soon as they did, a whole bunch of queens got them. The doctor who did them retired early."

"How much did they cost, if you don't mind my asking?"

"$8,000. I think you can get them cheaper, but I went to one of the really good surgeons. Duffy recommended him to me. When are you getting fake titties?"

"Oh, I don't have the money right now. Peyton and I are saving up for a house."

"That's so sweet. You're going to be like a happily married couple with a white picket fence."

"We'd like that." Latrine smiled, imagining her suburban spread. She pictured a modest two-story home with Georgian features to remind her of Edinburgh. Symmetry was a requirement. A Scottish-blue door in the middle to offset the red brick. A window above. Two windows on either side of the door. A green lawn that sloped downhill to their white picket fence. Peyton in the yard, mowing the grass in his kilt as she tended to her flowers in her Norma Rae do-rag.

"Well, as soon as you buy your house, you need to get fake titties."

"Are they really that necessary?"

"You saw how many of the queens had them at local competition. Ina Godda has them, and she keeps on winning."

"Right." Latrine tried to mask her rage at the mere mention of Evil Godda's name. "Hers look dreadful though."

"I heard a rumor once that she tried to breastfeed her nephew with them."

Latrine let out a cackle. "That bitch is nutters. Hey, if I ever get them, will you help me go pick them out?"

"Like totally," she said. "Shopping spree! OMG I think you'd be so much fun to shop with. You're like foreign and stuff. I bet you have different tastes."

"We do."

"Yay." Cunny grabbed Latrine's right hand off the steering wheel and held it. "I have an international friend. We can totally eat at the International House of Pancakes too. You can like point to your country's flag while we eat sausage and eggs."

"If Peyton were here, he'd say 'Cunny, this is the beginning of a beautiful friendship.'"

"That's really sweet. Did he get that from a greeting card?"

"No, it's uh… Nevermind. Want to listen to some more Celine?"

"Sure."

After ten minutes of driving and singing along to the soaring voice of the Canadian songstress, they arrived at Rhiannon's Reading Room, which looked like it was probably just a room in Rhiannon's house. The place was reminiscent of a barracks used to house war criminals in Cuba during the Cold War. It was a white concrete block bungalow with black bars on the windows. Her garden—if you want to call it that—was a few shrubs, some desiccated flowers baking in the heat, and a mass of light-colored pebbles overrun with weeds.

"This is the place?" Latrine looked at the address on the prize certificate.

"Love don't live here anymore, girl."

Latrine placed the van in park, and they got out, adjusting themselves and fixing their wigs as they crept toward the front door, both unnerved at what could be lurking behind it. Was Rhiannon into some strange fetishes? Was her house a manifestation of *50 Shades of Grey?* What was going on behind those windows with the shades drawn?

They approached the door and rang the bell, which chimed as a Middle-Eastern melody. After a moment, Rhiannon opened the door. Latrine and Cunny attempted a smile in spite of the ghastly attire that greeted them. Rhiannon's unruly hair cascaded down over a mass of glass beads hung around her neck. Latrine supposed the beads were meant to accentuate the salmon-pink gauze caftan reaching to the floor. Giant polished stones adorned her hands, but their bold purple hues clashed with her orange nail polish.

"Hello," said Cunny and Latrine in unison.

"My girls. I'm so excited to see you." Rhiannon opened her outer door and invited them inside. She kissed them on both cheeks like they were back in Europe, somewhere on the continent. They stepped inside and were instantly transported into what looked like the plush gypsy version of Mary Poppin's purse.

"Wow! This place looks so different inside," said Cunny.

Latrine couldn't stop looking around. What on the outside was a stark, unadorned, bleak shed of a house was on the inside a plush, colorful, warm den. The walls were covered in fabric of deep purple. The carpet—a deep shade of red, adorned with Asiatic patterns on its edges. The furniture—laden with plush velvet and satin pillows, all in various shades of red wine, like a cask exploded and drenched the room with a rare amontillado. Deep purple swags of fabric radiated from the giant amethyst-colored crystal chandelier hanging in the center of the room like an award-winning Chihuly exhibition.

"Can I offer you a spot of tea?" Rhiannon asked in a faux British accent.

"I think that would be quite lovely." Latrine echoed the inflection.

"I love when people talk all British," Cunny added. "Even though you're Irish."

Rhiannon knit her brow. "I thought you were Scottish."

"She's Irish," Cunny corrected.

"No, no. I'm Scottish. That's different from Irish." Latrine was smile-masking.

"Oh. Whoopsies."

They chuckled. A friendly chuckle. A guffaw of sorts. They were new friends. Latrine felt like if it were anyone else, she'd sever Cunny's head and mount it on a pike as her people have been wont to do throughout history.

They sat down to a lovely cup of Earl Grey being poured from a silver service into delicately painted tea cups. Rhiannon sat across from them at a small table near the glass monstrosity dangling from the ceiling. They sipped their tea delicately. Very posh, they were.

Cunny placed her cup down and cleared her throat. "When are we going to start the reading?"

Latrine smiled, a bit embarrassed of her American friend's brazenness. Interrupting tea was just not something that was done where she was from, despite her own growing impatience.

"We can start now." Rhiannon got up and brought over some sheets of paper and a deep purple velour pillow laden with sparkling crystals: her own personal version of the Crown Jewels, it seemed. Rhiannon's Rhinestones. Between the crystals was a silver pen she picked up—one of those expensive pens for which you have to buy special refill ink. Latrine could feel her skepticism nagging her from the inside, but she put on a smiling face of anticipation to match Cunny's.

Rhiannon looked up at the two of them. "Now then. Who would like to go first?"

"Me!" Latrine's hand flew into the air before Cunny could even open her mouth.

"Okay, Latrine. Close your eyes."

"Should she leave the room?" Latrine nodded in Cunny's direction.

Rhiannon narrowed her eyes at the suggestion. "I'm a seasoned pro, Latrine. I can do this with an audience. Now I'm going to use this pen to put me into a trance. You never know what can happen when I go into a trance. I see things. I see many, many things. Are you ready?"

"I'm ready." Latrine closed her eyes. She felt her heart pounding, rhythmically chanting her zeal—her wants, her desires. Warm positive energy coursed through her veins, and Rhiannon hadn't even started yet.

"Just relax. Breathe in through your nostrils and out through your mouth."

Latrine took a deep breath—in through the nose, out through the mouth, like she had a cold stethoscope flush against her chest. She heard the sound of Rhiannon's pen on the paper. She couldn't hear the pen actually leave the paper. Just long strokes. She thought what was being drawn might be circular.

"I'm picking up some positive energy here. I can feel it coursing through your veins."

Latrine's excitement started to build. Rhiannon was feeling the same energy she felt.

"I see big things from you. Positive things. I feel powerful energy coming from you."

Latrine was intrigued. She couldn't help it. She felt her knees bouncing and her face morphing into a smile. Positivity was the word she wanted to hear. Positivity was how she chose to live her life. Positivity was what she believed would save the world. She wanted to be a beacon of positivity. She wanted to hear more. She internally begged for more positivity.

"I can feel you working hard and then succeeding at it. Yes."

Latrine was on the edge of her seat, convinced Rhiannon was imbuing her with more positivity.

"I can feel that you need to live in the moment. You shouldn't be waiting on things. You should be living 100% for the present. The present is where your power is. Such power. Such awesome power. I can feel your power. Yes. Yes. Yes!"

Latrine echoed her. "Yes. Yes. Yes!"

"Such power. Yes. Yes! Yes!"

"Yes! Yes! Yes! Yes! Yes!" Latrine felt her whole body surging, rushing with heat, with energy, with excitement, with ecstasy. She saw herself dancing and twirling on stage. She felt the unceasing adulation from her legion of fans. "Yes! Yes! Yes!"

"No!"

Latrine opened her eyes.

Rhiannon deflated. "Let me try to get it back. I was seeing big things for you, Latrine. Big, powerful things, and then it all went black."

She closed her eyes and began waving the crystals around. Latrine kept her eyes open, remaining vigilant due to the sudden interruption of the reading, searching for whatever had caused Rhiannon to "no" her. Latrine looked down at the paper and saw that indeed her pen was making circular strokes—strokes in the shape of two breasts. A tale of two titties had apparently been read.

"Ah yes. I think that's it. I believe I see it again. Big things. Big things for you, Latrine." Rhiannon put the pen down, a less enthusiastic vocalization of what had just transpired. Without missing a beat, she turned to Cunny. "And now for you, Cunty."

"Cunny." Cunny sounded offended.

"Oh for stars, I apologize," said Rhiannon. Latrine normally laughed at such a schadenfreude type of moment, but she couldn't stop thinking about how quickly Rhiannon turned before her reading was finished. *It all went black? Was she going to die? Be in a coma?*

Just as she was about to gain the strength to ask for clarity, Rhiannon began Cunny's reading. She again drew in circular patterns, vertically first, then horizontally, like she was sketching a tornado or a whirlpool. "Oh my. What have we here?"

Cunny opened her eyes. "What?"

"Sh!" snapped Rhiannon. "Your eyes must remain closed."

Cunny obeyed. The reading continued. Rhiannon continued the circular pattern with her gleaming crystal. Latrine felt nothing coming from it, so she couldn't imagine Cunny was getting any-thing out of it either. Rhiannon didn't even look like she was into it. No heat. No fire. No passion. Nothing. Maybe a dead energy.

"I see… Brilliant things."

Cunny lifted her eyebrows, her eyes still sewn shut.

"You have such power. The pen is searing with energy. Powerful energy. Oh my! What force!"

Cunny's head circled in synch with the strokes of the pen: side-to-side at the neck, head over, head under like she was a Black American woman who had just been cut off on the road and was waving her finger and telling the guilty party what she could do with herself.

"Oh I see it. This is unbelievable. Bigger. Bigger. Unfathomably big. You're going to be huge, Cunny. You're going to be a giant, Cunny! Massive!" Rhiannon paused a moment. The pen paused. Cunny's head stopped moving. A breathless moment. And then the pen moved again, as did Cunny's head, like a cat watching a string swaying back and forth like a pendulum. "I see something else. What is it?"

Latrine was on edge. She wanted to shout *spit it out, bitch!*

"I feel a power overtake me. It's coming on. I see it. You, Cunny. You are marked for greatness! You are marked for greatness!" Rhiannon shouted at the top of her lungs while pounding the table. As her fists pounded, Cunny's head nodded up and down in synch so hard she feared she might get whiplash. And just like that, the pounding stopped. Rhiannon opened her eyes. "I don't know what that means."

Cunny opened her eyes again. "What?"

"That."

"That I'm marked for greatness?" Cunny asked.

Latrine was spooked.

Rhiannon stared off into the distance. "There was such a positive energy."

"I felt it," Cunny added.

"Such a positive energy. Then mystery."

"Mystery?" Cunny's face couldn't conceal her worry.

Latrine's face had already progressed to being completely freaked out. She felt compelled to speak up. "I'm a little curious about what all this means, Rhiannon."

But she ignored Latrine. She ignored Cunny. She sat back in her chair in a trance.

"I feel so empty now." Rhiannon's aura had aged sixty years. She bore the soul of a woman in a parched and decaying wedding dress sitting beside an open fireplace.

Cunny looked completely confused. Latrine placed a hand on her shoulder. "Are you okay?"

"I think so," Cunny said.

"We should go."

"Now?"

"Yes. Go." Rhiannon's voice was a wilted carnation compared to the flourishing fiery orchid from just a few minutes prior. And then she added, "Alone." Only that 'alone' had a little more force, just enough force to launch Cunny and Latrine out of their seats, grabbing their purses as they darted for the door.

"Alone." Rhiannon's voice increased in volume, as if possessed by some inner dynamism. It sounded more like a command than some unconnected expression of her state of being.

They slammed the door behind them, only to meet a rainstorm of biblical proportions. Without an umbrella and with an urgent desire to flee the premises, they decided to sacrifice their coiffed wigs and their *special care* attire and dash to the van. They got inside and slammed the door, completely worn out and breathing so hard they were only one step shy of hyperventilation. Latrine looked at Cunny.

"What the fuck was that?"

Cunny pulled down the visor and looked in the mirror, checking the state of her wig. "I have no idea. It was all going so well and then just splat."

"Splat?"

"Yeah, splat. Like it just… went splat."

"Let's get out of here." Latrine started the van and drove away.

They sat in silence the whole rest of the way back to Cunny's flat, listening to Celine's ballads to mellow the moment. Neither of them had the energy to say anything, and neither of them wanted to acknowledge what had just happened any further. Latrine pondered how they both received bizarre fortunes. She figured Cunny would be thinking the exact same things. *What could all of it mean? Big things? Living in the present?*

Then it dawned on her. 'Living in the present and not waiting for the future' was exactly what Peyton had been telling her all along. That was how to achieve the big things. For the first time in a long time—maybe ever—she thought Peyton was brilliant.

In that moment, she decided not to wait until the next year to try to compete. She needed to seize the day and take out the bitch who stole her spot. Twatla and Duffy needed to be shown just how much they underestimated her. She was the real Countess.

Chapter 3

Ina Godda the Diva always likened dress shopping to going through customs after a long international flight home: You just want get through it as quickly as possible, and you don't want anyone to catch your smuggling of various accessories and accoutrements. She never left a store without enacting what she called "Project Dynamite," though the plan did not actually involve the use of any incendiary devices. It was aptly named because she thought the project worthy of a fireworks show on Independence Day. She shopped for dresses at various boutiques and department stores, accumulating various fabrics she would drape over her arms as she continued to browse. When she was sure nobody was looking, she'd pilfer accessories from bins and clip them with old-fashioned plastic clothespins to the insides of the gowns. They would remain unseen while the checkout clerks folded the materials and placed them into a bag. They remained unfelt because of the garment's often sequin-heavy fabric or durable construction. She believed that although she resembled a wealthy American socialite shopping the Champs-Èlysées, she had a discount queen sensibility. Any diva who was blessed enough to compete so successfully in so many competitions, according to Ina Godda the Diva, must develop strategies for devising head-turning looks on a budget.

Ina Godda believed the responsibility of a diva included much, much more. A diva must have the sewing prowess of a royal tailor, the creative design talents of an Academy Award-winning costume designer, and the color palette of a Renaissance painter. A diva must know how to construct a gown from a stack of cocktail napkins, duct tape, and thread if she needs to, all the while possessing the enchantment to stop gay traffic during the

Pride festivities. That was why Ina Godda was firm in her belief that the gown she bought off the rack didn't mean she ever wore anything bought *off the rack*. A diva knew to view the off the rack piece as a fresh block of clay out of which to sculpt a work of art to rival Donatello—the artist from the Renaissance, not that frightful mess Donatella Versace.

Ina Godda prided herself on once purchasing a banal Jessica Simpson salmon gauze dress at Macy's that, after her design talent and ingenuity, metamorphosed into a shimmering evening gown of velour, sequins, beading, and rhinestones, which dazzled during her Courtney Love "Celebrity Skin" number. Her ironic portrayal of the grunge goddess was not undercut in any way by her resemblance to the cast of "Dynasty." She won the competition. Any diva should know how to craft a meaningful narrative with her clothes and choice of song. Drag Queenery was an artform, one she had mastered to such a great effect she believed she'd be endowed with the title of Duchess for another year, with another chance at the big prize.

She knew she'd made a great Duchess over the past year, and her placement in the top ten Dames was a badge of honor given the hefty competition from San Fran's, New York's, and Chicago's Duchesses. Those cities were home to whole Duchess Dynasties. She had no fears over competing against Cunny Corleone in the Regionals. After having spoken to her in passing over the previous year, they'd been cordial to each other, but Ina Godda believed she'd never had the misfortune of speaking with someone so vacuous. Cunny's sublimely toned periwinkle eyes did little to mask the vacant stare she had as she spoke and as she listened. Her mouth always seemed to be open ever so slightly, like she was trying to breathe lifeblood into every thought so as not to let them stagnate and rust in the vast recesses of her brain.

However, Ina Godda did believe Cunny had some redeeming qualities. She had bold tastes and a penchant for thrilling hair choreography. Good haireography could fool anyone—especially the judges—into believing the dancing was more substantive.

She feared the gays might fall for it, especially since those moves gave Willow Smith a career at the age of nine, whipping her hair back and forth in such frenzy that the strains of the terrible song itself went unnoticed.

Ina Godda got the inkling it wasn't just Cunny she should be afraid of. There was the strong possibility that another region could have another queen just like Cunny. Cunnys could be everywhere. Lifeless, insipid Cunnys. She knew she couldn't forget her worthy adversary from Atlanta, Ms. Blanche BuDois. She was unpredictable. Mercurial. Spasmodic.

It worried Ina Godda that the judges liked the crazy spirit. That sense of unpredictability. They liked to be on edge when a queen was performing. They liked to be surprised. That was where Ina Godda felt she was weak, and it was a virtue she needed to acquire. She scarcely won Duchess last year over Miss Blanche BuDois. If she returned, she'd provide a tough challenge—one that Ina Godda might not be able to conquer again.

Ina Godda was tense, and she needed something to calm herself down. She dug through her cupboards in search of some chamomile tea, but she found none. She lit a cigarette and took a few puffs, but it did little to calm her nerves. She contemplated meeting up with her Marco Polo, the beautiful dildo from the man of her dreams, for a midnight rendezvous. But no. What she needed to do was call Twatla to find out if she knew anything about Blanche BuDois. For once, Marco Polo just wasn't going to be enough to sedate her nervous energy.

She picked up her circa-1950 antique gilded rotary phone and dialed Twatla's number. It had several nines, so it took a few moments. Her nerves rattled the phone in her hand.

"Hello," said Twatla, breathing quite heavily, like she'd run to the phone. Ina Godda expected she did. Everyone raced to the phone when she called.

"Yes, Miss Twatla? This is Ina Godda the Diva calling."

"I know that."

"Miss Twatla, I was just wondering if you heard any news about the Countess of Atlanta."

"Let me put it this way, girl. You have every reason to be afraid."

Ina Godda took a deep breath, trying to suppress a desire to scream. "She won?"

She attempted in vain to plant her feet to the ground instead of bouncing her knees incessantly.

"Countess Blanche BuDois once again," said Twatla.

"And the runner up? What of the runner up?

"Sweet Jesus, are you nervous again, Ina Godda? Girl, you ain't got nothing to worry about. You're safe. You're gonna whoop some Blanche ass this year again, and you ain't gotta worry about the runner up. I mean, I like the queen and all. She's nice. But bitch smokes more crack than Whitney did."

"You really think so?"

"Yes, girl."

Ina Godda smiled. Her nerves were gone. A wave of relief washed over her. She heard Twatla smiling too. And moaning. She heard moaning. And squeaking. She couldn't fathom why she heard moaning and squeaking.

"What's that noise?"

"Would you like to say hello to Duffy?"

An image of hetero-sex flashed through her mind. The searing still frame of Twatla's mounting Duffy burned and branded her brain. What made the image even more scalding was the thought that Twatla might very well still be in drag. There were rumors Duffy enjoyed intimacy with Twatla when she was in women's clothing. A paroxysm of fright jolted Ina Godda, vomit nearly spewing from her mouth. For years, she heard rumors Twatla loved to show off how straight she was by video-taping herself with Duffy and then handing out recordings of them as Christmas presents. But Ina Godda thought the rumors to be utter fabrication given Duffy's status as a respected detective. To her knowledge, no video had actually ever surfaced. However, given that she'd actually at present suffered through a few moments of their intimacy, she had gotten an auditory glimpse of what her anticipated Christmas present might be. She issued an abrupt 'thank you' and issued a Twatla a fond farewell.

Ina Godda hung up the phone and breathed a sigh of imminent success. She believed it was the right time to treat herself. What better way to purge the stench of vaginal intercourse from her head than intimacy with her beloved? She walked down the hallway to the framed poster of her handsome stallion. Marco stared at her in all his pec-tacular shirtlessness. It was officially time for their special midnight rendezvous.

Chapter 4

Latrine burst into the door and saw Peyton sipping a glass of whisky, lost in a film. She stood there for a moment, trying to guess which one it was. It was period. It looked Shakespearean. *Elizabeth* with Cate Blanchett. The choice made her fairly certain he was in a low-stress mood because period pieces required patience. However, given the level of treachery in the plot, it wasn't a completely accurate gauge. The more accurate gauge would be the type of whisky he sipped.

"Ardbeg?" She actually hoped he was drinking something lighter.

"Glenkinchie 12-year."

Glenkinchie. Lowland whisky. Hints of lemon. No hints of peat.

"You're back." Peyton moved the glass side to side, his eyes glued to the telly.

"Aye. I'm back. Not an Islay whisky, right?"

"No. It's not an Islay night."

Latrine knew his drinking a more citrusy whisky likely meant he was amenable to conversation and in a more open-minded mood. He really started drinking the lighter Lowland brands after he met Latrine, something she could take pride in. He'd lightened up. She liked to think she tamed the wild Scotsman, but on occasion, when he was stressed, he still went for the Islay. It was a spectrum, really. Islay meant he was stressed. Lowland meant he was happy. Speyside meant he was horny. Highland meant he was spunky, and Campbelltown—well, that meant he'd cut a bitch. The current Glenkinchie made Latrine feel completely comfortable to raise the subject of taking out Ina Godda the Diva with the reassurance that he wouldn't get belligerent over the memory of what happened at the local competition or tell her *I told you so.*

Latrine stood there for a moment before it dawned on her that perhaps he had had more than one glass of Glenkinchie. After more than two glasses, the mood-ring-whisky-region approach to measuring his demeanor went straight out the window. Before she could muster the courage to steer the conversation in her direction, she turned down the volume on the film. She knew it was rude, but he'd seen it about six times.

"What's the look on your face?" he asked.

"You can tell?"

"Aye. I can always tell when your head's mixed up."

"Aye. My head was mixed up." Latrine sat on the couch beside him, resting her bare feet on the coffee table, her blue-painted toes glistening.

"Was?"

"I've made up my mind."

"About what?" Peyton took another sip.

"I'd like to take out Ina Godda, and I need your help."

Peyton issued a smile. It was the kind of smile that began as a hiccup, then elongated and raised the upper lip before lifting and widening the eyes. Latrine could see the whole facial transformation from genesis to actualization. She could feel the warmth radiating from his countenance. He threw back his glass of Glenkinchie—a brave gesture given its potency. When he kissed her, she got a hint of the lemon the bottle promised—her very own gay whisky tasting.

Peyton went to the liquor cabinet to pour himself another glass. He poured one for her too, which he handed to her on the way back to the couch. They raised their glasses in a toast.

"To winning Duchess Regionals," said Latrine, beating him to the punch.

"And to the $25,000 for the down payment on our new house," he added.

They sipped the whisky, savoring it in their mouths as long as they wanted to savor the moment.

"So how should we do it?" he blurted out after a wee bit of silence.

A montage of pranks and hijinks played in Latrine's head, a 3D movie of gay subterfuge, like a gay James Bond, but instead of the sexy siren Pussy Galore, it would be the Scottish-Vietnamese stud Dick Dat Mann.

"We could invite her to tea and put laxative in it."

Peyton took a sip of his whisky, focusing strongly on the idea. "I think that's a wee bit cliché. Besides, she'd probably be expecting something to happen if you were to invite her to tea anyway. She would keep watching you."

"You're right." Latrine took a sip, hoping its hints of lemon would bestow mental clarity upon her. "We could cut holes in the crotches of all her dresses."

"What good would that do? We break in, cut a couple of dresses up. She goes out and either buys more or sews them up. She's a drag queen; of course she knows how to sew."

Latrine felt a bit lost. Unintelligent, even. Peyton was more street smart than she was. He was more adept at getting things done his way—a born strategizer.

"Wait. So we break into her house." He took a pause, definitely on the verge of an idea. Latrine could see it forming in his eyes, his lips moving as if they were trying to figure out how to articulate it.

"So we vandalize the place?"

"No. Wait." He paused again. It was a few moments before she realized he was actually watching *Elizabeth* on mute. It was at the scene where the one bitch wore the dress that was poisoned before dying.

"We do something to her dress."

"Her dress?"

"Like that. We put something on her dress." He picked up the remote control and replayed the scene.

"No, Peyton. That bitch dies. We don't want her to die."

"But we can still do something to it."

"Well, how are we even supposed to know which dress she's going to wear?" Latrine threw her head back on the couch and massaged the area around her eyes in frustration.

"Aye. Good point. What if we do something to her Marco Polo? If she uses her Marco Polo before the competition, she'll be uncomfortable. She'll fuck everything up and lose."

Latrine perked up. "What are we going to do to it?"

She stared at him, watching him think, watching the wheels turn. But before she could let him finish processing the thoughts, the flash of an image from her Botany class at university played in her mind. It happened so fast, she involuntarily blurted out "nettles!"

"Nettles?"

"Aye, nettles. Do they have nettles in the U.S.?"

"I'm not sure, but I do know they have poison ivy." Peyton picked up his mobile as if to look it up.

"Poison Ivy. That's perfect actually. We coat her Marco Polo with poison ivy. Maybe she'll be so rashy that she won't even want to compete."

In that pause, she got an image of what poison ivy in the bum might feel like. A shudder crept up Latrine's spine, and it looked like Peyton felt it too.

"Ouch."

"Yes," said Latrine. For an ever-so-brief moment, she could feel Ina Godda's pain and suffering. It was almost enough for her to realize they might be going down the wrong path.

But then Peyton smiled at her. "You're right. That's perfect. I'm proud of you."

He lifted his glass toward her and took a sip of his Glenkinchie. Peyton liked the idea. That was important. Seeing Peyton happy made her happy. And the fact that he was proud of her? Even better. Any reservations about any malice in their attack dissipated.

Latrine stared at the film as it continued to play. "She was complicit in the injustice perpetrated against me."

Peyton smiled like he was pretending to understand what she just said. Latrine sipped her whisky, sucking her lips together to savor the taste. She thought about how diseased Ina Godda's mind was anyway. How totally nutters she was. She sat on her metaphorical throne like an inbred regent poised to drive her queendom into the ground. She was the updated version of King George's madness, unfit for rule. Her subjects didn't trust her to put on a good show. They didn't have faith in her like they had faith in Latrine during her debut. They wanted Latrine to win. The tepid response to the results said it all. The people wanted Latrine as their Countess to represent them at Regionals.

Chapter 5

Peyton picked up his mobile and looked up the number to Hamburger Mary's before placing the call.

A rather nasaly Southern red-neck drawl answered. "Hamburger Mary's. This is Trayla Park speaking."

Peyton wanted to laugh at the image of a banjo player from *Deliverance* flashing in his head, but he kept it in. "Trayla, my wife and I are coming to lunch today, and we're wondering if Ina Godda the Diva is working."

"I'm sorry. It's a little difficult to understand you. Ina Godda will be in at 11 today. She's working the lunch shift."

"Oh good. She's our favorite." Peyton wanted to vomit after he heard himself say the words out loud.

"Did you say favorite? That's really weird."

"Why?"

"Because she's nobody's favorite. She's creative and all, but she's a terrible waitress. People usually get her once as a server before they ask not to be seated in her section ever again."

"Oh. Well, we bloody love her as a waitress." It got easier to lie after he heard the truth.

"You're foreign. I guess the service is bad in Dublin, so you don't have too much to go on."

Peyton hung up the phone and tried to keep himself from hurling it at the ground.

"Let's go," he said to Latrine.

They climbed into the van and drove a bit out of town to find a wooded area. The Withlacoochee State Park sounded appropriate to harvest poison ivy for the bitch's man-coochee. The sounds of the violin solo in Celine Dion's "To Love You More" masked the silence. It was the only song playing for the entire journey. Latrine had it on repeat. Peyton looked over at his Love as she lip-synched with all her soul. He figured she thought herself as performing show-stopping karaoke every time, despite her single-octave range. A smile crossed his face whenever she reached the last note of the song, which had to have exceeded fifteen times by the time he pulled off the road. He followed a gravel road, focusing hard on where might be a good spot to find some poison ivy.

Finding an area with a wealth of undergrowth, he parked the car and unbuckled his seatbelt. "Let's go."

"Let me just finish this song. You know I can't just cut Celine off."

Peyton sighed and waited, not that he found it too much of a problem. He was used to it. After Celine belted her last note—and Latrine lifted her arms in triumph—they got out of the car and started walking.

"Did you bring the paper towels and plastic bags?" Peyton asked.

"Aye."

They walked a bit down a path. Peyton looked over at Latrine as she swatted bugs away, moaning and grunting like she was hiking around Loch Ness on a balmy summer day.

"What are these? Bloody midges?"

"Do they have midges in North America?" Peyton barely paid attention to her dramatics, looking down at the various vines and undergrowth covering the forest floor.

"How do you even know where to find this poison ivy anyway?"

"I just know."

"I don't think we're going to find any."

"Will you have a little fucking faith in me?"

Latrine paused. "I'm sorry. Of course I have faith in you"

Peyton realized he probably shouldn't have snapped, but his annoyance grew like Prince Harry's erection around a Vegas stripper. He didn't like to apologize to Latrine too often. It gave her too much power. She needed to know where her place was. She was there to look pretty. He was the leader.

A thin patch of weedy plants caught his eye, and he squatted down to study one particular specimen. He took out his phone, pulled up an image of the same plant, and placed the phone beside it to compare.

"These look like the ones," he said. "Hand me the towels and the plastic bag, will you?"

Latrine did as was requested. "Just mind yourself."

Peyton got to work harvesting the poison ivy, placing it in the bag and minding his hands and skin so as not to touch anything. After taking a few stalks of the stuff, they hiked back to the van and got back on the road.

"This isn't going to hurt her too badly, right?" asked Latrine after a few moments of silence.

"No. It'll just make her itchy for a few days and make it so she can't compete due to a rash in her arsehole and all over her bum."

The ride to Ina Godda's was fairly lengthy given how far out of town they had traveled. Latrine was quiet for most of the way. Peyton assumed she was nervous. His anxiety was building too: He feared she might lose her head and flake out. They pulled up beside Ina Godda's building and parked the van. All that was left to do was stake out the place to see which flat was hers and be sure she left.

"If we weren't trying to be so stealthy, I'd say to thank Cunny for telling us where she lives—even the building—without having to ask for it. The dafty's good for something after all." Peyton looked over at Latrine, smiling at his own joke. She didn't respond. Instead, she stared straight ahead.

Peyton could sense his fear was starting to play out. He needed to be sure she was cooperative. "Hamburger Mary's said her shift starts at eleven. It's not too far from here, so we should see her leave."

"I don't know which car is hers," said Latrine.

"I don't know either. That's why we got here early. To make sure she leaves."

They sat in an awkward silence.

Latrine reached for the dial. "Can we put some music on?"

Peyton smacked her hand away. "Are you gone batshit?" That'll bring attention over to us. We can't have her looking over here."

"I know that, Peyton. Just softly. Low volume."

"No!"

"Fine," she said.

Peyton noticed her pout. "Aw, don't get scunnered now."

"I'm not scunnered."

Peyton slammed his hands on the top of the steering wheel. "Jesus! What is taking her so long?"

"She's probably bouncing up and down on Marco Polo before work."

"Marco Polo's probably coming out of her mouth by now."

After a moment, Ina Godda emerged from her door. Peyton was in awe of what she wore in broad daylight. He assumed she thought she was Beyoncé or something. Clad in a hunter green sequined cocktail dress with a plunging neckline, enormous silver bangles clinked on both arms. Her hair was pulled back away from the face, complete with an explosion of massive curls in the back that must have taken all night to set. Her heels were at least twelve centimeters high, and they were platforms on top of it all. He turned to Latrine in shock.

"Hamburger Mary's must have a liberal dress code for their queens. Isn't all that fake hair unsanitary? And how the fuck does she walk in those?"

"I don't know. She must spill a lot of mimosas," Latrine said, her mood somber.

"Look at how she's walking. Like a slut."

Latrine played with a bracelet on her wrist. "I wish I had a dress like that."

"She's got a butt plug shoved up her bum for sure."

"She was walking like that when she was named Countess."

Peyton smiled. Latrine was perceptive. They both watched as Ina Godda got into her car. She opened the door and placed her handbag on the roof—a delicate operation. With a tug at her dress and a flick of her hair, it dawned on Peyton that somehow she had to drive in those shoes. He doubted she'd take them off. She didn't seem to be the type of queen who would carry a pair of flats as alternative footwear in her handbag. She got into the car and closed the door behind her. As she backed out, she turned her head to look behind her. Peyton and Latrine ducked down before they could be seen.

She drove off. They sat up. Latrine stared straight ahead.

"You're not chickening out, are you?"

"I'm just nervous."

"So you're chickening out then."

"No. I'm not."

"Good. Because I shouldn't have to remind you of why we're doing this. You're the Countess. You'll be the Duchess."

And with that, Latrine got out of the van and slammed the door behind her. She stormed toward Ina Godda's flat before stopping half way and turning around. It looked like the surge of energy was over and she was retreating.

"Are you fucking coming?" she asked.

Peyton was initially stunned at the profanity, but he was proud. He got out and followed behind her. "Lead the way."

And she did.

• • •

Latrine knew Peyton was right. Ina Godda never stood up for her. Instead, she sat idly by and participated in the pilfering.

They approached the door to her shitty flat just as some shirtless bloke in gym shorts with glistening pecs stepped outside to walk his dog. It was a Golden Retriever who growled at Peyton.

"Sorry about that. He isn't normally like this. Golden Retrievers are usually good dogs."

"That's okay." Peyton was trying to be as amiable as possible. Latrine froze.

The neighbor bloke nodded in the direction of Ina Godda's flat. "I don't think she's home. She usually plays her music really loud, and it just stopped a minute ago. I heard her door slam.”

His dog kept yapping at Peyton, its leash fully extended.

“Angus. Calm down.”

“Angus. Angus is a pretty dog,” said Peyton, approaching it. The dog barked ferociously.

“I seriously don’t know what’s wrong with him. Down, Angus.” Angus seemed to relax for a moment, sniffing around Latrine’s left shoe.

The neighbor bloke looked at Peyton. “Hey, if you see my neighbor, tell him or her or whatever to keep the music down. It’s really annoying.”

“What the bloody fuck?” Latrine took a step back as Angus lifted his leg, urinating on her shoes.

“Angus!”

Latrine grabbed Peyton and led him over to the van.

“I’m sorry, guys!” The neighbor bloke shouted after them.

They climbed back inside and waited for a moment. Latrine took off her shoes and threw them out the window. “I can’t believe I just got a fucking Golden Retriever Shower.”

She climbed into the back of the van and picked out a pair of standby heels. The dog had obviously sensed what they were about to do. It was a sign. They should just go home and forget the whole thing. She had to tell Peyton.

Peyton kept a watchful eye on the neighbor’s moves as Latrine climbed up front.

“This is wrong. We shouldn’t be doing this.”

“Shut your hole. Don’t be put off by that dog’s *50 Shades of Yellow*. We’re going to do this. Ina Godda’s own neighbor even hates her. Everyone hates her. She deserves this.”

Peyton kept vigilant as the bloke went back inside and closed the door behind him.

“Let’s go.”

They slinked up to Ina Godda’s door. Peyton reached into his trousers, took out a bobby pin, and began picking the lock.

Latrine figured he'd be a master at something like that. All the poor Weegees were. But for some reason, he encountered difficulty. She assumed it was the bobby pin. He wasn't used to maneuvering small things into tight holes. She tried her level best to wait patiently for a split second, but the thought of Ina Godda's neighbor coming out again started a panic, and she nudged him out of the way, squatting down on her knees.

"Give me the bobby pin, you spastic," she said with enough force to knock down the door herself. She didn't think he knew how much he was getting in the way. With just a few twirls of the pin, the door unlocked.

"If you don't win Duchess, I think you have a future in breaking and entering," said Peyton.

"I thought you said I was going to win."

"Of course you will," he said.

Latrine focused on the task at hand so they could get the fuck out of there as soon as possible. Her hands shook as they crept inside, making sure to close the door gingerly so the neighbor bloke wouldn't suspect anything.

Cold air and the scent of bubble gum assulted them. The bitch had the thermostat set at sixty-eight degrees Fahrenheit, which Latrine mentally translated into Celsius. Ina Godda must've figured herself for Joan Crawford or some aging starlet who needed the temperature at a specific setting to keep her skin taut.

The bubble gum oder came from a gumball machine loaded only with pink gumballs in her foyer. But it was a framed poster of a hot nude man with sparkly blue eyes and golden blonde hair that captured their attention. The autograph over his shoulder looked like a five-year-old scribbled it with sharpie.

"To my favorite queen—love Marco."

"That's her Marco Polo, huh?" said Peyton. "That's the man behind the myth. I bet Ina Godda never even got this poster signed by him. She probably scribbled it herself and told people he did it."

Latrine stared at Marco's crystalline eyes. His gaze reminded her of Peyton's when they first met. "He's pretty sexy actually. I can see why she gets nutters over him."

She could tell Peyton didn't like hearing that at all.

"Aye. He's sexy. But he's a gloryhole that's stretched to capacity."

"Jealous?"

"I'm not jealous of that no-talent bloke. I can fuck better than he can. I'm sure."

They segued into the living room area, complete with a disco ball hanging from the ceiling. The walls were a pepto-bismol pink, and the floor's linoleum tiles in a black and white checkered pattern over which a pink shag area rug rested. Her black and white couches and chairs were definitely rejects from the Ikea creative team, because nobody in their right mind would want those pieces. On the walls hung more images of her beloved Marco, including one in the form of an Andy Warhol-type painting. As a matter of fact, Marco hung among lithographs of actual Andy Warhol paintings. There were Campbell's Soup cans. Marilyn Monroe. Elizabeth Taylor. Michael Jackson. Jacqueline Kennedy Onassis. It looked like Studio 54 got the runs, and Ina Godda decided to call it her living room. It was all so tacky, but it definitely cost a pretty penny. Latrine tried to hide that she wanted Studio 54 to take a shit for her too.

At an opening in the wall to the kitchen, two barstools sat before a mini soda shop-themed counter with empty glasses for Coke floats. A jukebox stood in the corner, ready to turn the place into an American sock hop, or at least turn it into some mishmash of *Paris is Burning* and *American Graffiti*. Latrine thought it was cute. She wanted to turn her living room into a fucked up combination of two movies with no plot. After approaching the jukebox, she started flipping through some titles.

Peyton walked up beside her. "Any Celine?"

"No. Bitch has no taste."

"Let's stop wasting time then. Where's her bedroom?"

Peyton opened a door off to the side of the living room, where they encountered the sacred bedchamber. They walked into what appeared to be where the Amazon Rainforest went after it started disappearing. That room Latrine didn't want a copy of, and it snapped her out of the haze of wanting anything else Ina Godda had. Any trace of jealousy morphed into disgust over poor taste. An explosion of animal print numbed her eyes to the point of a migraine. It was a genuine feline fiasco. Her bed? Leopard. Her pillows? Leopard. Her carpet? More leopard. Her walls? Portraits of leopards. And on her desk? A stuffed snow leopard, which completely clashed with the rest of the fauna in the room. Wrong species of leopard.

"I think she likes cats," said Peyton.

"Dead ones."

"She's like Cruella De Vil," he said.

"That's dogs."

"Oh."

Latrine hurried to a door in the corner. "Focus. The closet's over here, I think. I bet she keeps her Marco Polo in the closet."

"No. I bet she keeps it in her nightstand." Peyton opened the drawers in both of them. "You're right. It's not here. I don't like it when dildos are in the closet. They need to come out."

Latrine rolled her eyes. Wit was never Peyton's thing.

Ina Godda had a walk-in closet the size of another bedroom. Latrine wondered if it was an actual spare bedroom she converted. The closet was organized into dragwear and non-dragwear, and it was color-coded according to the spectrum of the rainbow. Her shoes were arranged by height, with the tallest platform heels to the right all the way down to the smaller heels on the left. A sewing machine sat in one corner beside a well-organized boutique of ribbons, textiles, and every other type of accessory that you'd find at a JoAnn Fabric.

Latrine sighed aloud. She thought the bitch was ridiculous. Ina Godda didn't need that $5,000 prize money she stole from her for more gowns. She had enough gowns. Perhaps there was even some cotton growing out on the terraces to make her own on top of it all. Latrine could feel her aggravation building. She just wanted to rip those dresses down and tear them to shreds, but she knew that with her apparent sewing prowess, Ina Godda would just stitch them all together like a brand new Amazing Technicolor Dreamcoat.

"I don't think we're going to find it here," said Peyton.

Latrine had actually stopped thinking about Marco Polo. She stared at the fucking dresses. All of them. The mother-fucking dresses that Ina Godda didn't deserve. Latrine wanted the Studio 54 room. She even wanted the leopard room so she could tame it. She deserved those dresses. She deserved those heels. She deserved that fucking fabric. Her breath got shallower and quicker. The injustice. The sheer injustice. Who would right this wrong? Nobody. Nobody but them.

"I have another idea." Latrine grit her teeth. Her fists were clenched. "Let's go back to your original plan. Let's make like *Elizabeth* and coat her competition gowns."

Peyton smiled at her and walked over to her side, placing his hand on her shoulder like she'd just won something big. "Which ones do you think they are?"

"I don't even know where to begin, so we'll have to use the poison ivy sparingly," Latrine replied, trying to temper a bout of oncoming frustration.

"Let's think then. What color did she wear to the last one?" asked Peyton.

"Oh, fuck it. It's not about the color. Even if we limit the poison ivy we have to one, including eliminating the color from the local competition, she still has five colors of the rainbow from which to choose." Latrine grunted, allowing the frustration to come out but minding it enough so the neighbor bloke wouldn't hear.

"Keep your head!" Peyton shout-whispered to counter her outburst. "That just means we need to trick her into wearing a specific dress that we taint."

Latrine walked out of the closet and sat on Ina Godda's jungle-cruise of a bed.

"What if I invite her to a party and guilt her into coming? I can suggest it be a theme. Cunny can help me convince her to come," said Latrine.

"Aye. I could help with the invitation," said Peyton.

"No. She hates you. She wouldn't come if she knew you were going to be there. You can come, but I just can't tell her that."

"Fuck her then," he said.

"You know what? I'll invite her to tea at the Inverness Tea Room. I'll invite Cunny too. We'll theme it as Kentucky Derby. Every American queen watches the Kentucky Derby."

"Is it even the time of year for the Kentucky Derby?" he asked.

"Who cares? Let's see what she's got that she'd wear to that fucking thing."

Latrine reentered the closet and began flipping through a series of dresses of all kinds of materials and textures. Velvet evening gowns. Satin ball gowns. Taffeta wedding gowns. Indeed, the bitch was weird. She probably dressed in the gowns to profess her love to Marco Polo just before she fantasized about a honeymoon in which he ravished her. Ina Godda also had a pastel shade of every color in the rainbow and seemingly one of every light-textured fabric.

Peyton pointed. "Those ones."

"Aye. Anything pastel. The Kentucky Derby spectators wear pastel dresses in light fabrics with big hats draped over their heads. They definitely are taking after the Brits with that tradition."

"Aye. I imagine it's like participating in a royal wedding to them," he said.

"They wish they were us. Hand me a pair of gloves," said Latrine.

He gave her a pair of durable gloves made for hair-coloring. She put them on. He donned his own pair. They looked like doctors prepping for surgery. She held out her hand as if to request a scalpel.

"Poison?"

He handed her a few leaves of poison ivy, and she selected the first pastel dress she saw: a blue muslin. She rubbed the inside of the dresses liberally with the leaves before moving on to the next pastel.

"We're going to be here for a while, huh?" Peyton asked.

"Aye. A while. Maybe you'd better stay on the lookout for if she comes home. You're the sentry for the day."

•   •   •

Nothing got past the sentry. Peyton stood beside Ina Godda's bedroom door, listening out for the sounds of approaching heels. He looked back at Latrine, who toiled away in the closet. Only the sound of leaves rubbing against the different types of fabrics could be heard. It was a sound reminiscent of sandpaper—like she was sanding down Ina Godda's ego so the rest of the world wouldn't get splinters.

Peyton stood at the door.

He stared at the floor.

He kept standing there.

He stood there some more.

Being the sentry was boring. Peyton started looking around her bedroom, tinkering with things, gawking at the tacky ugliness of it all. Over her bed was a giant mirror, he assumed so she could watch herself as some bloke shoved it in her mantwat. The mirror was surrounded by the kind of lights you'd see in a dressing room backstage at the Parliament House. He opened and closed some drawers in her desk, wondering if it was where she kept her mythical Marco Polo. Instead, he only found some condoms and lube—befuddled that she wouldn't keep it in the most logical and convenient of places, by her laptop computer.

He looked around the room more, the constant sound of ivy brushing up against satin as background noise.

"Everything going okay?" Peyton asked.

"Aye."

Peyton walked toward her dresser. Figurines of various wildcats were arranged in a pack: Leopards, bobcats, cheetahs. They all surrounded an elephant figurine. Poor elephant. Didn't know what she had coming to her. To the left of the scene from *National Geographic* was an ornate gilded music box. It looked like something found at the Louvre, something that Marie Antoinette might have used to lull her kids to sleep. Peyton traced his finger over the gilded monogram "M." M? M for Marie? Was this actually Marie Antoinette's? That bitch could afford an antique Marie Antoinette music box? Marie Antoinette couldn't even afford a Marie Antoinette music box in her final days.

Peyton opened it up, and to his surprise, he heard no music playing. All he saw was a button. A button that stared at him. For a wee moment, he thought he saw a face on it, and the face smiled at him, begging him to press it. So he did. A series of soft, filtered track lights illuminated the dresser area. The area on which the pack of wildcats attacked the elephant lifted up and folded over with the cats glued firmly in place. The sounds of opera sopranos singing the chorus of "Ina Gadda da Vida" in perfect harmony filled the room, like he was listening to an electric Bach concert at Royal Albert Hall. Up from the recess of the dresser lifted a pedestal, on which sat, in all its splendor and glory, her precious Marco Polo.

Latrine rushed out of the closet, beckoned by the angelic surround-sound.

"What the fuck is that? Is someone here?" she asked before her eyes focused on Marco Polo. "Is that…?"

"It's got to be her Marco fucking Polo," Peyton confirmed. They stared at the thing for a few moments, unable to take their eyes away from it. It was actually very pretty—and husband-sized. It wasn't too big. It wasn't too small. It was just right. It was circumcised, with lovely proportions. It even had just the right amount of vein action on the sides.

"It's like silicon splendor."

Latrine's eyes burned with jealousy. Peyton couldn't tell if she was horny or angry.

"Are you okay?" Peyton asked.

"I'm feeling just fucking bonny," she said, gritting her teeth.

"Go ahead and finish up with her dresses. I'll put this away."

"No. Wait." She disappeared for a moment into the closet and came out with a fresh leaf in her gloved hand.

"I like the way you're thinking. It's a good thing I still have on these gloves; I bet this thing is freshly used." Peyton picked it up and held it about ten centimeters from his face, taking a whiff. He scratched off a little brown speck on the head with the tip of his glove. "Aye. Fucking freshly used."

"Give it to me." Latrine grabbed it from his hand. She coated the Marco Polo with the poison ivy, rubbing vigorously around the tip.

Peyton watched as she placed it back on the pedestal. "Put everything back to how you found it, and let's get out of here."

Latrine disappeared into the closet. Peyton pressed the button, and the angelic music returned as Marco Polo retracted down into its den. But it wasn't so simple. Marco Polo stopped before being completely retracted. Peyton pushed the button again. Nothing. His panic led him to say a small prayer. He pushed into the head with his glove, like he was checking for a pulse. He stepped back and studied the situation for a moment before trying the button one more time. The pedestal resumed its retraction and disappeared completely.

"That fucking music," Latrine said from the closet. "We're going to have to sneak out the back door and head in the other direction. The bloke next door thinks she's not home, and now that bloody music is playing. We can't be seen."

They grabbed their belongings and fled the flat via the back door. Peyton was pretty sure they were as unseen as pale Scottish ninjas against the White Cliffs of Dover. They climbed into the van and did not say a word to each other. Something had come over Latrine. Something strange. Peyton couldn't help but feel like she was finally taking out her anger on Ina Godda, and deservedly so. He looked at her. She seemed to be fuming. He thought he'd let her calm down a wee bit before saying anything to her. It was a new side of Latrine, a side he liked. He turned the key in the ignition, and they drove off in silence.

Chapter 6

Cunny was in the middle of brushing out one of her blonde wigs and jamming out to Kylie Minogue's "Get Outta My Way" when the doorbell rang. She seldom had visitors, let alone those who arrived unannounced, so the sound was a bit perplexing. After gingerly placing her wig on a mannequin head, she shuffled over to the front door in her favorite pair of white Hello Kitty fuzzy slippers, peering through the peephole.

She gasped, quickly opening the door. It was Latrine.

"OMG!" She kissed Latrine on both cheeks. "I'm so happy to see you."

"Cunny, you wee lass. I was just in the neighborhood, and I got a thought. May I come in?"

Cunny nodded and led her to the living room. Latrine took a seat, not really taking in the décor despite having never been inside her place. She looked more eager to dive right in and tell Cunny what she'd been thinking about.

"I was just straightening this wig to start fresh with it." Cunny picked up the mannequin head and continued to brush it out. "I'm thinking curls. OMG, can I get you something to drink? I totally forgot to ask."

"No, it's okay." Latrine smiled. "So, let me tell you about this fabulous idea."

Cunny stopped brushing for a moment. She hung on to her every word, watching like a dog waiting for a treat.

"I was thinking we should do High Tea. There's a fabulous new place downtown called the Inverness Tea Room. It's a little off the beaten path. It's on an upper floor of an office building, and it's got this lovely terrace where we can sit outside and sip all afternoon and eat scones and have the full tea service. What do you say?"

Out of everything Cunny could have anticipated, that was the least she'd expected. Her immediate thought was that High Tea involved smoking weed. She just couldn't connect why you'd have to get high to have tea. She thought that was maybe the origin of the whole 4:20 thing. Maybe 4:20 was when they served High Tea. Either way, Cunny didn't do drugs, but she tried to think about a way to break it gently to Latrine that she wasn't interested.

"I don't know. I'm not really into that." Cunny crossed her legs, her Hello Kitty slipper staring at Latrine while hanging off the ball of her foot, as if Hello Kitty herself were speechless at the suggestion. "I mean, I'm fine if other people do it. Just getting high was never my thing."

Latrine let out a cackle. "No, you wee lass. Oh, that's so cute. High Tea is something we do back home. We've done it for generations. It's very posh—very genteel. High Tea is when friends dress up and look fabulous and sip tea while eating little finger foods."

Cunny's mouth was open as she tried to picture it. She recalled a few fancy British movies and shows where people sat around and drank tea. It was always the rich people who seemed to be able to do it. No poor people ever really drank tea. And this place was tucked away in some office building downtown with a terrace? It must be a thing—a private, exclusive thing. Latrine must be able to get in because she's from that swanky part of Scotland.

Cunny smiled. "Okay. I'll join you since you can get us in."

"Oh, it's—." Latrine paused. "You know what? We should have a theme. Why don't we make it a Kentucky Derby-type afternoon?"

"Is it Kentucky Derby time?" Cunny was vaguely familiar with what that was. She knew it was at least American and not British, and she didn't want that to jeopardize their getting into the Inverness Tea Room.

"Oh, who bloody cares? Who needs it to be the Kentucky Derby to dress that way? In the U.K., we dress formally like that whenever we can. It's just that you Americans only see it fit on Derby Day.

Well, I say we bring it back into fashion year-round. Ladies and queens should dress like it's the Kentucky Derby every time they go to tea." Latrine's passion for the subject was convincing.

"I agree. We should have more occasions to wear a hat, LOL."

"Exactly. Oh, and Cunny?" Latrine leaned forward in her chair. "I think we should make it a threesome."

Cunny giggled. "I haven't done a threeway in a really long time."

"Not that kind, lassie. I mean we invite Ina Godda the Diva."

The giggling stopped abruptly. That was a game-changer. With the problems they had last time they were together, any pleasant afternoon tea was going to be ruined by a whole lot of attitude and snide barbs being traded back and forth between the two of them, and that just wasn't Cunny's favorite thing. She loathed bitchery between queens. But how could she back out and not hurt Latrine's feelings?

Cunny picked up the mannequin and started brushing the blonde wig furiously, avoiding eye contact with Latrine. "Do you think that's a good idea? I mean, you two didn't get along at the Parliament House. She didn't even want to come with us to Rhiannon's when she had a gift certificate and all."

Latrine got up and sat beside Cunny, placing a hand on her thigh. "I really want to make amends with her. I've been beating myself up about what happened between her and Peyton, and I think she thinks I'm partly responsible. I just want her to know there are no hard feelings. Besides, you said yourself you wanted to spend more time with her before you went to Regionals."

Cunny was torn. Latrine seemed to be pure in her intentions to invite Ina Godda, but the situation could turn ugly in an instant. It then occurred to her that it was very possible Ina Godda wouldn't even want to go, even with Latrine's elite connection to the Inverness Tea Room. That might be attractive for Ina Godda—easy admission to a new place that's exclusive. One thing was for sure: Ina Godda would never go if it were Latrine to extend the invitation. It had to be Cunny.

"You know what? Let me call."

Latrine smiled. "Oh, Cunny. I don't want to put you out. I can do it."

"No, no. I like putting out." Cunny got up and walked to the kitchen to grab her phone. Scrolling through her numbers, she realized she never stored Ina Godda's, but she remembered she had her business card somewhere, likely in her junk drawer. Sure enough, there it was, located beneath a pile of takeout menus stained with soy sauce.

"Are you sure you don't want me to call?" asked Latrine.

"Yeah. And you know what? It might be better if she doesn't know you're going."

Latrine looked stunned by the suggestion. "I really think I can handle it."

"I just have a bad feeling, Latrine." Cunny tried to say it as politely as possible.

Latrine let out a sigh. "Can you at least put her on speaker so I can hear?"

"Okay, but don't say anything. She might back out if she knows you're going."

Latrine looked perturbed, but Cunny was desperate to bridge the gap between the two queens. She began to see it as her mission. She'd be the peacekeeping troop, like those ladies who wear all that sexy camouflage and still manage to be fabulous. *OMG that should totally be a costume for the Grand Dame Competition.* Cunny dialed the number and put her phone on speaker. As the phone rang, she started to wonder if Ina Godda might think High Tea was beneath her. The thought of whether there was something higher than High Tea raced through her mind until Ina Godda picked up.

"Ina Godda the Diva. All the Diva to meet your needs." Her voice was vibrant.

Latrine suppressed a giggle. Cunny put her index finger up to her mouth to remind her to remain silent. Latrine mimed a zipper closing over her lips and flashed a sheepish grin.

"Hi, Ina Godda. It's Cunny Corleone."

"Oh." Ina Godda's energy died. "And to what do I owe this unwarranted encroachment of my time?"

"I was talking to a friend earlier, and get this—she said she can get us in to the Inverness Tea Room for High Tea."

"Cunny, darling. Anybody can get into the Inverness Tea Room. You don't even need a reservation."

The smile faded from Cunny's face. She looked at Latrine, shaking her head as if at a loss. Latrine mimed putting a hat on her head, jogging her memory about the Kentucky Derby angle. "Well, great then. I was actually thinking we should go and bond before we go to Regionals together."

"We're competing against each other. We don't need to do that."

"But I think it would be fun." Cunny's bright optimistic tone was becoming more plaintive and whiny. "I had this whole Kentucky Derby outfit picked out and everything."

"It's not time for the Kentucky Derby, Cunny."

"I know, but I really wanted to dress up and wear a great hat at tea. The Inverness Tea Room has this amazing terrace with a great view. Come on. It'll be fun. You have such a great sense of style. If anything, it'll be a nice day and a perfect chance to show off a fabulous hat and dress in that fierce way you always do."

Latrine gave her a thumbs up.

"But it's just you and me?" Ina Godda asked.

"Yeah." Cunny looked at Latrine. "I mean, other queens might be there enjoying tea, but it's just you and I in our own little tea party, looking fabulous."

"I'll see you tomorrow at three." Ina Godda hung up.

Cunny smiled at Latrine. She believed that since she'd gotten to know Latrine so well, Ina Godda would definitely want to heal any open wounds too—as long as Latrine really wanted to do the same. "Promise me that you'll be nice to her."

"I have no reason not to be. See you tomorrow afternoon." Latrine kissed Cunny on both cheeks and sashayed out the door. Cunny's face beamed with pride, like she'd gotten two soap opera vixens to join forces.

Chapter 7

Ina Godda had to admit she was a little surprised to get such a pleasant phone call from her direct competition. She counted her blessings for the plethora of dresses she had ready to go. High Tea was something she'd actually attended before. The experience of dressing up with the girls and sipping from dainty cups was always a diversion she enjoyed. The challenge in attending the meeting was going to be outdoing Cunny—to eclipse her in all her splendor.

She did suspect Cunny to be a worthy competitor in the future; however, that was a belief best kept secret. Were she to know, she might find it necessary to begin seizing the opportunity to exploit any areas of weakness she perceived. It didn't matter that Cunny wasn't the brightest of them. That type of predatory relationship was a fact of life in the competitive drag jungle. It was especially true in that particular competition circuit. Cunny would inevitably succumb to that backstabbery because it was behavior in which Ina Godda herself partook. She would fill each performance with what the other queens couldn't—or simply wouldn't—do.

Ina Godda did think it was lovely Cunny had extended an olive branch to try to get to know her, but she couldn't get too comfortable with her. Allowing her into her inner sanctum when she had no clout was a path she refused to take. She'd have to keep her at arm's length until she became a queen who was valuable to know. Twatla Tharp and Duffy MacDuff fit that bill. Twatla wasn't a competitive queen. And Duffy? She had a vagina. No competition there. Indeed, they were a glamorous and powerful couple. They frequently had the judges in the palm of their hands because, well, they typically hand-picked the judges themselves. Mutual friends, former drag competitors, members of the gay press. All people with whom Ina Godda was well-acquainted. Being friends with Twatla and Duffy meant being friends with a very important pool of people. She found it important to communicate with Twatla and Duffy quite often, making sure to have a girls' night once a week with them. It was also important to care about Twatla's football games when her testosterone surged from the month of August through to the Super Bowl. That was how to play the drag circuit. And she didn't dare admit those tactics to Cunny. No way.

She curled her wig for the day's tea, basking in the auspiciousness of her alliances, when she realized she had "The Young and the Restless" on DVR. She turned it on and took a trip down to Genoa City. Some of the actors, she often admitted to herself, gave Marco Polo a run for his money. She found it difficult to remain faithful to him at times, but she always made time for him as penance for her wandering eye.

As she continued applying her curling iron to her wig, she watched the hunks of Genoa City ravage their way through the female population, taking no prisoners. They were aggressive in that episode, asserting their control over their women, marking their territory like packs of lions. Two of the hunks began a fistfight over one of them, and Ina Godda was riveted, accidentally burning her finger. She unplugged the curling iron and stuck the finger in her mouth, soothing the burned spot. One of the men fighting was a beautiful red-headed actor whose name she had trouble recalling. He had a wonderful body. Tight, smooth, muscular, with just the slightest red happy trail. The fight got vicious, and Mr. Redhead's shirt was torn. She gasped. Her heart pounded through her chest at the sight of his erect pink nipple poking through, giving just the slightest glimpse of his smooth, milky pectoral. His bright blue eyes narrowed at his foe as the damsel in distress tried to stand between them.

"Don't come between them, Victoria. They're battling for your love, bitch."

Mr. Redhead lunged at his enemy, tackling him to the ground. They writhed and rolled around in the dirt, forcing the damsel to call for help. A few punches were thrown. Mr. Redhead ended up on top, in complete control of the other guy. He squeezed his neck. Such power. Such force. And just when Ina Godda believed Mr. Redhead was going to sink to the level of killing his opponent, he let go. His enemy began a coughing fit, and Mr. Redhead got up.

"You keep away from my girl," said Mr. Redhead. "Next time I see you by her, I won't be so nice."

Ina Godda was getting worked up. She turned off the television and could feel her erection throbbing and her bottom puckered. It was time to spend some quality time with Marco Polo before having to meet Cunny.

She walked into her fabulous closet and took out the day's dress and hat. After laying it her outfit on the bed, she sauntered over to her dresser and opened her Polobox, letting the pedestal rise before her. She genuflected in honor of her man. Looking at her watch, she estimated she had approximately half an hour with which to be intimate with Marco Polo. With the push of a button on her remote control, a movie screen dropped from the ceiling. She turned on a scene from the Marco Polo collection and began to disrobe. It was time to get down to business.

Chapter 8

It didn't take Latrine long to throw together her ensemble. She usually lamented the privation which had befallen her wardrobe, but she did own a basic and simple blue dress and matching hat. She had some white heels that fit both the ensemble and the occasion. She opted for a straight-haired wig for the day, relatively conservative. The sheer volume of big hair shouldn't dwarf the hat on her head. The hat itself was another story. Her initial choice was too drab and didn't make enough of a statement. It needed to be the type that would be seen at a royal wedding or the Derby itself—the type of hat that ended up in *People Magazine.* Latrine knew Ina Godda the Diva would be making hers as elaborate as possible, glue-gunning rhinestones to it at the last minute, so she needed to at least match her level of fabulosity. She understood it might be a moot point, though. Showing up in a pair of trousers and a t-shirt might be enough for the moment, given the circumstances. There was even a good possibility Ina Godda wouldn't show on account of a sudden rash. Or Ina Godda could just pull out at the last minute—something her lack of real live sexual partners never permitted her the chance to do—and not even try on any of the tainted dresses. Judging what Latrine had seen of her ego though, she'd likely make every effort to make an appearance just to be seen, admired, and feared by her competition.

Peyton strolled into the room and started getting undressed. "I have the perfect outfit for this afternoon."

Latrine walked over to him and put her arms around his shoulders. "Love, I didn't tell Cunny you'd be coming. Maybe it's best if you stay home."

Peyton pushed her arms off. "Are you gone nutters? You said I could go. I put in just as much work as you. I want to see the bitch go down. Besides, you said Ina Godda doesn't know you're going, so Cunny doesn't have to know I am. She can't tell me to leave. It's a public place."

Latrine smiled and nodded. "You're right."

The hat Latrine donned was turquoise blue, with a medium-sized brim. She went out to a local fabric shop the previous night and bought a darker blue ribbon and some faux baby's breath. The ribbon made for a nice bow, and the baby's breath created an idyllic bed of flowers on the brim. Latrine spent most of the ride admiring it in the passenger seat's visor mirror.

Peyton parked the van in the garage of the office tower that housed the Inverness Tea Room.

"Wait a moment." He rushed out and around the vehicle to open her door like a gentleman. Peyton himself was dressed quite lovely. He wore a button down shirt with a tie—of all things. His top matched nicely with a pair of pressed gray trousers and shiny shoes. On his head, not to be outdone, rested a thatched fedora. Not a smidge of his street-Weegee past was evident anywhere on his person—until he opened his mouth. He helped Latrine out of the van, closed the door behind her, and held out his arm to escort her into the building like they were walking down the aisle.

As they entered, Latrine basked in the splendor of the building. The expansive lobby was covered in polished marble and onyx, and her heels made a percussive clack-clack-clack that heralded her arrival. As they reached the lifts and pushed the 'up' button, Latrine looked down at Peyton. He looked up at her. They smiled in anticipation. The Grand Dame Competition was within reach. She grabbed for his hand, but he took hers instead. They were united, a force to be reckoned with.

They disembarked the lift on to the tenth floor lobby, home of the Inverness Tea Room. The establishment was reasonably busy for that time of day. It was still new, so word was likely beginning to spread around town of its location and concept.

They approached the hostess, who flashed a smile at them. Latrine breathed a sigh of relief. Patronizing a restaurant in drag that did not specifically cater to gay clientele always came with the risk of dirty looks and hostile attitudes. She never had a problem at that particular place, but she always feared the stares whenever someone was working whom she didn't recognize.

"How ya'll doin'?" the hostess asked.

"Wonderful." Latrine turned on the charm.

"Oh my god! Ya'll ain't from around here! Ya'll are from Europe, ain't ya'll."

Latrine was rather surprised at the thickness of her drawl. She understood they were in the South, but Florida was only technically south.

Peyton stood up tall. "We're from Scotland. Greatest country on Earth."

"Oh. Well, welcome to America."

"Thank you. We live here now."

"I see," she said, somewhat disappointed, like they'd somehow brought plague-infested mice with them and would be abetting the spread of pathogens. Latrine was actually surprised she'd been less receptive to their being Scottish than her being in drag with her husband.

Latrine didn't want the awkwardness of the moment to taint their anticipation for tea. "We're meeting someone."

"Oh, ya'll must be with the other drag queen. Right this way." The hostess turned and walked out toward the terrace.

Peyton grabbed Latrine's hand. "She looked at us like we were dirty. She must be mixing us up for being Irish."

They followed the redneck lady out to the terrace, and seated there was a glorious Cunny. She smiled for a moment before her eyes landed on Peyton. His presence gave her pause, but she seemed to shrug it off as a warm smile returned to her face. As she rose, practically in slow motion, Latrine got a glimpse of her stunning black-and-white striped floor-length dress. Her collar was adorned with a long string of exquisite pearls, the kind of pearl necklace a queen would be proud to show off, the kind that wouldn't wash off after a night of great sex. On her head rested her trademark blonde wig in perfectly curled ringlets, and on top of that was a massive white floppy hat with a giant black satin bow around the brim. From the center of the bow sprouted a gargantuan black flower. From head to toe, she looked like if Audrey Hepburn fucked the Cheshire Cat in a black-and-white porno. Latrine smiled and gave her a kiss on each cheek.

"You look bonny. Very old Hollywood."

"Yes! I totally look like Bonnie. A wee bit like Bonnie," Cunny said to Latrine. "Hi, Peyton. I didn't know you were coming."

She leaned over to kiss Peyton on each cheek. Cunny may have been a bit of a dafty, but she was picking up on the Scottish lingo and habits quicker than Latrine thought she would. They sat down at the table and looked at the menu.

Cunny leaned in to whisper. "Peyton knows to be nice, right? Just friendly tea."

Peyton seemed to overhear. "I am on my best behavior, Cunny." His enthusiasm was laced with an uncharacteristic bubbliness.

Cunny let out a sigh of relief. "Fabulous! Um, I didn't want to order yet because I didn't know what kind of tea you all would want. I'm not good with my teas. Tequila, yes. Tea, no. Do you think we should wait for Ina Godda?"

"Not at all." Latrine called the waiter over. "We'd like the High Tea special with service for four—the Earl Grey—and for our snack, we'd like the blueberry scones with clotted cream on the side."

Peyton grabbed her hand and kissed it. "Latrine knows how to do it."

"Aye." Latrine pulled her hand away, trying to quell any excitement Peyton might have over seeing Ina Godda lest he give anything away.

"Aye," Cunny said, playing along. "Well, it's three now, so let's give her a couple of minutes before calling her in case she forgot."

And just like that, Latrine could feel a presence behind her. All heads on the terrace turned to see Ina Godda the Diva, dressed as a statuesque living passenger on the *Titanic*. It looked like she decided the Kentucky Derby theme would be relocated to Edwardian England instead. She wore a burgundy-wine colored wool sweater buttoned all the way up to her neck, with long sleeves. She sauntered in, seemingly in slow-motion, like she was a clothed Venus emerging from a shell in a Botticelli painting. A satin bustle trailed behind her, exploding from her fitted waist. The brim of her hat orbited her head like the rings of Saturn, if Saturn had a field of giant purple orchids growing out of the side of it. Giant purple stalks of faux leaves sprayed out from beneath the orchids, flapping in the wind as she drew closer. For a moment, Latrine felt like the ship was sinking, and Rose was waiting for Jack Dawson on the Grand Staircase. Just like that, she began panicking. She couldn't remember if she actually rubbed the poison ivy on that sweater and that skirt. She had so many. They all looked alike. Did she make it over to the burgundies in her closet? And she was wearing wool in that weather. Nobody in their right mind would wear wool when it was that warm out. Then again—nobody was quite like Ina Godda the Diva.

None of it fit in with Latrine's plan. She looked at Peyton. He was content with eagerness over what he thought was coming. She pondered how to break the news she didn't hit that ensemble.

"Wow! Look at you!" Cunny got up to kiss her on both cheeks, but Ina Godda's attention had landed on Peyton and Latrine. Ina Godda braced Cunny's arms, whispering in her ear, her eyes glaring at them.

Latrine could hear Cunny whisper. "They're being so nice. They totally want to bury the hatchet and just have some tea with you. Really."

Ina Godda rolled her eyes and took a deep breath before lifting her head so her chin beamed with snootiness. Her shoulders were thrown back, extending her neck. She glided over to the table and stood over them like they were urchins and she was a rich bitch from a Charles Dickens novel.

"Hello, Latrine." She then leaned over to Latrine for an embrace, but Latrine didn't want to take any chances.

"No, no. I have a sore throat. Don't get too close."

Ina Godda backed away immediately. She looked over at Peyton and forced half of a smile.

"Peyton." She nodded her head at him in feigned politeness.

"Ina Godda." He mimicked her tone.

Latrine stared at her for a moment, a fake smile plastered on her face as she recalled definitely only hitting the pastels. She was nowhere near that outfit. Her heart broke at the thought of Ina Godda remaining in the competition. Ina Godda was still going to go to Nationals, and knowing Twatla and Duffy's shadiness, Latrine knew she was still going to win. She wouldn't even get her chance to show her stuff. Again, Ina Godda robbed her of a title. She continued smiling at Ina Godda, a glint of fire burning in her eyes.

"So what is with the sore throat, Latrine? Peyton's nether region tainted with some unflappable STD?" Ina Godda looked up from her menu to glimpse Peyton's reaction.

"I only have my eyes on the one and only Latrine." He was being pleasant, though it was likely he wanted to hurl insults back at her.

"Latrine, did you get that ensemble at Lane Bryant? I think it's time to lay off the clotted cream."

Latrine could feel her heart pounding. She could feel herself wanting to lunge across the table and shove her hat down her throat. How she longed to serve that fucking ugly vulva a poison ivy salad with a side of ether. A deep breath was needed—perhaps a few. Peyton's smile evaporated, and he looked like he was about to push her over. Latrine put her hand on his for gentle reassurance. Neither of them vocalized a response. They weren't going to take her bait and turn that tea into a bitchfest. They were, however, going to sit in awkward silence.

"It's quite a lovely day." Cunny tried to feign British poshness to break the ice.

"It is," said Ina Godda. And with that, the pregnant pause seemed to last longer than *Gone with the Wind*.

Latrine and Peyton reclined in their chairs, mouths completely closed.

"I don't know; it's a bit hot out here actually," Ina Godda continued, after a moment. She took a matching burgundy-wine fan adorned with feathers out of her bag and fanned herself like she was in a Restoration comedy. Latrine wished she had one that was bigger and more ornate.

Much to their relief, the waiter came bearing a tray of silver tea service for four.

"Oh, you ordered already. How nice." Ina Godda was definitely being sarcastic.

"The scones will be out in a moment," the waiter said before walking way.

"It really is very hot out here." Ina Godda tugged at her buttoned up collar and fanned herself with increased rapidity.

Peyton shrugged. "I feel fine."

"Are you okay?" Cunny asked.

"I'm fine. It just seems to be getting hotter and hotter." Ina Godda adjusted her bra.

"Would you like to play mother?" Latrine asked her.

"I would love to." Ina Godda scratched a bit above the breast. Latrine figured it had to be either coincidence or stress, the itching. She stole a glance at Peyton, who watched her like a vulture circling his prey. He wasn't being particularly subtle about it, so Latrine kicked him under the table, causing his voracious smile to fade a bit. She realized how she would let him know that wasn't one of the dresses she tainted: a text message.

Ina Godda lifted the teapot.

"No cream for me." Latrine took out her phone, indifferent to the obvious impropriety of texting at the table. "No sugar either. Masks the Bergamot in the Earl Grey."

Latrine noticed a slight quiver in Ina Godda's pour, which seemed to increase as she poured for Cunny and Peyton.

"Are you sure you're okay?" Peyton asked.

"I'm fine. Never better," Ina Godda replied as she poured her own cup. She leaned back in her chair and brought the cup up to her lips. They all followed suit, trying to avoid watching the slight twitches and spasms she was subtly trying to hide. One twitch, however, spilled some hot tea on her dress.

"Oh Goodness," Ina Godda cried out at the spill. The next thing Latrine noticed was the full cup of tea crashing to the floor and shattering, Ina Godda leaping out of her chair and scrambling about, clawing at her sweater, ripping what she could. Her hat and wig flew off, exposing a nylon cap on her head—a true humiliation for any queen in public. She twitched her bum around, trying in desperation to back it into the arm of the chair in which she sat, all the while ripping at her bra, unleashing her silicon-enhanced breasts for the world to see. A giant rash stretched across the valley between them.

Cunny's hands covered her mouth. Peyton's mouth was agape, and Latrine was pretty sure she looked completely shocked herself.

"Itching! Get this shit off of me!" Ina Godda screamed with barely intelligible articulation. She began flailing about the terrace, ripping her skirt to pieces, sending them flying toward the other patrons who watched on in utter consternation. She moved in a zig-zag pattern over to the railing of the terrace before leaning on it to catch her breath, her upper torso completely exposed. She tugged off her girdle, standing stark naked except for a dance belt that was layered with duct tape. A massive rash had spread all over her bum and between her thighs. Latrine thought she even saw a little under her nose. She must've just been intimate with Marco Polo right before she left her flat. She must've used it in more than one place. That was the only explanation.

She scratched at her bum with more vicious fury. In the apparent haze of her itching, she leaned into the railing, a rod positioned firmly in the vicinity of her arse crack. She backed into it, moving her bum in a circular motion, gaining relief from the rod and railing. She backed into the railing with force, with desperation, with yearning, oblivious to the stares from the patrons. She whimpered as though gaining some form of reprieve from the railing itself. The tension on the terrace was palpable. A waiter attempted to help Ina Godda, but she just kept pushing herself up against the railing, ignoring his extended hand.

And then there was a creaking.

And before Latrine or anyone could do anything to help, the railing gave way, and Ina Godda the Diva plummeted over the side of the terrace, falling ten stories to what had to be certain death.

Latrine's hands covered her mouth. That wasn't supposed to happen. She was just supposed to be too rash-stricken to compete. Either from the clothes or from Marco Polo or both. But since it was just Marco Polo, Latrine would have thought that she'd just be unable to attend Nationals because it infected her with some strange toxin, which she would blame on Marco, severing her ties to him and burning his dildo in effigy for closure. She was just supposed to be itchy and incapacitated to the point of needing to stay home. Not that. Not allowing herself to back into a railing that, after anally raping her, gave way and forced her over the edge.

Cunny burst into tears. Latrine hugged her and cradled her in her arms, trying to pretend she was completely in shock, which she was—somewhat. She looked at Peyton. He walked over to the edge, along with a few other gawkers, peering over to see. He stared for a moment before looking back and walking back over toward her.

Latrine looked up as Cunny continued to use her shoulder to blot her tears. "How bad?"

Peyton put his hand on the nape of her neck. "It's pretty bad."

"I need to look." Latrine gently pushed Cunny away.

Cunny wiped away what seemed like an endless stream of tears. "Why?"

"I need closure." Latrine hugged Cunny again tightly. "Do you want closure too?"

"No. I can't look," she said.

"I understand." Latrine broke free. "Peyton, can you get her to sit down for a moment?"

Peyton sat Cunny back down at the table. Latrine slowly approached the edge of the terrace. The feeling was reminiscent of the night she came out to her parents. She climbed to the top of Salisbury Crags, a line of vertical cliffs that overlooked Edinburgh. There were no guard rails to protect anyone from falling over the edge. She stood up there and contemplated jumping for a brief moment, but it was that view, that majestic view of Edinburgh with St. Giles and the Sir Walter Scott Monument dominating the skyline, that made her come to her senses. The wind tussled her hair. A refreshing light sprinkle of rain pattered on her face. The whole of Edinburgh seemed in the palm of her hands. And if her parents were the only thing blocking her success there, she could move to the U.S. and dominate the scene. Peyton would be proud of her, and she could do it without anyone's criticism. It was the moment she seized control of her destiny. She had taken advantage of the path that was rightfully hers.

Latrine peered over the edge. Below, ten stories down, lay the lifeless body of Ina Godda the Diva, bruised and battered, twisted like a pretzel. A few people who were in the Rock Close Garden below approached the body, pointing and covering their mouths. She could hear police and ambulance sirens in the distance rapidly approaching. After a deep breath, she returned to the table and sat down beside Cunny and Peyton, taking a sip of her tea. There was nothing else she could do. She sat in silence, observing the confused and bewildered patrons and staff of the Inverness Tea Room, ready to move forward.

Chapter 9

Duffy was at the station when she got a call for a possible suicide investigation in the Rock Close Garden below the Inverness Tea Room. It was a strange place for a suicide. She didn't know why anyone would just jump from the ledge of the Inverness Tea Room. It was only tea. How bad could it be to precipitate a jump? She called Detective Ross, whom she was sure was taking an afternoon siesta somewhere, and told him to meet her at the crime scene.

When she arrived, she was surprised to see Detective Ross had already cordoned off the area and was already wearing a pair of latex gloves. She did her best to corral rubber-neckers away from the scene as she walked toward the body. Detective Ross rapidly approached her with his hands up, as if pushing her back along with the rest of the crowd.

"Whoa, whoa!" said Duffy. "We have a job to do here."

Detective Ross rested his wrist on her shoulder, his latex-laden hand hanging off her back. "I really think it's best if you leave this one to me."

"Uh-uh. Who do you think you're talking to? We investigate together."

Detective Ross took a deep breath. "It's not pretty over there."

"Of course it's not. It's a body."

"It's not just a body."

Duffy could see a look of concern in his eyes—a look of concern *for her*. She didn't do well with pitying looks. After pushing his wrist off her shoulder, she hurried to the corpse. It was partially unclothed, pale white skin seemingly afflicted with some kind of rash amidst some serious bloody lacerations. It seemed a wig cap stretched over the head of a mangled body, positioned exactly where it was when it fell. Nobody had touched it. There was a made-up face. It was definitely a drag queen. A drag queen she knew.

Reality smacked her. Duffy fell to her knees, her hands covering her mouth. Detective Ross rushed over and put his arms around her, ripping off his latex gloves. She couldn't cry. She couldn't feel anything. She just stared.

"Let me take this one. Go home to your husband."

"No," she said. Then, after a pause: "I need to do my job. She would want me to do my job here."

Duffy looked up at the spot from which she fell. The railing on the terrace of the Inverness Tea Room was broken. It lay in pieces amidst the rocks in the garden.

"This was not a suicide."

Detective Ross helped her back onto her feet. "We can't rule it out yet, but I know you're right. Do you need to call Twatla?"

"I'll tell her when I get home," Duffy said. "I'd like to be there when I tell her. Let's go check out the scene up there."

They walked into the building and took the elevator up to the tenth floor. As the elevator doors opened, Duffy noticed that the Inverness Tea Room was not, at the moment, the placid, trendy tea spot it normally purported to be. It had confused patrons and gawkers who had come to witness the spectacle.

As they walked out to the terrace, they found Peyton Dingwall, Latrine Dion, and Cunny Corleone, the latter two of whom were dressed in full drag, like they were attending the Kentucky Derby. Cunny rose from her chair and darted over to Duffy, throwing her arms around her and weeping.

"Oh, Duffy! I can't believe it!"

Duffy stabilized her footing after nearly being taken down by the force of Cunny's embrace. "Neither can I. Here. Have a seat."

Duffy eased her back down and pulled up a seat beside her. "Can I ask you a few questions?"

Cunny tried to speak, but she couldn't get the words out. Duffy placed a warm hand on her thigh. "It's okay, girl."

Cunny blotted some tears with a napkin. "I have a horrible headache. All this crying."

"Would you like an aspirin? Latrine carries aspirin." It was an oddly pleasant statement coming from Peyton, whom Duffy equated with a class of Scottish street peasants.

"Allergic," Cunny mumbled.

"Latrine, can I ask you a few questions?" said Duffy.

Latrine began to cry and waved her hand all around.

Duffy studied her a moment before moving on. "Peyton?"

"I think we're all a bit worked up right now." Peyton placed a concerned hand on Latrine's back.

"We completely understand. Why don't you all head home?" Out of the blue, Detective Ross reminded everyone of his presence.

Duffy glared at him.

Without missing a beat, Peyton got up. "I can take them home."

Peyton helped Latrine up as she dried her face with a napkin. In turn, Latrine helped Cunny up, and the three of them walked out of the café, arms linked as if in some sort of solidarity.

Duffy turned to Detective Ross, casting sideways glances at the posse as they boarded the elevators. "Why did you do that?"

"Do what?"

"Let them go. They're key witnesses. They're the only other ones in drag, and the victim was clearly in drag too."

"I was trying to be sensitive. You all are part of the same community. They've just lost a friend. Of course, they're going to be grief-stricken. We still have time to question them."

"You just gave them time to corroborate stories," said Duffy.

"What—do you think they pushed her off in front of all these people?"

Duffy shrugged. "Let's find out."

They approached the hostess. Duffy took out her badge and flashed it.

"Ma'am, we'd like to ask you a few questions about what happened here today."

The hostess looked up from wiping off some laminated menus with a Windex-soaked cloth. "Awful, isn't it? Just awful."

Duffy was unfazed by her thick Southern accent. "How did the victim go over the edge of the terrace?"

"Oh he was just flailing around like something bit him—like there was a rattlesnake biting his legs or something."

"His legs?" Detective Ross asked.

"Yeah, like kicking about and ripping off the dress and everything." The hostess waved some of the menus around as if to demonstrate the hysteria before putting them down on the podium. "Then he started rubbing his butt up against the railing really hard. I guess it was so hard that the railing just gave way, and he fell over the side."

Duffy stared at her, trying to visualize the bizarre scenario. "Okay. And did the victim say anything while that was happening?"

"Naw. Just a lot of cursing, I think. I couldn't really make out what he was saying."

Duffy looked at Detective Ross before continuing. "And the other drag queens. Were they with her when it happened?"

"Yeah, they were all sitting at the same table. The one in the blonde wig was here first."

"Cunny," Duffy clarified.

"Pardon me?" The hostess' tone sounded like she was offended.

"The drag queen. Her name is Cunny," Detective Ross offered.

"That's rude and just plain disgusting."

Detective Ross knit his brow, perplexed. "What? The name?"

"That's irrelevant." Duffy didn't want to any ignorance to stymie the investigation. "The other two. They came together?"

"Oh yeah. The Scottish ones. I think they're illegals. They said they live here now." Her voice had dropped to a whisper, as if she were revealing some incriminating news.

"This isn't an immigration case," said Detective Ross.

"They came together then." Duffy was trying her damnest to keep the interrogation on the right track.

"Yes. They did. They went over and sat with the one who died."

The hostess' voice returned to full volume.

"So Ina Godda was here first then?" Detective Ross asked.

"What?" she asked.

"May I?" Duffy held up a hand to Detective Ross, recognizing that talking to the woman might throw the investigation into a tizzy so early on. "They ordered. What did they order?"

"I don't have the authority to check the computer. I just take people to their tables and talk to them while I bring them menus. Sometimes I talk about the specials if we have any."

Duffy sighed. "Okay. We need either a waiter or the manager to help us out."

"Let me go find him." The hostess turned and disappeared into the kitchen.

Detective Ross looked at Duffy and puts his arm around her. "Are you sure you want to keep going with this right now? Don't you want to get home? I can take care of it. Really. We can start asking questions tomorrow."

"I can at least talk to the manager. I can at least start to get answers," said Duffy.

"I can too."

Duffy took a deep breath and nodded. He gave her a hug, and for a brief moment, she could feel the tears well up in her eyes. He broke away and walked over to a nearby table, grabbing a napkin and holding it out for her to take. She blotted her eyes and looked up at him.

"Let this be the only time I do this during this investigation," said Duffy. "I don't need any of that conflict of interest shit coming down."

"Deal. Now go home. Tell Twatla. Call me if you need anything," Detective Ross said softly.

"I want details tomorrow morning."

Chapter 10

Twatla reclined on the sofa, her feet with their canary yellow painted toenails pointed toward the ceiling. The remote control continued its tyrannical rule over the television as she flipped back and forth between *Sports Center* and a rerun of *The Young and the Restless* on cable when Duffy burst through the door.

"Can you turn that off?"

Twatla sucked her teeth and looked up at her with the *no you didn't* look on her face. Duffy's eyes had a glint of melancholy in them. Twatla hit pause on the soap and sat up. Duffy sat down beside her.

"We had a victim that fell off the ledge of the Inverness Tea Room."

Twatla tried to picture the floor plan. She'd been there once before. "Fell off the ledge? Like the terrace?"

"Right. The terrace." It was Duffy's first time there herself.

"Fell? Or jumped?"

"We haven't ruled anything out."

"Okay." Twatla searched her face. "You look upset. I don't see why you're upset about this. You see this kind of thing every day in Orlando."

"We know the victim." Duffy took a deep breath. Twatla's heart felt like it had sucked all the blood in her body up as a reservoir while she danced on the precipice of anticipation.

"It was Ina Godda the Diva."

Twatla's jaw dropped. She threw back her head. *Oh sweet Jesus.* It couldn't be true. They had just spoken the other night. Ina Godda was excited for her prospects. She was revved up and ready to go. The title of Duchess was assuredly hers, with a strong possibility of placing in the top ten at Nationals again. Sure, she had her normal insecurities, but no more than any other queen—any other person—had. It just didn't make sense. It did not compute.

"How is this possible?" Tears formed in Twatla's eyes, and Duffy became an amorphous mass. "She definitely couldn't have jumped."

"No. I believe she fell." Duffy reached over to the end table and grabbed a tissue, handing it to her. "It looked like she was leaning against the railing and rubbing her backside against it. Witnesses say they saw her ripping her dress off and that her skin was red. I noticed what looked like a rash on her body when I saw it."

Twatla blotted around her eyes. "So was it some kind of allergic reaction to something? Was she sick? Was it the shingles?"

"I don't think you can get the shingles at her age. She wasn't that old. At least, I don't think she was."

Twatla took a deep breath.

"Are you going to be okay?"

"Yeah. Sweet Jesus, I just need a moment to take this all in. You know what? Let me turn this shit off." Twatla hit the power button on the remote control. "We're gonna head up to the church and pray for her."

"You know how they feel about you," Duffy reminded her. "They're not exactly welcoming of your lifestyle."

Twatla stood up. "They can suck on my Spanx. And you know what? They can gawk at me all they want this time, because I'm going in full drag."

She marched to her closet in search of the appropriate all-black dress to accompany her straightened wig. She donned her Spanx in record time and threw on a simple black pencil skirt with white trim. The matching tailored jacket she got for half off from White House Black Market would work nicely to compliment it. She slid into a pair of black pumps and threw on her wig. Just some simple eyeliner and mascara would do. No need for the eyelashes, since she'd probably cry them off anyway.

A toned-down burgundy lipstick seemed most appropriate. She applied a little foundation and concealer to even out the skin. After one last look in the mirror, she was ready to go.

She walked out to meet Duffy, who had definitely decided just to wear what she wore to work. It wasn't that difficult for her actually in that situation since she normally wore a black or navy pants suit to work every day. Such was the life of a detective.

Duffy issued a small grin. "That was record time."

"We are going to be praying for the loss of our friend. This is one time where being conservative is appropriate. Anything elaborate and time-consuming would just be out of place—even for Ina Godda the Diva." Twatla grabbed her purse as Duffy stuffed her wallet and keys into her pocket.

When they got to the church, they were fortunate in that it was relatively deserted. A few parishioners inside turned their heads as they walked in. The thing about being a drag queen with a strong faith connection was that whenever they headed into a house of worship, they inevitably got the stares, the glares, and the gossip. Occasionally, they even got kicked out, which of course always prompted her to launch into a litany of psalms and verses about acceptance and judgment that would make even the most illustrious preacher cower. Duffy was great about standing by her side. Sadly, the worst of it came from her proud sisters. They gave her looks like she was about to turn their men to the Down Low or something—extreme judgment. Duffy always grabbed Twatla's hand to reassure them—and Twatla—that she wasn't going to let things get ugly.

They took a seat in the vicinity of their normal vantage point, reflecting on the life of a fallen sister. A good friend. A great person. Ina Godda had a heart as warm and vast as the Painted Desert.

Twatla pondered what the funeral should be like. It couldn't be any ordinary service. It had to be spectacular. It had to be worthy of someone with the name of Ina Godda the Diva. It had to be so flashy and dazzling that the astronauts in the International Space Station could look down at the earth and think interstellar warfare had been declared. Every queen whose life Ina Godda had ever touched should be there to participate in a day of music, fashion, and reverence—all in good taste, of course. Duffy was going to be invaluable in planning. She was organized. She might even offer some inspired suggestions.

But Twatla would get the final say.

Chapter 11

Peyton finished dressing in his light blue button-down shirt and khaki trousers. Never in his life did he ever think he'd become a person who sat behind a desk all day and sold tickets to a basketball game, but there he was. Actually, before he left Glasgow, he barely knew what basketball was. He understood it much better as he got older, though he didn't really follow it all too much since being in the US. It was nowhere near as exciting as football or rugby, or even cricket. Men bounced a ball and tossed it into a basket. Then they bounced the ball to the other end and tossed it into the other basket. And those bloody players were all the size of giants—the kind his grandparents characterized in their stories of ancient Scotland, with the exception that most of the giant players in the US were black.

Peyton walked out to the kitchen, all buttoned up and ready to eat his cereal, when he encountered Latrine sitting at the table, looking like she hadn't slept for even a few minutes. She was out of drag and in a pink robe, massive bags under her eyes. Even worse, she'd gotten the whisky out—single malt whisky. The Glengoyne eighteen-year. It was serious.

Peyton knew he needed to tread lightly. "You couldn't make up your mind about whether to drink the Highland or the Lowland, so you went right for the one in the middle, huh?"

"I couldn't sleep." She stared at the glass. At least she had the sense to use the Glencairn glasses and not drink from a bloody tumbler. Scotch whisky was always best drunk from the Glencairn glasses. The shape allowed for the full aroma and full experience of the whisky.

Peyton went to the cupboard and took out a bowl, filling it with dry cereal. "What's on your mind that you're drinking a Glengoyne eighteen-year at eight in the morning?"

"I don't know. I just couldn't sleep." Her voice had the raspy texture of a vacuum cleaner inhaling a trail of mud.

Peyton poured some almond milk over his cereal. "You want me to make you some pancakes before I go?"

"No. I'm supposed to meet Cunny for lunch."

Peyton shoved a few spoonfuls in his mouth. "That's not for a few more hours. You should be eating something when you're drinking a Glengoyne. If I had more time, I'd make you a Scottish breakfast." The chewing and talking combination yielded a drizzle of cloudy liquid from his mouth.

"The Queen Mother used to drink Glengoyne, and she lived to be 102." She didn't seem to be making much sense. Peyton pondered the relevance of her random fact before he dropped his bowl—still half full of cereal—into the sink.

"Okay. I will see you when I get home tonight." He bent down and kissed her on the forehead before heading into the foyer. "Just lay off the whisky soon."

The doorbell rang. Peyton turned around and looked at Latrine. "Is she coming early?"

"No. I wasn't expecting her until noon." Latrine sat up. "Go tell her I'm not awake yet and to come back at the right time."

Peyton walked toward the front door and opened it. There stood Duffy and the beautiful man she was with the day before at the Inverness Tea Room.

"Oh. Hello, Duffy and Hot Bloke from yesterday." Peyton's eyes dropped down to the latter's package area.

"Detective Ross."

"Ross." Peyton looked up and smiled. "Good name. Scottish."

"If you say so."

Peyton's eyes migrated up to Duffy as he stepped outside the doorframe, closing it behind him. "What are you doing here?"

"We were just wondering if we could ask you a few questions."

"Some other time. I'm on my way to work." Peyton opened the door to retreat inside.

"We'll only be a few minutes," said Duffy.

Peyton pushed the door closed on them. "I can't be late."

Duffy placed her palm firmly on the door and pushed back. "Then we'll call your office for you and let them know you were participating in a criminal investigation. I'm sure they'll understand."

Ross lent his strength to the resistance. "We'll make them."

Peyton could feel his knees starting to buckle, and not because he was nervous in any way. It was because Ross was powerful and strong—like he could lift and bench press him.

"Come in then."

Peyton escorted them over to the kitchen, where Latrine had just taken a sip from a freshly poured glass of Glengoyne—to which she had at least added some water.

He cleared his throat as Duffy and Ross rounded the corner into the kitchen. When Latrine caught a glimpse of them, she spit her mouthful of whisky all over the table and her pink robe, launching into a coughing fit.

"What are you all doing here?"

"We didn't mean to interrupt your busy morning," Duffy said. Latrine shot her a dry look, like she understood that Duffy was a shrew and that practically anything that came out of her mouth was straight from the Cunt dialect of Bitchish English. However, she did quickly mask her dry look with a smile, realizing the authority standing in her kitchen at that moment.

Latrine cleared her throat and wiped her mouth. "That's okay. I was barely getting started."

Duffy took in her surroundings. "Your kitchen is cute."

"Thanks. I laid the tile myself," said Peyton.

Ross looked down at the floor. "Even as a renter? They let you lay the tile?"

"How do you know we rent?"

Ross waved his hand dismissively. "That's not important."

"We just weren't going to say anything to the landlords. We think it's an improvement, and they'd be happy with it," Latrine chimed in.

Duffy leaned against the counter, her arms folded across her chest. "You're probably right." She continued to look around the kitchen from her stationary position.

An awkward silence. Ross cleared his throat. "How long did it take?"

"Oh, all day. A long time, really." Peyton giggled.

"I wiped his brow all day and then serviced him after," Latrine said.

Peyton's nervous giggle stopped. Normally Latrine was a little bit shyer about revealing details about their sex life, but after thinking about it for a second, he figured she was trying every tactic she could think of to get Duffy and Ross to leave off while still making it seem like she could be pleasant and open with them.

Duffy glared at Latrine. "Let's cut to the chase. We want to ask you a few questions about Ina Godda the Diva."

"Go right ahead." Latrine seemed to be inviting Duffy to play. "I mean, there's nothing really to say. She pranced around the Inverness Tea Room like a bloody bat out of hell and fell right off the terrace."

"That's just it. That behavior is uncommon for Ina Godda," said Duffy.

"Not really. Have you ever seen her dance to The Pointer Sisters?" Latrine took a sip of her whisky. "I saw a video on YouTube of her routine to 'I'm So Excited' that made me wonder if she was on cocaine."

"Aye. And yesterday she seemed so excited that she just couldn't hide it. She was about to lose control and I think she liked it." Peyton's nervous giggle returned. "You may want to check and see if she was on any drugs."

"The autopsy is pending and will take a week or so," Duffy said.

"That's after Duchess Regionals," Latrine added.

"Very good, Latrine." Duffy's condescension was unmistakable. Peyton could tell why Latrine looked like she wanted to bitch slap her. He wanted to hit her himself after that snarky remark, but they had to be nice. They couldn't get Duffy angry. She seemed like the type of person who would find every reason not to let Latrine compete even though she was entitled to with Ina Godda out of the way.

"Witnesses have said that she ripped her clothes off and rubbed her posterior on the railing before it gave way," said Detective Ross.

Peyton stood behind Latrine's chair, resting his hands on her shoulders. "Aye. She did."

"Any thoughts as to why?" Detective Ross's tone mimicked Duffy's condescension.

"No." Peyton threw it right back at them.

"We're just trying to determine if anybody said anything or did anything to make her upset—so upset that she'd fly off the handle and start doing all of these strange things that seemed out of character for her," Detective Ross stated.

"She was nutters." Peyton's giggle returned, and Latrine followed suit.

"Totally nutters,"

"I'm glad you all think this is funny," Duffy said.

Peyton straightened his face and looked at the ground. "We don't think it's funny, Duffy. We're just trying to help."

Duffy pushed herself off of the counter and stood up straight. "This is not helping."

Latrine seemed to take it as a challenge. "Any other questions?"

"That's all for now. We'll be in touch." Duffy left the kitchen first, followed by Detective Ross.

Peyton looked over at Latrine, who poured herself another glass of whisky. She didn't add any water. He wiped his brow—a few beads of a sweat had built up on it. "I have a feeling they'll be back."

Latrine didn't say anything. She just sipped her whisky. Peyton decided to let her be, giving her a light kiss on the forehead before heading out to work.

• • •

Duffy and Detective Ross closed the door behind them and left Peyton and Latrine's apartment. That they were withholding more than their fair share of information was at the vanguard of Duffy's thoughts. The look on Latrine's face when they walked in the door revealed a guilty conscience. Either she said something to Ina Godda or she did something to Ina Godda to make her fly off the handle. It was unconvincing and illogical that she would flail around like she was impersonating Tina Turner in one of her routines—all the while stripping off her clothes in a classy, public setting, especially when said clothes were a dress as elaborate as that one.

"What did you think?" Duffy didn't even bother to look at the expression on his face.

"Definitely not sitting well with me."

"Not at all."

They climbed into Detective Ross's car and sat down. Duffy took out the file and flipped through some of the documents they'd acquired from various sources on the Dingwall-Macbeths as Detective Ross drove away. He put on his eighties flashback alternative music, and the world suddenly became emo. Duffy looked down and noticed an envelope marked "Immigration Services" on it.

"What's this?"

"Oh yeah. I picked that up last night. I knew they'd be applying for some form of work visa, so I found a record of it." His head moved to the rhythm of The Cure's "Love Song."

"Brains and brawn." Duffy opened the envelope, unfolding the papers. "Alastair? Alastair Macbeth? That's her name? That's her real name?"

"Apparently it is."

"I never thought I'd say that Latrine Dion was a step up." Duffy let out a cackle of a laugh. "I need to call Twatla."

"Isn't this supposed to be a confidential investigation?"

Duffy hit Twatla's number on her phone. "She won't tell a soul."

"Alastair Macbeth," she said, before Twatla could even say 'hello.' "That's the Scottish bitch's real name."

"Alastair Macbeth?" Screeching and hooting and hollering erupted from the phone. Twatla thanked Jesus and every other spirit in the Judeo-Christian tradition for cursing the banshee with so tragic a name. Duffy looked over at Ross who had a grin plastered on his face, a slight chuckle slipping out. Twatla's laugh was contagious.

Duffy told Twatla she'd see her later and hung up the phone. "There. That was a welcome reprieve to the tragedy, was it not?"

Detective Ross still had a smile on his face. "You're right."

"How much longer until we get to Cunny's apartment?"

"It's just down this road, I think." He slowed down to get a look at the numbers on the buildings.

"I think Cunny will be far more cooperative. I know she's getting closer to Latrine, but she's so dense, I think we could probably pry out the information we need without her even realizing she's spilling the beans." Duffy closed Latrine's file and put it aside.

Detective Ross parked the car. Duffy led the way up to Cunny's front door, ringing the bell. She answered, clad in a pink terrycloth robe. *Those queens and their pink robes.* Her makeup was undone, her face unshaven, and her hair—well, manly.

"OMG! What are you guys doing here?" Cunny tried in vain to close her robe more as if to indicate she was underdressed for such esteemed company.

"We'd like to ask you a few questions about what you saw with the Ina Godda incident." Ross sounded too business-like.

"I know you're probably still really upset about it," Duffy said in a softer tone. "But it would really help us to put some pieces together. We would really appreciate it."

Duffy's tactic in those situations was never to make her valuable witnesses think they were under investigation in any way. With Latrine, it was different. She was really suspicious to her from the get-go and needed to be treated that way. She needed to make her more fearful. Plus, Duffy hated her. It was appropriate to indicate subtly that she'd get her and her little dog too, even if just for the thrill of making her shake in her boots for a little while. Cunny had some genuine emotion at the Inverness Tea Room. She was naïve and easily vulnerable. If Duffy got Cunny to trust her and think she was showing concern for her emotional well-being, they'd get the information they needed.

Cunny showed them in, and they sat down in her living room. The furniture looked like it was square out of the Ikea catalog, and Duffy felt like she literally just took the catalog and ordered the entire room as is, installing it in her apartment. She even had a few books on the shelf that were in Swedish, which was funny because A) The bitch didn't know any Swedish for sure, and B) The bitch didn't read books for sure. Her wax fruit on the table was placed on top of a stack of *People*, and a mannequin head sat beside it with a wig adorning it. She had a curling iron plugged in and resting off the edge. Duffy had the sudden and palpable fear the iron was going to damage the layer of lacquer on the table. She wondered if Cunny knew that, or even if she knew that wood was flammable.

"You'll have to excuse me. I was just getting this wig ready for lunch today."

"I hear they've got a lot of fiber in them." Detective Ross, it seemed, was taking Duffy's cue for a softer line of interrogating.

Cunny laughed. She laughed hard. She laughed so hard she started snorting and gasping for air, leaning back on the couch, curling iron in hand. Duffy watched the curling iron as if it were a Molotov cocktail about ready to strike the poor, unsuspecting couch and burst it into flames. She wondered if Cunny had any spatial awareness or any awareness—of anything. After her laughter began to die down, Duffy cleared her throat to try and refocus the conversation.

"You are so funny, Ross." Duffy felt the need to acknowledge what had made Cunny so comfortable and ripe for questioning.

"He is. Funny and cute," Cunny said.

Duffy motioned for Ross to take a seat beside her on the sofa. "We figured that since we knew you, you'd be willing to help us out."

"Oh, of course! I definitely want to help out. I definitely want to know what happened to Ina Godda."

"How did you end up at lunch with Ina Godda, Latrine, and Peyton?" Duffy asked.

"Oh, it was Latrine's idea. She wanted to try to make nice with Ina Godda. I think she felt bad about what happened in the dressing room at the Parliament House."

Duffy was perplexed. She didn't remember there being any altercation of note that night in the dressing room. "What happened?"

"Peyton and her were kind of going at it with each other. You know, being kind of catty."

"Oh. Catty how?" Duffy stole a glance at Ross.

"Oh, you know. Being all snarky and what not with each other. Mocking each other and stuff."

"Can you be more specific?" Ross took out a small pad and stylus from his inside suit pocket.

"I mean, I don't really know for sure. We tried to get Ina Godda to come with us to see Rhiannon the next day, but she didn't want to." Cunny stopped working on a lock of hair and pointed the curling iron up at the ceiling. "I think maybe Latrine was feeling bad about that or something."

"So Latrine was really just trying to be nice by inviting her to tea?" Ross asked.

Cunny tipped the curling iron at him like a teacher holding a yardstick. "Yes. Definitely."

Duffy took a deep breath. An awkward silence permeated the room as the line of questioning started to reach a turn. "So what exactly happened at the Inverness Tea Room that made her go all nuts?"

"We all got there first." Cunny resumed her curling. "We talked for a bit and ordered tea and scones. Then, she walked in. She was really confident too. Definitely dressed to try to show us all up. She sat down after greeting us and then we got to talking a little. Small talk stuff. And then the tea came. Ina Godda played 'mother'—whatever that means—and then before I could even blink, she dropped the mug of tea and started itching and ripping at her dress."

"Just out of the blue?" Duffy asked.

Cunny nodded.

"Did she complain about itching or anything?" asked Ross.

"You know, now that I think about it, she was complaining that it was hot out on the terrace. But, I mean, that was kind of expected because of what she was wearing. You know, one of those fancy sweaters all buttoned up to her neck like in the olden days."

"And by the end she had ripped it all off?" Ross stuck the stylus in his mouth and turned the page.

"Yup."

"And did you see like a rash on her or something? Any kind of marks?" Duffy asked.

Cunny looked up at the ceiling like she was trying to visualize the moment. "She did have some red marks on her, but she was twitching so quickly and rubbing her ass so violently against the railing that it was really hard to see."

"So after she ripped her clothes off, she rubbed her rear against the railing *before* it broke?" Ross asked.

"Right. It was… It was… just so awful," Tears formed in Cunny's eyes. Duffy handed her a tissue from a box beside her couch and took the curling iron from her hand, unplugging it from the outlet.

"I think we have all we need for now." Duffy placed the handle of the curling iron on the table, making sure the hot part didn't come in contact with anything. She gave Cunny a hug before leaving.

As they walked to the car, Duffy shook her head. It was just such a strange situation. It was strange to interrogate someone about the death of a close friend. It was tough to suspect people who were in a competition that was supposed to be fun. It was unhealthy to have to treat everyone as if they were colluding in some grand scheme.

"We need prints from Ina Godda's apartment." Ross opened his door. "Let's hit that next."

Duffy climbed into the passenger seat beside him and buckled her seatbelt. "One thing's for sure. Everyone we've talked to so far knows we mean business. I think they all know we won't stop until we find out the truth about what happened."

Chapter 12

A strange door. One might say queer. Latrine had to open it to satisfy her curiosity. Turning the knob revealed a white blanket of haze, like steam emerging from a street-level subway vent on a winter day. She felt her muscles tense, as on the verge of cumming. Sheer ecstasy. Several doors lined the hallway, evenly spaced. All at once, they swung open. A phalanx of drag queens, clad in flowing medieval gowns, marched out. Flanking the hallway, they stood at attention, staring into nothingness. Latrine crept forward, remaining vigilant. There was nothing friendly about these ladies. Ahead of her lay what looked like a glowing orb. She couldn't tell. She kept edging forward. The queens' heads remained stationary. Eeriness took control of her limbs. They started to quiver. Her hands started to shake.

And then, before Latrine—was the orb. Only it wasn't an orb. It was a—Could it be a—

"Is this a dildo I see before me?"

Latrine approached it. It couldn't be. She looked around. The eyes of the stoic queens stared in her direction. "What are you bitches looking at?"

They continued to stare.

"Is this a joke?" Latrine turned around to see the queens no longer standing in succession, but edging closer to her. Strange grins were plastered on their faces. Not before long, she noticed one of the queens was the bitch Twatla, leading the group's slow stride toward her. They locked eyes with each other. Twatla smiled coyly.

To her right, Latrine could make out another familiar face, one whose face was softer than the severe features of the other queens. She gazed into her eyes, animated by some form of satisfaction, some form of lust. The face emerged from the mist, and she recognized it as that bitch Duffy. Duffy smiled at her, her jaw dropping like she was about to lick her chops. As Duffy lurked closer, Latrine noticed the queens forming a ring around her, forever a rosie with a pocket full of posies. Twatla couldn't help herself. Her mouth opened, her eyes drunk with lust. Did she want Latrine? Did she desire her? Did she want to ride her? Did she want to press her open mouth to some orifice of Latrine's fabulous body? Latrine believed in that moment Twatla was gay— no man would don a dress and a pair of fake breasts on a nightly basis and call himself straight.

"Clutch it." Twatla's voice was filled with wanton desire.

"Go on. Clutch it," Duffy added. The queens all stared at her like bitchy medieval children of the corn. She turned around and looked at the dildo, glowing like an ember in the night sky. It pulsed. It throbbed. It begged to be held. The chorus of "clutch it" continued in staggered succession behind her, waves of coercion crashing into her shoulder blades as they tightened into knots in her upper back. She cracked her neck to ward off the fetus of fright growing in her stomach. The acid churned and spewed a geyser-column of fury into her throat. She turned around to face them one last time, unsure if she should grasp the glowing dildo before her. They nodded. She paused before extending her arm with hesitation and wrapping her manicured fingers around the glowing phallus.

The energy. The sheer energy shot through her body, pressure building in her groin. The queens were in ecstasy. They moaned. They groped themselves. Even Duffy did, which Latrine found quite disconcerting. Latrine soon realized it wasn't just the queens grunting. It was the whole room—the whole hall expanding and contracting with delight, sheer delight at her holding it. An involuntary smile formed on her face, the kind you get when other look to you in praise of a fabulous performance of your favorite Celine up-tempo. Utter satisfaction. She looked down at the dildo in her hand.

"What the fuck?"

Blood. Blood on her hands. Blood on the dildo. Where had the dildo been? Which bitch bled on the dildo? Latrine dropped it to the floor, and it bounced once before lying there, lifeless. A lifeless dildo. Covered in blood. She looked up at the queens, whose smiles had widened and expanded like tooth-filled Venus Flytraps.

Twatla chuckled. Duffy chuckled. Twatla looked at Duffy. Twatla and Duffy chuckled. The queens chuckled. The chuckles grew. Chuckle. Chuckle. Chuckle. Ha. Ha. Ha. Ha. Ha. Ha. Hahahahahahaha. The room shook with uncontrollable laughter. Latrine stared at her hands, smeared with blood. She looked down at the dildo lying in a lake of red. Her breathing grew shallow. They laughed harder. She doubled over, her hands pushing into the sides of her temples. The laughs continued. No more ecstasy. No more delight. Only laughter forever more.

"NOOOOOOOOO!"

Latrine screamed aloud as she sat up in the bed. Peyton remained asleep beside her, unfazed by her outburst.

She shook him. "Peyton? Peyton, wake up. Wake the fuck up."

"What?" he asked, his eyes heavy.

Latrine clapped her hands together, and the lights turned on. "We killed Ina Godda."

Peyton, still lying prostrate, slammed his fists down into the bed. "Are you gone bats?"

"We did. We killed her."

"What's this 'we'?" Peyton sat up and folded his arms.

"I had a dream. There were drag queens. And doors. And there was a bloody dildo. Like how Twatla's cock must look when Duffy's on her period."

"You need to lay off the melatonin." Peyton clapped his hands, and the lights turned out.

Without missing a beat, Latrine did the same. The lights turned on. "We poisoned her."

"No." Peyton glared at Latrine before she got out of bed to pace.

"We poisoned Marco Polo—her lover. All she wanted was to stick him in her arse."

"She did stick him in her arse. And you didn't know that she was going to itch her arse all over the bloody Tea Room and then fall over the railing to her death."

That's right. I didn't know that. She stopped. She looked at Peyton. He looked at her, hopeful. He was perhaps a little tired, eyes glossed over and unfocused but still sincere.

Latrine sat down on the edge of the bed. "We did not know that."

Peyton fluffed her pillow and motioned for her to lean back. "You didn't."

"We didn't know that she was going to die."

He patted the pillow again. "Most certainly, you didn't."

"We're innocent."

"You're innocent."

"Take that, you bloody dildo." She clapped her hands and fell back into the pillow.

Chapter 13

The past couple of days were hard. Twatla missed Ina Godda. Her smile. Her sarcasm. Her attitude. She was truly one of the most spectacular queens to have ever graced a stage. Edge. Creativity. An adoring fanbase. She really had it all, but the secret Twatla knew about Ina Godda was that under her confident and educated façade was an insecure, lonely queen. Her solitude was mostly a product of her own doing. She had every opportunity to date and to make friends, but she was just so damn competitive it often caused a lot of misunderstanding. People got the impression she was arrogant and conceited and weird. In reality, she really had every right to be. She won more competitions than anyone Twatla knew, and maybe anyone she would ever meet in the future, even with talent like Cunny Corleone coming down the pike.

She often hid her insecurity, appearing to be a ball-buster, appearing to be the kind of queen you didn't want to mess with, appearing to be—well, let's face it—a bitch. Twatla knew differently. The challenge now was figuring out how to create a funeral to convey her warmth and her spirit that also still paid homage to her superstar image. Did Twatla go big and fabulous or small and intimate?

Twatla sipped a cup of tea in her quiet living room, nothing but the distant hum of a lawnmower buzzing outside. She paused for a few moments, closing her eyes, trying to envision what would be the right way to honor her memory.

Aww heck. Who am I kidding?

Of course, it needed to be a spectacle. They needed big queens, big hair, big music. They needed glitter and a gospel chorus. They needed to thank Jesus for giving them one of the greatest queens to ever walk the Earth. One of the greats was being welcomed into the Kingdom of Heaven where she'd be partying along with Whitney and Judy and Liz and Joan.

Twatla picked up the phone and started making calls. Florists. Fashionistas. Singers. Queens. Gays. Even lesbians. Everyone would have to come to the send-off.

A few hours later, the whole thing seemed to be coming together. Twatla created a workspace on the kitchen table. Flanked by notepads and electronic gadgets, she had an earpiece in her ear reminiscent of Janet Jackson on tour. Crumpled up scrap papers surrounded her like she was in one of those *Cathy* comic strips where the title character got flustered. Duffy strolled in, apparently home from work, and planted a kiss on her forehead.

"So I think the funeral is all ready to go," said Twatla.

"I didn't know it was your responsibility to plan it." Duffy opened the refrigerator and took out their Brita filter.

"Well, who else would? She has no family that even talks to her anymore."

"Have you tried those numbers I gave you?" Duffy poured two glasses of water—one for Twatla. "Ross and I tried contacting her closest relatives, and we just got a lot of voicemails."

"Same here." Twatla paused for a moment. The sadness that Ina Godda probably lived in complete isolation was palpable. She thought for a moment about how that probably inspired her to be the best queen she could be. "Well, you know what? We will put the invitation out there to them. Ina Godda is going to go out in such a blaze of glory that she will feel this love from Heaven."

Duffy walked over to her and put her arms around her neck, handing her a glass of water. "You're amazing."

Chapter 14

Latrine simply did not know what to wear. What did you wear to a funeral for a person who had it coming? She half thought about not going, but that would have been just daft. Not going made it look like she wanted her dead. Latrine didn't want her dead. Injured? Yes. Incapacitated? She'd take it. Dead? Well, no.

She imagined the funeral would be filled with gays dressed to the nines and queens dressed like it was Fashion Week in Milan. There'd be more black-sequined dresses than in Liza Minelli's closet. Seeing so many queens out in the daytime, overwhelmed by the sunshine of which their nocturnal habits and vices deprived them would be interesting to watch. She would most certainly be impressed if they didn't recoil from the brightness and crumble from the rickets they'd developed. It would also be interesting to see if any of those Miss Havishams exploded in a spontaneous combustion of tears, bitter misery, and retrospection as they wept for someone whose pitiful existence yet glamorous façade so closely mirrored their own.

Latrine decided to wear a black veil over her face. It'd be easier to grimace at the spectacle she anticipated would be thrown in Ina Godda's honor. She'd also wear a black cocktail dress—wholly appropriate for the occasion. Simple black dress. Curled brunette wig. Hat with a veil. Black pumps. She couldn't go wrong. Peyton decided to channel his Scottish roots and wear a formal kilt. Black and red tartan with a fitted blazer. It was one of his best. Latrine actually bought it for him on the Royal Mile in Edinburgh before they left. She hoped he'd wear it when they got married, but breaking it in for a funeral wouldn't hurt. She actually felt closer to him that day than ever before and got the slightest inkling he might propose to her.

They hopped into the van, and Latrine turned up the Celine song of the day, "Because You Loved Me." It never ceased to give her strength when she was weak. Peyton kept quiet.

Cunny reported back to Latrine all of the juicy details about everything she'd been hearing. The wake was closed-casket, which Cunny attended. Apparently, they couldn't get the skin right, and Twatla demanded she not be seen. It was also pretty apparent Twatla had trouble finding a funeral venue. She settled for a non-denominational church across town to which she'd never been. Originally, Latrine wasn't planning to go either to the wake or to the funeral out of fear of being recognized, but Cunny's description gave her the impression it was going to be a spectacle. Latrine realized that she needed to make an appearance, not only because it could get suspicious if she didn't, but she also realized that if indeed it turned out to be anything like what she said, it could be the event of the century—short of her winning Duchess and progressing to Grand Dame.

Peyton and Latrine drove past a cemetery, the spot she imagined Ina Godda would be buried. Leave it to that bitch to take up valuable parcels of real estate. It was a staunch belief of Latrine's that when she left the Earth, she would be cremated, with her ashes spread right down the middle of the St. Lawrence River: Half in Canada and half in the United States. That way, she could honor Celine's motherland and the other half of her could be dumped in Peyton's new homeland.

As they approached the church, Latrine glimpsed the masses of people in attendance. She had no idea Ina Godda the Diva was that well-known. They circled the car park three times, only to find no spaces available. A spot was free down the street which entailed hiking uphill in heels. Peyton and Latrine walked into the church and into the nave, assuming that was what those big assembly rooms were called in those non-traditional churches. In Scotland, most churches were hundreds of years old and followed a cruciform pattern. The non-denominational church definitely ascribed to the Heathen School of architecture. They found a couple of spots available in a pew toward the rear of the room and walked over. Latrine got a good glimpse of the crowd, and what she saw was like a bag of skittles upchucked right before the eyes of the Baby Jesus hanging over the altar. A rainbow of fruity flavors speckled the room. Oranges, Reds, Yellows—in all shades and hues. Every possible outfit and costume—from *Breakfast at Tiffany's* to *Gone with the Wind*. And there was Latrine, in a simple black cocktail dress with a black veil. The writing was on the wall. The veil had to go.

Feeling slightly mortified to be so underdressed, she found the fact that Peyton wore the more appropriate attire to be highly disconcerting. As she was about to sit, she got a text message from Cunny that read *I'm here. Where are you?*

Latrine looked around for a moment. Then, she spotted her— dressed as Marie Fucking Antoinette. She wore a huge hoop skirt of periwinkle satin replete with ruffles bursting from the center. She had so many ruffles, the periwinkle hue seemed to blanch into nothing more than peri-wrinkle. Her bodice was fitted with a lace corset. Her makeup—powder white with pink blotches on her cheeks. Her hair—a massive gray wig—was out of this world, or if not that high, at least nearly out of this room. It must've been about five feet high, and she walked like she was balancing a stack of books on her head—a runway model in training. As she walked toward them, all Latrine could think was that Cunny would want to sit beside her. The fear of her hoop skirt cramming her in was all she could think about. Those anxieties segued to the thought that any attempt to remain incognito was most certainly dashed as that colossus of gray hair was going to be a beacon of attention for miles on end.

Cunny sat beside Latrine just in time. The ceremony started. The procession lined up at the doors in the rear of the church. The opening electronic chords of Cher's "Believe" filled the room, a hokey attempt, Latrine thought, to get the crowd to ponder the profundity of the song's chorus. A giant disco ball dropped from the ceiling as the funeral march began. Twatla led the pack, accompanied by Duffy. As they marched down the center aisle, the casket appeared, draped with a rainbow flag, flanked by eight shirtless pallbearers. Each of them wore a long tie around his neck, each in a different color from the rainbow, which matched their square-cut boxer briefs. Their heads were bowed in some kind of hunk solidarity.

Latrine felt her jaw drop.

One of the shirtless men was far superior to the eight tasked with carrying the coffin. A blond crew cut, massive muscles, violet boxer briefs. Latrine had a feeling she knew who it was, but it was too coincidental. As the man looked up, she was nearly blinded by the shimmering crystalline blue eyes juxtaposed with his sun-kissed skin. Marching behind the coffin, tears in his eyes, was none other than Marco Polo—*the* Marco Polo. Of dildo fame. For a moment, she needed confirmation that it was all actually happening—that it was actually real and not some strange dream with dildos and laughing medieval queens. She looked down at Peyton, and he looked up at her, pointing in the direction of the legendary porn star.

"OMG!" Cunny shouted. "It's Marco Polo!"

Marco looked up, and for a moment, the music froze like a buffering YouTube video. He glared at Latrine—just Latrine, eyes piercing her and haunting her like she'd just wounded an animal and was pointing a rifle at it for the final kill. A slight shiver crept up her spine before she came to her senses and realized she was daydreaming. Marco never looked at her. He never even looked anywhere but straight ahead.

The procession reached the altar, and Twatla approached the microphone. She was clad in a salmon-toned evening gown with a massive afro wig. Her bodice was adorned with sparkly rhinestones, kind of like she went crazy with the Bedazzler. She droned on and on about how grateful she was for everyone to be there and how grateful she was to have known Ina Godda, and blah blah blah blah blah. Latrine looked at Peyton and rolled her eyes slightly, ever vigilant to see if anyone—including Cunny—

saw her. They were all wrapped up in their grief. Cunny had the waterworks dripping from her face like a torrential downpour at the top of Ben Nevis. The other funeral attendees were in various stages of their own tear-tempests, from monsoon-like sobs to little drizzles.

And before she knew it, the most magical spectacle of the day happened. A gigantic chorus of gay men and large black women gathered at the stairs to the altar in rainbow-colored choir robes, and the opening piano chords to Donna Summer's "Last Dance" played. One of the gays stepped up to the mic and began the solo ballad portion of the song. The choir behind him hummed dulcet harmonies in the style of a bluesy spiritual. And then he held out that note—the note right before the disco portion. It resonated through the rafters and every nook and cranny of that church. The disco ball started spinning, the crowd leapt to its feet, and the place erupted into a Studio 54 nostalgia party. Cunny joined right along with them, the sheep that she was. Peyton nudged Latrine to stand up, reminding her she had to look like she wanted to be there.

All Latrine kept thinking about was how after that tribute to a fallen queen, she would get to take her spot. She would get to be the object of worship—those people would all be celebrating her, and she'd be alive to see it.

The choir sang a few more disco anthems and club favorites, and the ceremony was over. Outside, Latrine stood with Cunny and Peyton, making sure she was seen with a tissue blotting her eyes as much as possible. As Twatla and Duffy walked over to them, her knees started to jitter. Cunny threw her arms around them. For a brief moment, Latrine thought they just wanted to say hello to her, but they quickly moved on and headed in her direction. Latrine forced a smile and blotted her eyes with a tissue.

"Latrine. Peyton," Twatla said in a curt manner.

"Twatla. I'm so sorry for your loss." It felt like the right thing to say. Everyone else had been saying it all day. Latrine hoped it sounded genuine.

"Thank you." Twatla's face was emotionless. "We have a bit of business to run through with you."

"Okay." Latrine worried Duffy would launch into questions again, but she remained silent for a change.

"Since Ina Godda is no longer able to represent our community in the Duchess Regionals, as runner up, you now qualify to attend and represent us." Twatla turned to Cunny and continued, "That means that I now officially endow you with the title of Countess, Miss Cunny Corleone."

Cunny smiled through her tears, reassuring Latrine that it was okay for her to smile. Though Latrine may have appeared tactful on the outside, on the inside, she danced a jig and screamed with excitement. It was bound to happen because she was entitled to it, but Latrine didn't think the title would be passed on at the funeral. The universe had its way of telling her she was doing the right thing—like choosing to show up.

Latrine expressed her gratitude and condolences once again to Twatla and Duffy, who seemed completely nonplussed. Twatla turned to Cunny, and right in front of Latrine, grabbed her arm. "Ina Godda would have wanted you to win. She saw potential in you."

Duffy apparently loved the dig at Latrine's expense. Her smirk revealed her vagina was so wet over it that it needed to be stored in a sealed container with dry rice overnight.

Cunny's mouth was agape. "I didn't think she liked me."

"Oh Lord have mercy, no! She thought you were great. That tude was a total façade, girl. If she came across with an attitude, it's because she knew you were great. You are marked for greatness." Twatla gave her a hug before walking off with Duffy in tow.

Cunny looked unsure of how to take the news. Latrine hugged her, squinting her eyes at Peyton. She recalled Rhiannon's reading and her premonitions. She no longer thought them odd.

Cunny was marked for greatness. Marked for greatness, my arse.

Chapter 15

Cunny didn't know how to take it all. She'd miss Ina Godda for sure, and it was sad she couldn't go with her to Regionals, but the prospect of Latrine getting to go with her made her ecstatic. She couldn't stop herself from daydreaming about shopping together and dressing their wigs together and doing each other's makeup. It was going to be such amazingness.

That, and she was the new Countess.

She stood in her closet after the funeral, pondering her routines, thinking through what she needed to pack. Twatla told her there was an opening number and a closing number that all contestants had to learn. Each competitor was also allowed two individual numbers to perform to. Cunny took that to mean there should be one ballad and one up-tempo. But she wasn't going to do that. She was going to do something different. If you wanted to win, she believed, you had to do what nobody expected you to do.

She would perform to do two up-tempos.

The first planned number was "One Day in Your Life" by Anastacia. She would don her brunette wig with the chunky blonde highlights. The ensemble would be a patriotic theme since Anastacia sang the song at the World Cup one year. She'd wear a red-sequined crop top tied below the breasts. No ponytail. A mountain of thick curls held in place with a blue-sequined headband. Blue-sequined bracelets. White mini-skirt. Red belt. Blue six-inch platform heels. She would be Miss America, Countess, Duchess, and Grand Dame all in one.

And that was just the first number.

The second would be even more retro. She'd perform death-defying hair whipping to Deborah Cox's "Absolutely Not," staying true to the song. She never really liked how Ina Godda the Diva would go against what the lyrics of the song said. She never understood that. Cunny would dress exactly as the song prescribed. Blonde hair in a high pony tail—perfect for whipping. Satin pink Chanel mini-skirt, loose at the top like a sixties go-go dancer. White knee-high boots with six-inch heels. She'd pirouette like an Olympic figure skater doing spins, amazing the judges so much they wouldn't be able to control giving her perfect tens across the board.

Cunny would be named Duchess. Latrine would come in second. And when Cunny won, she had a perfect plan for what she was going to do with that prize money. She was getting bigger boobs.

• • •

Latrine was quiet the whole trip home from the funeral, the hum of the van's decaying motor filling the silence. Peyton assumed she was worried about what Twatla and Duffy said to Cunny and that they might be in cahoots with her to get her to win Duchess. They'd used their weight before to get the judges to see it their way. They could do it again.

As they walked into the door of their flat, Latrine ripped off her wig and tossed it to the floor. She chucked her heels across the room, nearly toppling a bottle of his Glengoyne 18-year.

"Hey! Mind yourself!"

Latrine threw herself on the sofa. "I'm just so fucking scunnered."

"You have every reason to be."

"Pour me a whisky." She lied face down, so her command was muffled. Peyton wasn't used to taking orders from her, but in considering her vulnerable mood, he strolled over to the mini-bar and put some ice in a glass.

"You sure you don't want some mead instead?" he asked.

Her head lifted off the cushion. "This isn't fucking *Beowulf*. Give me the good stuff."

If he knew it was possible, he'd think she was on her period. "You want a Speyside?"

"I want the heavy stuff. Break out the Bruidcladdich 18-year."

Bruidcladdich. Islay whisky. She meant business. Peyton poured her a few ounces into a Glencairn glass and handed it to her. He retreated to his Glengoyne 18-year.

He plopped down beside her head as she continued to lie prostrate. "You need to find out her routines."

"Whose?"

"Cunny's."

"I'm not worried about her routines." She sat up, her voice candid. "I'm worried about more cheating. I'm worried about not getting what I deserve."

"You just keep a close eye on her. Maybe she's more honest than Ina Godda is. You never know."

And with that, Latrine shot the whisky. No whisky ever got shot, much less a heavy Bruidcladdich 18-year. She got up and put her pair of heels back on, tossing on her wig and straightening it as she walked toward the door.

"Where are you going?"

"I need a reading. I need to see Rhiannon." Latrine grabbed the keys from a wall peg and disappeared out the door.

Peyton had a faint fear about needing to stop her before she got in the van, especially after shooting whisky. There was no need for anxiety. She was a big girl—a big Scottish girl.

• • •

Latrine was sure Rhiannon was at the funeral, though she didn't see her anywhere at the church. All she knew was that bitch better not have stayed for any after-party. The sky opened up as she drove. Rain pummeled the van so hard it was nearly white-out conditions. They got a lot of rain in Scotland, but it was rarely torrential. Perseverance through the storm was paramount. Cars pulled off to the side of the road, turning on their hazards. *Fuck that.* There was no time for that. She made it to Rhiannon's and parked in her driveway. No sign of any car, though it was possible it was in the garage. The drawn shades in her house obscured any light, so there was no way of knowing if Rhiannon was home.

Latrine opened the van door as she opened her umbrella to avoid getting her wig and her dress wet. So much for that. The wind blew the rain sideways, attacking her like a hail of bullets. She made a mad dash for the front doorstep and rang the doorbell.

After a moment, Rhiannon answered. "Latrine? Oh my stars, look at you! You must be frozen. Please come inside." She opened her screen door.

"I'm so glad you're home," said Latrine, shivering, beads of rain dripping down her face from her drenched wig.

"Let me get you some towels." Rhiannon hurried down a hallway. Latrine took off her wig and wrung it out. A pool of water dampened the plush carpet. It looked like Latrine pished on it.

Rhiannon walked back in with a stack of towels. Latrine pointed to the spot on the rug.

"That's okay," Rhiannon said, wrapping her up. Latrine's makeup ran as she stood there in a wig cap. Looking as pathetic as possible, she half-hoped playing the sympathy card would garner a free reading.

"Can I get you some hot tea?"

Latrine didn't answer.

"Are you okay?"

"It's just—it's just that I miss Ina Godda so much." A whimper climbed through her trachea and out her mouth. The crying remained unaccompanied by any real tears, but the running makeup masked the act.

"I know." Rhiannon rubbed her shoulders.

Latrine wiped her eyes. "I feel so lost."

"You do?"

"Yes. So, so lost."

"Well, have a seat. Let me get a good sense of where you are." Rhiannon hurried over to her table and pulled out a chair.

Latrine lowered her head and raised her shoulders, a feigned effort to come off as demure. "No. You don't have to do a reading. I just wanted someone to talk to that I can trust."

"No, I insist. It's on me."

"Okay," said Latrine, as if her arm were suffering from a giant twist.

Rhiannon sat her down at the same table as before and walked over to a credenza to retrieve her plush pillow laden with the silver posh pen surrounded by crystals. She reached into a drawer and took out a few sheets of paper before sitting down across from Latrine.

"Mmmmmmmmmmmmmmmmm," Rhiannon hummed, as if trying to find a frequency. She closed her eyes, and the pen started moving on the piece of paper. "Yes. Yes. I see things."

Latrine closed her eyes. "What do you see?"

"Things."

Why so vague, bitch?

"I see some wonderful things."

It was clear to Latrine what they could be. "The Duchess Regionals?"

"I see a beautiful dress." Rhiannon's voice had such musicality to it.

"Yes. That makes sense," said Latrine with anticipatory excitement. "What of the dress?"

"The dress is… Burgundy. Kind of like on the *Titanic*."

Latrine froze and opened her eyes.

"The dress is tattered and torn." Rhiannon's tone was changing.

Latrine let out an uncomfortable laugh. "But the competition? What of the Duchess Regionals?"

"The competition," Rhiannon allowed the pen to draw what looked like either diamonds or kites. "The competition. Mmmmmmmmmmmmmmmmmmm."

The frequency stretched for what felt like ten bars of slow classical music. *Will you hurry the fuck up already?*

Rhiannon placed her pen down. "Do you really want to know?"

"Yes. Yes, of course. I really want to know."

"I don't think you want to know."

"Really. I do," Latrine affirmed. "What do you see?"

Rhiannon opened her eyes. "You're about to be eclipsed."

"Eclipsed?" Latrine paused for a moment. "Is it Cunny?"

"Cunny is unique. Cunny is special." Rhiannon looked at Latrine, wide-eyed. The possibility crossed Latrine's mind that she intended to say Cunny would be bestowed the Duchess title. It hard to be the reason she hesitated to tell her.

"So it *is* Cunny." An air of genuine despondence lay in Latrine's voice. But rather than looking at Latrine with pity and a tender sense of compassion, her comment was met with an accusatory stare.

Rhiannon grabbed her hand. "Perhaps you're too wrapped up in this competition. This competition spells darkness for you. You should take a step back."

"I plan to win," said Latrine in defiance.

"Oh you will do well." There was a pause. Rhiannon leaned back in her chair. "But at what cost, Alastair?"

"How did you know my—"

"This competition is poison. It's riddled with poison. Poison everywhere. Poison in everything. But you already know that, don't you?" Rhiannon's judgmental glare sent shock waves down Latrine's spine.

She leapt up from the table. "I should be going."

"So soon?" It felt like a passive-aggressive comment.

Latrine tried to be warm to her to leave a good impression, but she really just wanted to scram. She threw her arms around her for a quick embrace. "Thank you so much for the reading."

Rhiannon was unresponsive for a moment before patting Latrine on the back, keeping her there for an uncomfortable moment. "Don't lose this." The patting migrated to Latrine's head, causing her to break free.

"I won't." She tried to smile. "I have great support at home. Peyton is wonderful."

"He'll love you even more if you forget about buying that house."

Latrine paused. She didn't want the house; Peyton did. Rhiannon had her visions confused. That was the issue. Wires were crossed or something. It was a botched reading. Would Cunny win or not? She was even more confused, but there was no way she was sticking around for more answers.

The rain stopped. Latrine climbed into Peyton's van and turned on the music. The remix of Celine's "I Want You to Need Me" would accompany her home and help her to sort out her thoughts.

• • •

Latrine stormed in and slammed the door. Peyton waited for a fucking eternity wondering what happened to her, what with the rain coming down in buckets outside for the better part of an hour. Her walk toward him was slow and deliberate, her wig dripping in stringy knots like she tossed it into a pool and never let it dry. A manic expression widened her eyes.

"It's been fucking pissing outside. Isn't that dress dry-clean only?"

Her expression remained vacant as she sat down beside him.

"Whoa, whoa. You're dripping wet. Don't sit on the couch if you've got wet clothes." Peyton started to get up to look for a towel.

"It doesn't matter," she said. He lowered himself back down.

"What's gotten into you?"

"Cunny is the next Duchess." Her voice was soft, defeated.

"That's what she told you? That was what she said at the reading?"

"Aye. But she didn't say it. She implied it. Then she looked at me like I'm hiding something. Like I killed Ina Godda."

"Then she should know it was an accident." Peyton placed his hand on the nape of her wet neck.

"But she knew we were involved. I could tell. So chances are she's right about Cunny."

Peyton got up to pour a glass of whisky. "Want some of the Glenkinchie?"

"Glengoyne 18-year. Neat."

The stress of her dilemma was sprawled across her face. Her eyes were heavy with disappointment. He handed her a glass.

"Maybe it's not my year," she said.

"It's definitely your year." Peyton clinked his glass with hers as if to toast her. "You are poised and ready to go. You're doing choreography for your new routines and you've got all these ideas for new outfits for the competition. Of course it is your year."

"But if she's going to win anyway, why bother trying?"

"Rhiannon is most likely wrong. You need to try."

"Rumor is Cunny's the strongest contender."

Peyton took a sip of his drink. "So, you need to take her out."

Latrine snapped out of her funk and looked him in the eye for the first time. "I can't do that. She's my new friend."

"She's your competition." Peyton took a sip of his Glenkinchie and looked straight forward for a moment. There was the possibility Latrine wasn't quite seeing what he saw just yet, but her yearning for the title grew stronger by the minute. It had to be the case, or she wouldn't be so devastated by Rhiannon's reading. Peyton bit the inside of his lower lip, waiting for the moment to say just the right phrase. And with a deep breath, he said it. "Accidents happen."

Chapter 16

Things were just not going well in Genoa City. It was like all the hunks were in bad moods. They were wreaking havoc. Naturally, that meant they were all badasses in rare form, a trait that never ceased to get Cunny all hot and bothered. She took out her fan and watched as Tommy seduced Faith after he confronted her about sleeping with his brother. Cunny's only hope was that his brother would walk in on them, see them together, and join in. She had no qualms about its being incestuous or whatever. They didn't have to touch. With each pass of the fan before her face came the wish that daytime television would take more risks.

Her cell rang. Latrine's name appeared.

"Hey, you Scottish bitch."

"Hey, you American cunt."

"Of course you had to interrupt 'Y and R,' didn't you?"

"What's 'Y and R?'"

"OMG. WTF. BRB. Crying," said Cunny. "The Young and the Restless is only the most amazing show on the planet. I have to get you hooked. You'll totally feel like you live there, and the guys are super hot."

Latrine let out a laugh. "Well, if you like it, then I'm sure I will. Anyway, I was wondering if you'd be up for going shopping tomorrow. We'll make a whole day of it. Lunch and everything. Wear comfortable shoes. We've got a lot of stores to hit and a lot of fittings to do."

"So no heels?"

"No. You know what? I don't think we should go in drag tomorrow. I think we can cover much more ground if we're comfortable. Tomorrow we'll look like men."

"I have boobs, remember?"

"Right. Then let's make it low key. No elaborate dresses or anything. Jeans, maybe a nice top. Tame wigs. Light makeup." Latrine was always so pleasant, even when she was giving orders.

They said their goodbyes. Cunny hung up the phone and unpaused the television. Turned out it'd all been a setup. Tommy's brother knew Tommy would confront Faith and used her to trap him. Tommy's brother raised a gun at Tommy, but Tommy grabbed Faith and used her as a human shield. And then it went to commercial.

Cunny grabbed the remote and recorded the next day's episode. It was worth convincing Latrine to stop by her place after their shopping spree to watch it together.

Chapter 17

Latrine left the house dressed in a simple wig—no curls or elaborate hairstyles that day. She wore some stretch pants with an off-the-shoulder loose-fitting top, like in *Flashdance*, which she'd forced Peyton to sit through about thirty times by that point in their relationship (not that he minded). Her heels were something new: steel stilettos. Steelettos. Real metal. They were less likely to break, she heard. Perfect for a heavy shopping day.

With Peyton's help, she had attempted to lay out a route to maximize the danger. The pattern of stores in that day's itinerary was designed to push Cunny into harm's way. It was a shame he had to work; Latrine figured he'd probably enjoy watching Cunny get injured in some way. At least someone would get some joy out of it all. Latrine had been going back and forth in her mind all night. She really did like the girl, but she stood in the way of something very important at that stage in Latrine's life. And for that, she didn't feel bad. Latrine acknowledged she definitely had her way of being annoying, like when she continued to talk ad nauseam about things that didn't quite make sense, or when she peppered her speech with those fucking text expressions. Maybe it'd do some good to knock her out of her wits for a short period of time.

Latrine sat silently in the passenger seat, a habit that had become commonplace. Peyton droned on about tips and tactics, and she nodded along to make it look like she was paying attention. She played with the hairs at the end of her wig, massaging them with her thumb. There was still a chance she could make this a safe shopping trip—just two girls out on the town.

Peyton dropped Latrine off at Cunny's flat on his way to work, and she came to the door in a curly blonde wig, black leggings, twelve centimeter heels, and a black off-the-shoulder top. She looked just like Olivia Newton-John in *Grease* when Sandy decided to become a slut to impress Danny Zuko.

Latrine smiled. "You want me to take you to the Drive-in Movie?"

Cunny knit her brow. "Drive-in Movie? I thought we were going shopping."

"No, it's from… Ah, nevermind. You ready?"

Cunny stepped out of the way, like she was inviting her inside. "I have yesterday's episode of 'The Young and the Restless' recorded so we can watch before we go."

Latrine stared at the space inside her flat. It was warm, inviting—home to a friend. A pang of guilt fired through her veins. Her Adam's apple rose high in her throat before she regained the courage to take decisive action. A smile crossed her face. "That's going to have to wait. I have a very tight schedule planned. We have a great number of places to hit before lunch."

The smile faded from Cunny's face as she shrugged. "Let me get my purse then."

Attempts to block out their friendship and treat the whole afternoon like business were going to prove difficult. Latrine walked over to Cunny's car, the sun beating down on her pale skin as Cunny closed her front door and followed behind.

After they climbed in, Cunny put on "It's All Coming Back to Me Now."

"Did you put this on just for me?" The thoughtfulness wasn't making things easier.

Cunny backed out of the car park. "You're the only queen I know who chooses Celine above anyone else."

"Surely, I can't be the only one."

"No, really. You are."

Latrine looked out the window and sang a few bars to herself. She closed her eyes as a montage of a burgeoning friendship between her and Cunny played in her head. The images were tinged with sepia, a world of amber and garnet. Playful smiles on their faces as they held hands and skipped down the street. Moments of them dancing together on stage. Cunny lifted Latrine in the air as they spun around on a cold, barren ice rink—until Cunny's face was replaced with Peyton's.

Latrine opened her eyes. As Cunny drove through picturesque neighborhoods, Latrine saw the world in saturated colors. Red-brick houses with symmetrical architecture. Green lawns. Flowerbeds of zinnias and marigolds.

Latrine tried to shake off her nerves. As the song wound down, she let her eyes wander over to Cunny's breasts. They were lovely implants. Full, round shape.

"Which doctor did your titties?"

"Oh, Dr. Lennox. He's the best."

"Dr. Lennox?" said Latrine. "Scottish name. Of course, he's the best."

"You thinking about getting titties?"

"No, not really. Not yet anyway," said Latrine. "Just window shopping, I guess."

"You should really go in for a consultation. It's free, and he does this computer thing where he takes a picture and then he puts it up on the computer and you can play with the sizes and shapes and all. OMG it's fabulous. I could see what I look like with double-Ds."

"But you didn't get them, right?"

"Double-Ds? No. I got Cs. I'm a 16C. I thought they were just the right size, but now I want the bigger ones."

"You want to go bigger? They look big to me."

"Wanna feel?"

"What? Me? No. I'm not a breast gay." Latrine let out a nervous laugh.

"This is just for medical reasons. You need to feel what they feel like before you commit."

It was the smartest thing she'd ever said to Latrine. Cunny reached over and cupped Latrine's hand around her right breast, pushing down hard and massaging it. They did feel real, not that she had anything to compare it to, really. Latrine was impressed. She reached over and grabbed the other breast. Cunny, completely unfazed, drove intently down the road. Latrine weighed both of her breasts in her hands, playing with them like a teenage boy would do with a prostitute right before he was about to lose his virginity.

"They're well done," Latrine said.

"Right?"

Latrine wanted them. She really wanted them. If she got them, she figured she could be pretty much invincible. She would win Duchess every year like Ina Godda had. That would be $25,000 a year for who knew how long? She might even withstand the competition to win Grand Dame and the $100,000. It was time to set up an appointment with Dr. Lennox.

First things first, though. She needed to be decisive and keep her eyes on the prize. Cunny had the boobs, and they were an obstacle to her winning. Any pang of guilt for the day's scheme drained from her body. Cunny parked the car, and they got out, tossing their purses over their shoulders like divas on a mission. Latrine led her to a busy intersection, walking her right out into traffic. A car skidded from its brakes being slammed, and obscenities were yelled at them from behind the relative safety of a windshield. To Latrine's surprise, Cunny hadn't even batted an eyelash, completely unaware of the close call she had as a pedestrian.

Latrine led her to a boutique called Rhinestone Rendezvous, which sounded like the perfect store for a drag queen to stock up on the essentials. Cunny's eyes were instantly drawn to a multi-toned blue sari studded with blue rhinestones. Its different shades of blue bled into each other, so it looked like a giant wave pounding the beach.

"I want this."

"It looks like something that would be in my closet," Latrine said.

"I saw it first." Cunny was channeling her inner five-year-old.

Seemingly before she even finished her thought, Cunny's attention was diverted to another mannequin with a salmon-toned evening gown, not-so-shockingly studded with rhinestones. An *ooh* barely escaped from her lips before Latrine heard: "OMG, look at that one," as she darted over to another mannequin. It wasn't too long before Latrine realized they were in some sort of rhinestone-encrusted drag queen pinball machine where Cunny was the new Pinball Wizard with the supple wrists.

She walked over to the far wall, which was adorned with a veritable topiary garden of mannequins, all clad in elaborate gowns embellished with beading and sequins. Finding the right moment to knock a display over on her was tricky; the mannequins looked heavy—like they could do some serious bodily damage. Latrine figured it for Cunny's version of going to a sculpture museum. The mannequins were posed with different postures, much like the different levels in a very interesting tableaux or diorama. She moved from mannequin to mannequin like she was comparing the work of DaVinci to the work of Michaelangelo. As she proceeded down the line, she'd gotten her body angled away from the last one, allowing Latrine the perfect opportunity to improvise an accident.

She grabbed the foot of one of the mannequins, knocking it into the one beside it that was bent down on one knee. She hoped it would knock over onto Cunny, making her trip over the clothing rack beside her and sending her face smack into the floor. Instead, to her horror, pulling the foot of the mannequin did not cause the mannequin beside it to fall forward; it toppled the entire row of mannequins like a set of drunk-bitch dominoes, causing every shopper to turn and look in their direction. Cunny remained unfazed—and she didn't even trip and fall.

Latrine realized she hadn't completely thought through the physics on that one. A more sure-fire way of taking down Cunny looked like it would come from being outside.

"Cunny, you wee lass. Let's head over to Skin and look at some of the more racy ensembles. We need to make a mad dash for it.

I want to see if they have this one piece left that I had my eye on the other day."

"You feeling frisky, you Scottish bitch?"

"Indeed, I'm feeling frisky, you American arreola."

Latrine led her out the door by the hand and picked up the pace to give the illusion they were in a hurry. They darted down the street and approached a public square replete with skateboarders and roller-bladers criss-crossing in every direction like comets. They scurried right through the middle of the square, Latrine's own eyes carefully darting back and forth to ensure she was out of the line of fire. She pointed up at the tops of the buildings.

"I love the design of that tower."

Latrine shot a glance over her shoulder at Cunny, who had a vacant smile on her face, completely enraptured by the beauty and majesty of the buildings. Out of the corner of Latrine's eye, she could see a rollerblader speeding in their direction and hopping up on a stairway railing like he was skating through a parkour course. He dismounted from the railing and hurled at Cunny, full force. His rapid approach didn't even disturb her; she continued looking up at the buildings against the blue sunny sky as the poor rollerblader skid to try and dodge her, tripping over a planter that broke his fall. Latrine saw a few of his mates skate over to help him and could hear him shouting obscenities in their direction. Latrine just kept racing them through. Part of her wanted to stop because it might be an opportunity for a hate crime and a perfect opportunity to knock Cunny out of the competition, but the knowledge that she could be a victim too kept her marching ahead.

The frailty of Latrine's plan slowly became evident. Attempting to improvise traps in public was close to an impossibility, but she forged ahead, hoping that Skin provided the opportunity to incapacitate the bitch.

They walked in the store, and Cunny instantly had her eye on a red lace bustier worn by an anorexic-looking mannequin.

"OMG!" she shouted.

As she darted over to the mannequin, Latrine noticed a Roomba vacuuming the floor near her and gave it a swift kick it into Cunny's path, hoping it'd trip her. Instead, Cunny cleared it by a mile, like she was jumping hurdles at the Olympics. She fondled the material on the mannequin, so much so it bordered on molestation. Latrine looked around the store for any potentially perilous encounters. She saw racks and racks of panties, bustiers, bras, and teddies of every material. An entire section of the store was devoted to leather. There was even a section with mesh underwear for men (with no men trying on any at that moment unfortunately). To the rear of the store, she noticed the door to the stockroom was open, and it looked like they'd received shipments of boxes.

Latrine stood behind Cunny and whispered in her ear. "Psst. Let's go check out the new merchandise in the back."

"Why? There's so much out here to look at."

"Don't be bash. Let's go take a look. We might be able to slip something into our purses."

"I don't want to steal." Cunny's voice increased in volume slightly.

"Shh!" Latrine looked around. "We're not going to steal. We're just going to see if they have some new styles in. Don't you want to be the first to see so you can be the first to buy when they put it out on the racks?"

"You have a point," said Cunny.

They crept back to the storeroom, keeping vigilant that nobody could see them. The store wasn't that busy. The only clerk in the store Latrine spotted was actually on the phone at that moment. Perfect timing. When they got into the storeroom, a bunch of boxes were on the floor, ready for the picking.

"Oh my God, Cunny. Look at this!" Latrine held up a beautiful satin nightgown with lace around the boobage area. "This would be perfect for you."

She handed it over to Cunny, who also held it up, caressing the material like it was a hieroglyph etched into the Rosetta

Stone. As Cunny gazed at it, Latrine pretended to trip and fall into an adjacent free-standing set of metal shelves, stacked from top to bottom with boxes. With Latrine's feeble attempts at a stunt dive, the entire unit came crashing down to the ground. Boxes opened. Lingerie was everywhere. Cunny looked down at her as she remained upright—like a lone palm tree in a leveled rainforest—clutching that damn nightgown. "Are you okay?"

Latrine looked up at her from the floor, mulling over the possibility that like a pussy, Cunny had nine lives. Nine fucking lives. She helped Latrine up just as the clerk came rushing in.

"What the hell are you doing in here?"

The bitch couldn't be more than twenty years old, and Latrine was fairly certain they had interrupted her attempt to get laid on her lunch hour.

"Excuse me," Latrine spit back. "You were obviously too busy on the phone to help us, so we came back here to look for ourselves."

"You're not allowed back here." The bitch had a haughty, valley-girl accent.

"The door was open, and I don't see any sign that says 'no admittance' or 'employees only.' Did you see a sign, Cunny?"

"No, I didn't."

"Cunny? What kind of a name is Cunny?" The bitch was throwing shade at them.

Latrine looked at her name tag. "What kind of a name is Sophia? Because that name means wisdom, and if there's anything you don't have, it's wisdom."

"Good one," Cunny said.

"And on top of that, you're lucky we don't call the manager and tell her that you were rude to a customer and you had your ear glued to the phone instead of attending to our lingerie needs. Better yet, you know what? We really should just get out of here. Your store is for skanks and wankers. Come on, Cunny."

And with that, they marched out of the store with their heads held high. While they were able to dodge trouble on that one, Latrine was seriously out of options, and she was seriously starving.

"Lunch?"

As they strolled to the restaurant at a notably slower pace, it looked like Latrine was not terribly cut out for a James Bond lifestyle. Not everyone could be as dapper and collected as Sean Connery when plotting things. She accepted that she didn't get the cool and collected gene inherent in her people's lineage. She told herself it would be okay; she would just have to hope Cunny caught the flu or something before she left the next day. The bitch would probably take an aspirin and be just fine, resilient as she was.

And then it hit her.

When they were at the Inverness Tea Room the day of Ina Godda's accident, Peyton offered Cunny an aspirin. She said she was allergic. Latrine didn't quite know what that entailed, but it had to mean that she'd get some kind of a reaction to it that might mimic the flu or food poisoning or something that involved vomit. And it just so happened that Latrine carried aspirin with her for when she and Peyton drank too much whisky.

They sat down to lunch at a Thai restaurant known for its spicy and delectable dishes—dishes that required a constant cleansing of the palate. The waitress brought over some glasses of tap water and asked them if they were ready to order.

"I'll have the Shrimp Pad Thai. But spicy. Very spicy." Latrine smiled like she was already savoring the taste.

It seemed to sell Cunny on it. "Oooh. That sounds good. Make that two."

Maybe the trick to setting a trap was not to actually set the trap. It was allowing the other person to behave normally, then pouncing when she was at her weakest.

Cunny picked up her purse. "I'm going to go freshen up a bit."

Latrine smiled again and watched her get up. *Good things come to those who wait.* She never was one for aphorisms, but that one was very much apropos. She looked around to see if anyone was looking. None of the other patrons paid any attention to her, and for once, Latrine relished that observation. She reached into her bag, pulled out a bottle of aspirin, and dropped a pill into her water. It took a bit to dissolve. That worried her. *Would one do the trick?* She called the waitress over and asked for a Diet Coke, demanding that she bring it immediately. The waitress returned quite promptly with the drink, and Latrine dropped a few pills into it, stirring a bit.

After a moment, Cunny returned. Latrine pointed to the glass. "For you."

"Oh, but I cut soda out of my diet last year. I'm just a water girl with the occasional juice and alcoholic beverage."

"You may need it after the Pad Thai."

"True." Cunny smiled as she sat back down, placing her purse on the floor beside her.

The move had the effect of revealing the top of her cleavage. "Your titties look fantastic today. I really can't stop looking at them. They're remarkable."

"Do you want to touch them again?" Cunny reached under and lifted them high. "You can touch them as much as you like."

"Maybe later." Latrine really wanted to touch them again, but doing so would draw unnecessary attention to them.

Not before long, the waitress brought their orders; lunchtime rushes meant they had orders prepped and ready to go a lot quicker. She dove into her food with the hopes that Cunny would too. However, Cunny happened to be showing much more restraint compared to the primitive eating habits of Latrine. Latrine continued to shovel noodles into her mouth, slurping them like it was a mere bowl of pasta, completely knowing she was really risking a five alarm fire in her mouth simply to goad Cunny to follow suit.

Not before long, Latrine felt the prickling of embers lining her lips—a burning sensation igniting like lightning striking a desiccated forest. The fire spread from the rim of her lips to the valley of her mouth. A searing, incendiary explosion of peppers and heat, the likes of which would dwarf the Great Fire of London, blew through her mouth as if fanned by the gusts of a tempest. She reached for her glass of water and chugged it, releasing a dam that sent a tidal surge to her tongue.

But the reprieve was merely temporary. The fire returned with a vengeance. She held up her glass, looking around in a state of panic for the waitress.

"OMG Do you want some of my water?" Cunny held up her glass.

"No, no. That's for you. You're going to need it," she said. The waitress came over and refilled her water. "You should just leave the pitcher."

Cunny was well into her plate of Pad Thai, and she hadn't touched her water or her Diet Coke.

"You're not thirsty at all yet?" asked Latrine.

"Actually, I don't think it's that spicy."

"It's like a group of agrarian Brazilians are slashing and burning the rainforest in your mouth. How can you think it's not spicy?"

"I just don't, LOL." Cunny giggled. That LOL and OMG business peeved Latrine. Her American friend really severed their bond by uttering every Americanism that had perverted the English language. She felt like reaching over the table, grabbing her by the mouth, and pouring that aspirin-laden Diet Coke right down her gullet. Every time that fork dove into the plate of Pad Thai, she hoped for some twitch, some spasm, some paroxysm of a conflagration that would yield a desperate need to quench her fucking thirst. *Will you drink, you American fucking cunt?*

Latrine sat there, her zeal for her meal slowing down to merely picking at it. A slight case of depression set in as the time passed. Cunny contentedly ate her noodles with measured bites, not showing any inclination whatsoever of a need to drink any liquid of any kind. Latrine held up her hand to get the waitress's attention.

"Can we get the bill? Separate checks, please."

Cunny put down her fork and wiped her mouth with the napkin from her lap.

"You don't want any of your Diet Coke?" It was a final attempt to convince her to drink.

"Nope. Not thirsty. Actually, I have to confess something."

Maybe Cunny had figured it out. Latrine held her breath. She felt her heart race and her palms drench. "What's that?"

"It became kind of a challenge not to drink. Sure, I could've had some, but when you asked me if I needed some water or Diet Coke and then you got all desperate to have more and more water, I wanted to see how long I could go before I needed some. And as it turns out, I don't need any." Cunny lifted her purse onto her lap. "But what I do need is a mint. I think there was some garlic in that dish."

Latrine stared at her with utter contempt for a moment as she dug through her purse for her Altoids. If there were a way to bitch slap her or prick her implant with a fork, Latrine would do it. If she could kick her in the face, she would do it. If she could ram her chopsticks down her nose and scoop out pieces of her unformed brain, she would do it. But she took a few breaths and remembered to play nice.

"So. Where to?" Cunny asked.

Latrine put her elbows on the table and rested her head in her hands, massaging her temples. "I'm getting kind of tired actually. Too many carbs. Carb coma."

"OMG me too."

Grr.

"I need a little caffeine actually," said Cunny.

Latrine perked up. "There's a Diet Coke sitting right in front of you."

"Oh, not soda though. Tea! Do you want to go back to your place and have some afternoon tea? I was having such a good time before the accident the other day. I really think everyone should have tea in the afternoons. It's just so relaxing and nice. And you can dress up and be fabulous and everything."

Latrine had to admit, she kind of liked her again after that.

Some of her Scottish heritage had infiltrated her culture and branded her naïve and impressionable brain. An uncontrollable smile formed on her face. "You know, I recorded that soap opera you were telling me about. I was going to watch it with Peyton."

"OMG, I *have* to watch it with you guys."

"Well then let's head back to my place, and we'll have some tea and chat a bit before Peyton comes home. Then we can all watch it together."

"Yay!"

They loaded into Cunny's car and started the trip to Latrine's. She still fluctuated about what to do, though the opportunity to create an accident evaporated. They'd be in her house with her stuff. If anything happened, Latrine would clearly be the one to blame. That was true for poisoning, dunting her head, knocking her knee. Everything. Except if she did it herself. Latrine wondered if she could convince her to drink some whisky. They had enough whisky to have a full-on whisky tasting at her flat. They could even use the Glencairn glasses. Latrine realized she could pitch it as an authentic whisky tasting since she was on the cusp of understanding and embracing Scottish culture.

They got back to Latrine's flat. Latrine opened her door like a tour guide.

"I love your place." Cunny explored the place with zeal and rounded the corner into the kitchen. "OMG I love the tile."

"Peyton laid it himself."

"Fabulous work."

"So I have a proposal," said Latrine.

"Yes. Yes I will marry you."

"That's good to know." Latrine couldn't hide a small laugh.

"JK."

I know. I know you were just kidding, you dafty.

"So as I was saying," said Latrine. "Instead of tea, why don't we have a whisky tasting?"

"Oh no. No, thank you. Last time I had Jack Daniels was

when I was twenty one and I got so sick. That stuff is disgusting." Cunny grimaced and clutched her stomach.

"Jack Daniels?" Latrine seethed at the suggestion that bourbon was anything like Scottish whisky.

"Yeah. I think I had some Maker's Mark that night too. I don't know what we were thinking." Cunny continued to look around, seeming to marvel at the sun's rays shining onto the tile.

Latrine was determined to be a good hostess, or at least to appear that way. She reached into the cabinet and took out two Glencairn glasses.

"OMG those are so cute! What kind of glasses are they?" she asked.

"They're special glasses. For whisky. Scottish whisky. Scotch, as you call it here in the U.S."

"I love them."

"Well, they really make the whisky tasting a unique and memorable experience. Peyton and I have dozens of brands from all over Scotland. The Highlands, the Lowlands, Speyside, Islay, and even a Campbelltown."

"I don't know what any of that means," she said.

"Well I can teach you, you wee lass. We can drink out of these fabulous glasses and try all of them. It'll be fun," she said, pouring a wee bit of Bruadar. "Try this. It's a good one to start with. It's a blend with honey and sloe gin. We can start with the blends and then move on to the single malts."

Latrine held the glass out to her. Cunny grabbed it, her pinky flying high.

"Now, don't shoot it. What you do is move it around in a circular motion like this." Latrine guided her hand. "Then you take your nose and dip it into the glass, inhaling and taking in the scent. What does it smell like?"

"It smells really sweet."

"Very sweet. Now you just take a wee bit of a sip."

Cunny tilted the glass back and sipped. Her eyes lit up with a smile plastered across her face.

"That is so yum." Cunny took another sip before finishing off the glass.

Latrine moved on to another blend before she poured her some of the Speysides.

And the Highlands.

And the Lowlands.

And the Islays.

And even their Campbelltown.

And Latrine was drinking right alongside her. And things were getting blurry. And they were laughing. And they were singing. And they were drinking and carrying on. Latrine turned on her phone for some music and attached it to her… put it near her… played it through her speaker. The sounds of Celine's "That's the Way It Is," filled the room.

"I never really cared for this one," Cunny said, sipping her… what Latrine thought was her… she thought it was her ninth drink. Latrine thought she… she thought she was starting to feel it. She thought even a bitch like that cunt can't even who can't even can't even drink a fucking glass of water because the fucking Pad Thai was too fucking hot.

"Mariah could sing it better," said Cunny.

"Bitch, no. Go lick a have a lick a cunt," mumbled Latrine. "That bitch Mariah can't sing for shite. She can hit notes. Big whoopdie fucking cunt."

"Listen, you Irish bitch—"

"Scottish! I'm The Scottish Bitch. Get it right, American Pie."

"Scottish. Whatever." Cunny held her glass up to her mouth beside her up to her mouth like a micro like a microphone. "This is what Celine sounds like."

Cunny sang a few off-key bars of "My Heart Will Go On."

Latrine took off her steeletto heel and used it as a micro *hiccup* as a microphone too. She sang the first line of Mariah's "Hero," trying to sing like trying to overpower her.

And then they were dueling fighting divas singing their hearts out. Cunny kept going singing and Latrine kept singing going too.

Cunny continued to belt, taking liberties with the lyrics. "I aaaaammm. Celiiiiiiine Dion and my husband molested me like alllll the Irrrriiiish Prieeeests molest the kidddds."

And then Latrine's steeletto landed in Cunny's chest.

And then there was blood.

And then there was a knife in Latrine's hand.

And then there was Cunny on the tiles.

And then there was a knife in Cunny's chest.

And then there was more blood.

And then Latrine picked up the phone to call.

Latrine picked up the phone to call Peyton.

• • •

Jesus, Peyton's phone rang off the hook. People wanted tickets. People wanted to return tickets. People wanted to make his day fucking miserable. Those people did nothing to quit the stereotype that Americans were a needy race of people.

His mobile phone rang. It was Latrine. He declined the next incoming call in his work queue and answered it.

"Yes, Love?" Peyton kept his voice low.

"Peyton?"

Peyton hunched over in his cubicle and put his hand over his mouth as he spoke. "Was there an accident?"

"Aye."

He paused. "Big?"

"Aye."

He couldn't breathe for a moment. "How big?"

"Dead."

His stomach lurched toward his throat. A gush of perspiration flowed down his face. Pools of sweat began forming in his pits.

"What do you mean 'dead'?"

"She's here. On the floor. Dead. There's blood."

"Where?"

"At our flat."

"Fuck. Did anybody see?"

"No."

Peyton took a deep breath.

"Here's what you're going to do. Go grab a bunch of blankets from the closet and wrap her up. Put some plastic around her wound. Make sure no blood shows through. Put her in a corner. Try to clean up some of the blood on the floor. I'll be home as soon as I can."

"Okay." Latrine's voice sounded distant. Unconnected.

"Love?"

"Yes?"

"Breathe. Stay calm. I love you." He heard the phone click on the other line.

That was not supposed to happen. Things went way too far. But they had to act. They had to act accordingly. They couldn't get caught. Peyton stared at the faux wood grain on his desk as the sounds of incoming calls at other cubicles created a cacophony of irritation.

Peyton snuck out of work without telling his boss where he was going. If he asked later, Peyton would tell him he had the runs and spent the rest of the day in the bog. He jumped in the van and drove away, paying careful attention not to speed; he couldn't get pulled over by the police. That would be disastrous. His thoughts reeled from the stress and the anxiety. He tried to turn on the radio, but nothing helped. Thankfully the drive home wasn't too long. He parked the car and made a mad dash for their flat.

"Latrine?" He slammed the door behind him. "Latrine?"

No answer. A smeared bloodstain coated the tile in the kitchen. He looked around the apartment for any sign of her and any sign of the body. Nothing in the bedroom. Nothing in the bathroom. Nothing in the living room. Nowhere to be found.

Just the stain.

Nothing but the stain.

Peyton took out his cell phone and dialed her number. It rang. And rang. And rang. No answer. Voicemail picked up. He tossed his phone on the table and noticed all the whisky was in the kitchen. It was normally in his liquor cabinet in the living room. Shards of glass lay on the floor, more on the counter.

Peyton took out a broom and dustpan and swept the floor. The house was silent. Still. Absolutely no noise. He heard the sound of his own heart beating. He heard the deep breaths he was taking. He heard every fucking bodily function. The blood stain on the tile looked like streaks of rust painted across the floor. It'd gotten into the grout. How the bloody hell was he supposed to get that shit out of the grout? *His beautiful tiles.*

He grabbed a bucket, filling it with some water and some cleaning detergent. He donned a pair of dish gloves and went to town on the floor, scrubbing and scrubbing and scrubbing, nothing but the pang of desperation to keep him company.

The thought of where Latrine went plagued him. It would be the normal thing to go out and look for her, but it wasn't like he could launch a search party or anything. He had no idea where she would have gone to. It was definitely to dump the body; that's for sure. But where? Where would she dump the body? And was she even thinking clearly? It didn't sound like it.

An hour passed. Peyton was done in. He was pure done in. He sat back and looked at what was left of the stain. It had been reduced from streaks of rust-colored guilt to discoloration in the form of a brown birthmark across eighty centimeters of tile or so. The grout was doomed to look like shite for the rest of their time biding there.

An area rug was needed. Taking some action to move one would occupy the time instead of sitting there like something pathetic. He headed into the living room and moved the coffee table, rolling up the Oriental carpet. It was unfurled in the kitchen, covering up any last vestige of the stain. Perfect. Bloody perfect. He reached into the cupboard and took out a glass, pouring himself some Glenfiddich. Standing on the carpet, the whisky gave him a necessary buzz.

· · ·

Latrine drove around Orlando in a daze, driving so slow in some neighborhoods Miss Daisy would complain of boredom. Her brain was a numb cocktail of shock and whisky, but being the professional drinker she was, she managed to stay alert enough to avoid hitting anyone or anything. Given the threat imposed by the ominous afternoon sky, it seemed most people were huddled indoors to wait out the impending thunderstorm.

She turned on the radio and filled the piercing silence with the sound of whatever pop diva came on the radio. Like a sign from Heaven, Celine's "The Power of Love" engulfed the car with lush melody. Classic Celine. It had just totally made her day. She sang at the top of her lungs, belting out every note and sustaining every vibrato she could. The power of love had given her life.

It was actually mid-vibrato when she realized she was driving Cunny's car on I-4. If she took the car back home, they'd connect Latrine with her somehow. It would have to be stashed somewhere. Another sign from Heaven came in the shape of Jesus' earthly amusement park: The Holy Land Experience. It was Orlando's own recreation of ancient Israel for the Jesus People to come and watch daily crucifixions of an actor in a loincloth with great abs.

Upon pulling into the parking lot, Fake Jerusalem was besieged with a torrential assault of rain, rendering the place devoid of any theme park pilgrims who would most assuredly not ever experience a deluge at the real site. Latrine pulled down a side access road and put her car in park. Without any hesitation from the sheets of water pummeling her windshield, she opened her car door, dashing around to her trunk. Heaving Cunny's body over her shoulder, she carried it to a dumpster and tossed it in before jumping back into the car.

A nearby neighborhood offered her refuge to wait out the storm unnoticed. When the rain abated, Latrine wrung out her clothes and abandoned the car in a strip mall parking lot close to a bus stop. It wouldn't be a glamorous trip, but Orlando's Lynx bus service would be graced with a soggy, shoeless, stained Scottish queen on the way home from a long day of work.

Chapter 18

Peyton heard the door open. Latrine skulked into the kitchen, dragging her feet. Her wig was off. Her makeup ran down her face. Brown spots stained her dress.

"You didn't let anyone see you like that, did you?"

"Just on the bus." Latrine shuffled her feet right over the area rug without any regard for it. "I was so soggy nobody wanted to sit near me. It just looks like I dropped shepherd's pie on my dress."

"What happened?"

She took out a glass from the cupboard and got water from the tap. "I killed her is what happened."

"How did you end up killing her? I thought you were going to just let her have an accident."

"That didn't work." Latrine sat down at the table beside him. "I need one of those."

He poured her a glass of Glenfiddich.

"Now, I want you to tell me what happened."

"I had been trying to get her into an accident all day. I tried knocking things over on her. I tried leading her into traffic. I tried dropping an aspirin into her drink." Latrine's voice was sullen and raspy. "We came back here because she wanted tea, but then I thought it might be worth it to get her drunk off of whisky and then she could fall or I could trip her or something. But then I think she kept insulting Scotland and then she insulted Celine. And then I don't remember what happened after that. I just remember her being on the floor, and a bloody heel and a bloody knife in my hand."

"So you lost your head for a wee moment and then came to your senses."

Latrine stared at her drink as the glass sat on the table.

"Where did you go for the past couple of hours? Where is the body?"

"Jesus' dumpster."

Peyton furrowed his brow.

"In a dumpster at the Holy Land Experience."

"So you didn't remember what happened here, but you remembered how to navigate your way around Orlando. Bloody brilliant," said Peyton. "Why there? That place is crawling with Born-again Bigots."

"It was raining like a white-out. Nobody saw me. I stashed the car and took the bus home."

"But—." Peyton slapped his palm to his face. "You need to dispose of the body for real."

"Okay. So let's go bury it. Right now." She didn't sound even remotely serious.

Peyton got up and paced. "It's not raining anymore. Shit. You didn't leave any evidence of yours anywhere on the body, right?"

"I don't think so. I did wrap her in some old blankets like you said to."

"You better not have used any of my good tartan fabrics."

"No. Just some old ones from Marks and Spencer. The ones we got on sale back home."

Peyton massaged her shoulders. "Aye. That's a good lass. Did you dispose of the weapon?"

Latrine rolled her head back as the tension was being squeezed out of her. "I think I threw the heel and the knife out the window. I really liked that pair of steelettos."

"As long as there's no evidence to connect you to the body."

"Shouldn't be."

"Good. Now go get yourself cleaned up. We should get some sleep." Peyton kissed her on the forehead. She left for the loo. He stared at the carpet and rolled it back to check the tile. The stain seemed to have grown back. A slight hyperventilation developed in his lungs, so he quickly covered it back up and turned out the light before heading to the living room to pour himself a Bruichladdich. Islay whisky would be the thing to calm him down before bed.

Chapter 19

When Duffy finished her shower, Twatla sat at the edge of the bed holding Duffy's phone. Her sleep mask was pulled up so it rested on her forehead. She looked pissy.

"Duffy, you've got to keep this ringer turned off. When you leave, then you can turn it on."

"It's my job. Crimes don't all happen between nine and five." Duffy stripped off her towel and put on her bra and panties. "So who was it?"

"Detective Ross Hashanah."

Duffy started to put her navy blue suit on. "That means someone died."

"Great way to start the day. 'Good morning. We have a corpse for you to look at. It's only been rotting here for a week. Not too bad'," said Twatla.

"I'll call him back after I eat." Duffy looked in the mirror and straightened her jacket.

"Oh, you're eating breakfast now?" The phone rang again in Twatla's hand. She held the phone up for Duffy. "Must be an important corpse."

Duffy pressed "accept" and put the phone up to her ear. "Ross, it's way too early. I haven't had any breakfast or coffee, and I'm not even completely dressed yet."

"Did you have to even give him that mental image?" Twatla lowered herself back into bed and got under the covers.

"You need to head over to the Holy Land Experience." Ross had a slight edge in his voice. "I'm on my way there right now."

"Why in Jesus' name do we need to go there?"

"A body in the dumpster."

"I'm on my way." Duffy hung up.

"Who is the lucky corpse?" Twatla asked from under the darkness of her sleep-mask, her body resting in the middle of the bed flanked by pink satin pillows.

"Maybe an Israelite." Duffy kissed her on the forehead and jetted out the door. So much for breakfast.

The drive to the location felt routine. Ironically, the Holy Land Experience wasn't an area immune to crime. The site had long been rigged with a brigade of security cameras to fight the petty theft of Baby Jesus figurines. But nothing looked out of the ordinary as the faux Jerusalem skyline became visible. The gilt top of Solomon's Temple glistened in the morning sunshine as Duffy drove down a side access road. Surprisingly, only a handful of detectives and police were at the scene.

Ross approached her as she got out of her car.

Duffy grabbed a pair of latex gloves from her center console. "What have we got?"

"We don't know yet. We need you to identify the body."

Duffy's heart dropped. Her throat filled with the massive lump rising in it, and she didn't even know who it was yet.

"Another queen?"

Ross nodded and led her toward the body, but she stopped. "Then why couldn't they wait to get the body to the morgue?"

"They wanted you to help with the investigation." Ross put his hand on her back to push her gently in the direction of the crime scene.

A tear dripped from her left eye. "Why do I have to ID her? Didn't she have any identification on her at all?"

"Nothing. Either he was robbed out here or taken here after being killed."

"You know just about everyone I do."

"I get them all confused. I only met him a couple of times. *Her.* I only met her a couple of times. I can't be sure. You've known her for longer."

He took her hand in his, placing his other hand over it. "Come on. I'll be right beside you."

An elderly man in a suit stopped them. "Detective Ross, you said you'd have no more people out here. I can't have this getting out. If the public found out that a body was found on our property, especially this type of body—"

"She's OPD," Ross said, nudging the park's manager to allow Duffy to pass.

"This type of body?" Duffy asked the manager. "THIS TYPE of body?"

"Not now," Ross growled, pushing her firmly from behind.

As they approached the dumpster, she could make out what looked like black heels.

It was a good thing Duffy didn't have any breakfast. Her heart sped like the rushing current of a riptide. The palms of her hands were covered in sweat, which she was sure must've been grossing out Ross. Duffy saw a queen in black leather with blood caked around the breast area. And then she glimpsed the face, blonde hair adorning a lifeless pallor.

Her knees gave way as she sank into a posture befitting the location.

Ross knelt beside her. "We just need you to identify the body. Then we can go."

"It's Cunny Corleone," Duffy whispered.

"Do you know her real name?"

"Her birth name is Richard Little." She shook her head and looked him in the eye. "Two in one week, Ross. Two in one week."

"I know. This confirms our suspicions about Ina Godda the Diva's death."

"I need to call Twatla."

"This is an active investigation. It should remain confidential."

"Ross. This is a matter of safety. Twatla could be in danger."

"Look, this is definitely a conflict of interest for you—"

"We have a big competition this weekend with a whole bunch of queens. They're going to be scared shitless, let alone be in mourning."

• • •

The phone rang. Twatla reached over, pulling up her eyeshades onto her forehead. "Girl, a queen's gotta get some sleep!"

"It's happened again." There was a choke in Duffy's voice. "Another one dead."

Twatla ripped the eyeshades off her head. Breathless, she felt beads of sweat forming on her forehead. "Sweet Jesus. Who?"

The pause sounded like Duffy was trying to find the words. The anticipation that it might be Latrine sent a surge of conflicting emotions through Twatla's body. The heartache of another living soul lost was tempered with the mental satisfaction of knowing it was somebody whose shot at Duchess shouldn't have ever materialized.

"It's Cunny." Duffy's voice was hollow.

Twatla opened her mouth, but couldn't speak. She visualized Cunny's beautiful, vacant stare. Her sweet, innocent demeanor. She immediately felt that profound sense of loss when the Lord took someone so young—someone with so much promise and talent. Twatla choked a bit, and a cascade of tears rolled down her cheeks. She planted her feet on the floor and sat on the edge of the bed, wiping her eyes with dogged determination. "Was it another accident? Cunny's not too bright. What happened? I can handle it."

"It wasn't an accident." Duffy paused. "She was stabbed."

Twatla gasped. Her blood ran cold. *Murder?* There was somebody out there killing queens in *her* competition. This was personal. If she was the mother hen, there was a fox in the coop. "I'm heading over there."

"No. We've got it covered."

Twatla stood up, pacing around the room, her robe flowing behind her like a cape. "Sweet Baby Jesus, don't you go locking me out of this. I need to be able to put on a strong face for the girls and I can only do that if I know what the hell is going on. I need to know everything."

"Okay." Duffy knew Twatla meant business. "I'll try to get home for lunch and fill you in."

"I'm coming out the door now."

"No!"

"I'll be up there as soon as I can." Twatla hung up before Duffy could give her any more domineering shit.

Twatla threw on some sweats and darted out to the car without getting into drag, without laboring in the mirror, without any hint of femininity. The fear they might have a serial killer on their hands was palpable. The safety of all her girls was in jeopardy. She worried about her own security. She started to think about the danger faced by whoever would take Cunny's place at the competition. How was she even going to name someone to her spot when they were only two days out?

And then she got a bad feeling. It hit her like a ton of shit-colored bricks.

What if the killer was lurking among them? What if it was someone they knew? If it were one of the queens, surely it would have to have something to do with making it to the Duchess Regionals. The only runner up who was named was already going to the competition. Cunny had moved up a spot and taken the Countess title. Latrine moved up a slot to qualify alongside Cunny. So why kill Cunny? The motive just didn't make much sense, unless someone was so desperate to win, they'd kill off anyone who posed a threat. If that were the killer's M.O., then it was very possible there would be more deaths to come. Twatla gripped the steering wheel with a potent mixture of anxiety and anger.

Twatla made it to the Holy Land Experience in under twenty minutes. Duffy speedwalked to intercept her and locked her in a tight embrace.

"You shouldn't be here."

Twatla broke free. "That bitch."

"I know what you're thinking," said Duffy, as if a warning were the next words out of her mouth. "There's no proof yet that Latrine's the one behind this."

"Just two dead queens who were better than she'll ever be. Isn't that enough?" Twatla noticed there was no crime scene tape. No sign of a body. It must've been taken away.

Duffy put her hand on her shoulder. "It's just speculation. We don't know enough about Latrine's relationship with either of them, especially Cunny. Look. For all we know it was a hate crime."

Twatla crossed her arms. "A hate *losing* crime."

"It could have been Peyton."

"That fucking little murderous leprechaun."

"We can say they're persons of interest. We will investigate them for sure. But that's all we can do right now. They're just not charged with anything." Duffy turned Twatla's face toward hers. "You need to be clear on that."

A crotchety voice interrupted their conversation. "Excuse me—," the park manager spoke directly to Ross, blatantly ignoring Twatla. "I don't want any of these people here."

Twatla's mouth dropped. "Who the fuck is this saggy testicle?"

"The park manager," Duffy said. "Mr. Ratzmanoor."

"Detective Ross, we can't have this becoming a shrine to decadence and debauchery."

Twatla scoffed. "Too late for that."

"You said you'd keep this quiet," Mr. Ratzmanoor continued. "We don't want any media attention."

"I said I'd do my best. I never made any promises."

Twatla turned on Ross. "And why in the wide world of jockstraps would you promise that?"

Ross ignored her and looked to Duffy. "Detective MacDuff," he said in an overly professional tone to remind Duffy she was on-duty.

Duffy got it and snapped back into detective-mode with a, "Ms. Tharp, enough."

Twatla was too flabbergasted to speak; she didn't know if she was more annoyed or turned on by Duffy's bad-cop act.

"Do what you need to do and get out of here. We open in a few minutes." Mr. Ratzmanoor's finger waved at them like they were misbehaving schoolchildren onthe playground.

Duffy held up her hand to the bastard. "We're leaving."

Twatla edged toward him, a murmur of hostility in her voice. "Listen, you wrinkly bigot. I know for a fact the guy playing

John the Baptist gives mercy fistings on the second floor of the Parliament House every Tuesday night. The hands welcoming people to the Kingdom of Christ are tainted with taint."

"We're going." Duffy dragged Twatla by the arm to preempt the developing Crusade.

Twatla continued shouting the whole way. "I'm going to start a Holy Gay Days where we all dress in red and get down on our knees before Jesus. Jesus will love us. He already does. You'll see!"

Ross shook his head as he followed them to Twatla's car. He didn't make any eye contact with Twatla. "Duffy, can I talk to you for a moment?"

"What's this 'keeping it quiet for the Father, Son, and Holy Bigot' shit?" Twatla was amped. "And anything you say to her, you can say to me. I'm her home secretary."

"This is a confidential investigation," he said.

"Just like how it was confidential when you wanted me to create your iDate profile?" Twatla asked. "The one that got you all those dates? I even posted some of that bad poetry you've been writing."

"You've been writing poetry?" Duffy asked with a small smile.

Ross grit his teeth. "Okay, fine. I will just go ahead and announce the tip I received to everyone that wants to fucking hear. Turns out Latrine Dion and Cunny Corleone went out on a little shopping spree together yesterday. We've got some work to do."

"Are you tagging along?" Duffy asked Twatla.

"As your home secretary, I think it's of the utmost importance that I know every detail."

"Don't you have to pack for the competition?" Ross said.

Twatla led them back in the direction of their cars. "Oh, honey. I packed for that last week. We're all ready to go. I even have the choreography and blocking done for the opening number. Right now, I'm a warm gun ready to get my fill of ammunition to get this bitch arrested and out of this competition."

"Absolutely not." Ross lifted his index finger like he was giving an order. "She can't know we suspect anything. Everything needs to play out as normal until we get an arrest warrant."

Twatla wanted to bite off his finger and spit it back at him. "She's dangerous. I'm going to protect my girls."

Ross sighed. "I understand that you want to protect them, but we can't let anyone even hint to her that she's being investigated. Don't tell anybody."

"You won't need to worry." Duffy's tone was softer. "You know I'll be there. Ross is coming too. We're going to be keeping an eye on her. She won't do anything out of line. Think about it. If she is guilty and she did it to win this competition, she wouldn't want to ruin it."

"Girl, you'd better be right. Lord have mercy on that Scottish bitch."

Chapter 20

They were leaving in two days; Latrine simply had to work on her routines. She visited her choreographer, Francisco Castro, a doll. Sure, his language skills were impaired by broken English, but he knew how to choreograph a routine. He was kind of cute too, in a once-was-a-twink kind of way, especially when he showered Latrine with compliments about how scrumptious her arse looked in a pair of stretch pants.

Latrine's first number in the competition would be Celine's "A New Day Has Come," which was going to stun them with its ethereal fabulousness. Celine's soft, delicate vocals floated over the strings before they soared into the rousing chorus. As soon as Francisco put on the song, her body craved movement. Her torso spun her body into a pirouette. She leapt around, casting her hands skyward, getting completely lost in the music.

Francisco had to tap on her shoulder to get her to focus, handing her a pen to serve as a makeshift microphone. Latrine donned her four-inch heels and her practice wig to get a good feel for how the outfit would move during the routine. He choreographed spins, arm movements, pliés, and even one hell of a jeté—in heels. They went through the routine about six or seven different times, each time getting better and better, stronger and stronger. She succumbed to the melodies, getting even more lost in the whimsy of the dance, leading her even more musically astray with every run-through.

After they'd exhausted rehearsal on the first song, they moved on to the second. The curated selection was Celine's "Misled," which would reveal her naughtier side. Her planned costume would include a blonde wig. High ponytail. Black leather gown. Black pumps. And OMG a fabulous red belt that cinched the waist. A Cunny reincarnated. When she twirled, the leather would fly up to reveal a pair of red-sequined hotpants. Francisco put on the track, and Latrine surrendered herself to the music once again. Francisco had it choreographed where she had a combination of something called "krumping" mixed with some jazz. She would pirouette while "popping." Her legs bent into pliés while stomping. She groped the area where her fake titties would be and flung her ponytail. In that moment, during that song, she was giving Celine a run for her money—so fucking sexy she was going to burn that auditorium to the ground.

• • •

Peyton sat at his cubicle, bouncing his knees. Conversations with ticket-buyers were terse. He couldn't eat. He didn't sleep at all, which made him wonder how Latrine was able.

Latrine killed someone. She actually killed someone. She said her head was mixed, but she actually plunged the knife into Cunny's heart. Her friend. Her fucking friend. Something was different about Latrine. The competition must've been getting to her head—the stress. It was pressure he felt guilty about encouraging.

He needed to call her, tell her that she didn't need to go through with it—that she should call Twatla and tell her that she was bowing out of the competition. He declined his queue and called Latrine on his mobile. He got up and walked away from his cubicle to avoid whispering again. This was a conversation that had to be clear and candid. But the phone rang. And rang. And rang. And went to voicemail.

"Love, call me back as soon as possible," he said. He hung up, standing in the stairwell, caressing his mobile in his trembling hands.

But she didn't call back.

Normally when he called her and she missed it, she called him back immediately. Not that time. He knew she was working on her routines for the competition, but she should've still heard the phone.

He called her phone again. Still no answer. Straight to voicemail.

Peyton headed back to his cubicle and sat down. The impact of plopping down on the chair compressed his spine, sending a shooting wave of pain to the top of his head, a tightness that circumnavigated his skull and pierced his temples. He threw up his hands to either side of his forehead, massaging in circular movements. Whisky would help. If only he had his flask.

Out of the corner of his eye, he could see his boss making his rounds through all the cubicles. He put his headset back on and turned on his phone queue. He took a call, listening to some bloke drone on and on about needing a refund for his season tickets. His eyes never left his mobile, which lay lifeless on the desk before him.

Chapter 21

Twatla assumed Duffy wanted to drive her home instead of riding shotgun with the Rossian Revolution so they could come up with a strategy for dealing with Latrine that weekend. Duffy was a consummate professional, but she also knew her girl well. Twatla didn't play when it came to a threat, so if that Scottish bitch was going to try to mess with her and her competition, the wrath of her backhand would be felt. It was known to disfigure.

But Twatla had to remain calm. She had to breathe. She had a show to put on—an opening number to teach, an opening number that was supposed to include Latrine. Directing with Latrine beside a bunch of queens who all pegged her for guilty might have negative implications. They might fear her and demand the opening number be cut. If the rumor mill got out of control, the queens would all stay home. If she didn't have a show, then the Scottish bitch would win because the auditorium had a no-refund policy, and the show would have to go on anyway. Latrine could win if she was the only bitch there.

Twatla looked a Duffy, a panic flashing across her face. "How can I warn the other contestants?"

Duffy threw a sideways glance at her. "Should you be doing that?"

"Either way, they're going to figure out this bitch is crazy. I need to reassure them they're all safe."

"I support your decision, but remember she's just a person of interest right now. We're not leveling any accusations just yet." There was a sense of rational judgment in her tone.

"Right." Twatla paused for a moment, staring at the road as it stretched before her, taking in the miles and miles of scrubby-looking forest and aborted fetus billboards. "Why do you think she's doing this?"

"To win, of course." Duffy's eyes left the road for a moment.

"But don't you think that's a little ridiculous? I mean, do you think there was something else? What if she suspected they were all sucking Peyton's dick or something?"

Duffy chuckled. "Right. Latrine just got really defensive over his foreskin."

"How do you know he has foreskin?" asked Twatla.

"He's Scottish. I assume he has foreskin. Anyway, look. I understand that you want to keep the girls safe and you have a competition to run. Just remember that you can't reveal any details about the investigation."

It was Duffy's subtle way of implying she'd turn a blind eye to Twatla's calling the contestants. She pulled her phone out of her purse and scrolled through a bunch of numbers. Her thoughts were frazzled. Focusing on who to call first caused a dull pain in the back of her neck. She took a deep breath and dialed Blanche BuDois' number. The call rang over the car's speakers.

"Make it fast, Twatla," Blanche said as she answered. "I've got sequins to sew."

"Hey girl. Listen." Twatla paused, not knowing how to phrase what she needed to say. "I don't want you to be alarmed, but…"

The thundering bass of gay club music could be heard in the background. "But? Alarmed about what?"

"Cunny and Ina Godda have been killed it seems." Twatla said it slowly, her tone despondent. "Their bodies have been found."

Duffy put a reassuring hand on her thigh.

Blanche turned down the music. "I just talked to Cunny the other day. We were going to meet for drinks when we got to Tampa."

"She's not going to Tampa, girl." Twatla paused. "She's dead."

A piercing scream nearly blew out the speakers, lifting Duffy's hands off the steering wheel and up to her ears. The car swerved. Twatla felt an empathetic surge of tears drip from her face. After a moment of uncontrollable—and surely ugly—crying, Blanche seemed able to regain some composure.

Twatla took a deep breath. "The person of interest is a contestant."

Blanche blew her nose and cleared her throat. "What do you mean? There's a deadly queen going around killing other queens?"

"I have to be specific, Duffy. This is going to cause panic."

"I don't know what you're talking about." Duffy waved her hand, giving her assent.

"The person of interest is Latrine Dion," said Twatla.

Blanche was silent for a moment. "Who the fuck is Latrine Dion?" It was a sober, clear articulation of the question.

"She's this girl from across the pond with a leprechaun for a husband. Listen, Blanche. She's not officially been accused of anything just yet. She's just a person of interest," said Twatla, in part to placate Duffy.

"So what does that mean?" Blanche asked.

Twatla looked at Duffy for approval as she continued. "It means we can't do anything. We have to let her compete until there's enough evidence in the investigation."

"So what you're saying is that she can compete and participate and smile and dance, and we all have to sit there and pretend we like her and that she didn't just kill two of the most talented queens in the competition?" Blanche's voice revealed a developing sense of fear and panic.

"No. I'm not saying you have to pretend to like her or that you even have to be nice to her. I'm just saying that she gets to compete. You don't even have to acknowledge her presence if you don't want to." The thought occurred to Twatla that Blanche was looking for some reassurance of her safety. "Don't worry. We will have police at the hotel and at the auditorium. I've got your back."

Chapter 22

Fucking. Long. Day.

Peyton needed his whisky.

He needed his Latrine.

He dragged his feet through the front door to find her parked in front of the telly, legs spread eagle, attaching some kind of chrome studs to a black pleather dress with a glue gun. A soap opera played. He assumed it was "The Young and the Restless" again, which he thought was odd given who introduced her to it.

"What took you so long?" Latrine didn't even look up to acknowledge him.

"It was just a bad—"

"What do you think?" Latrine held up her dominatrix-inspired leather gown that looked like Barbarella brought out the dirty side of Julie Andrews in *The Sound of Music*. "It's for my second number."

"It's good."

"Good?" she asked with disbelief.

Peyton plopped down on the sofa and rested his head on a throw-pillow. "I tried calling you. I really needed to chat."

"I was busy. All you can say is 'good?'" Latrine rose to her knees and held up the outfit.

"Lovely. Beautiful. Listen, I think we should chat about this competition a wee bit."

She placed the gown neatly on the ground before getting back up to her knees. "You want a blow job?"

"No, not right now." Peyton couldn't believe the words that had come out of his mouth. He'd never have declined a mouth on his cock before. "You look really busy and I don't want to interrupt your flow."

"*I* want a blow job, you fucking eejit." Her voice was fierce as she stood up. "Now get your ticket-selling arse over here and give me one."

Peyton didn't know quite how to handle the demand. It had never happened that way before. He stood up from the couch and ambled over to her. With a push on his shoulders, he fell to his knees so his face was level to her crotch. The unbuttoning of her trousers let loose an erect penis which flung out at him like a slingshot. With her thumb and forefinger clasped around its base, she smacked him in the face with it a few times.

"Do you want it?"

"Yes." It was an empty affirmation. Hollow.

He opened his mouth and slowly worked his way down the shaft with the timidity of a first-timer. She pushed his head down on it farther and farther until he was gagging. After a few minutes of that, she pushed him to the floor and pulled down his trousers. Without any lube, she pummeled and plowed his bum like she was marking her territory. He turned his neck, noticing her eyes were glued to the telly. The episode of "The Young and the Restless" left her entranced while mindlessly fucking his arse into oblivion. Peyton was completely numb to every push, every thrust, every moan, every smack. It was like Miss Celie getting pummeled by Mister in *The Color Purple* on their wedding night. No emotion. No expression. No pleasure.

After what seemed like thirty minutes of fucking, Latrine dismounted him and resumed her dress-making as though she'd had a schedule to keep. "Be sure to get your packing done tonight. We're leaving right when you get off work tomorrow."

Peyton didn't acknowledge her. He shuffled into their bedroom naked and fell down on the bed. After taking a deep breath, he managed to scooch himself under the covers and drift off to sleep.

A strange door. Some might say queer. Very fucking queer. Peyton turned the knob and opened it slowly. A haze of mist crept out, like morning fog in the Hebrides. Up ahead of him, he saw a stage. A spotlight shined down on what looked to be a microphone. He got closer and closer to it. From the shadows emerged a figure. He couldn't quite make out who it was, but he could tell she was staring at him. She motioned with her fingers for him to come closer. As he did, he saw she was clad in a bright red caftan with shimmering sequins embroidered on it. Her hair was pulled up into a French twist, with curly tendrils framing her face.

And then he realized who it was. It was Ina Godda the Diva herself, glaring at him, beckoning him to come closer like a Siren. She was singing "You Make Me Feel (Mighty Real)" by Sylvester—or at least she was doing a good job of lipsynching. It was strange seeing a dead bitch singing a song about being real, but it was charming, he had to admit. But then, without much of a segue, the song changed, and she started sing-talking. A strange, pulsating beat with matching pulsating lights that punctuated the strange cadence of the song told him that he was "Walking in the Rain." Her rhythmic talking really did hypnotize him to keep "Walking in the Rain." So Peyton kept walking. He kept walking toward the stage. In the rain. Only it wasn't raining. And then he realized it isn't Sylvester anymore; it was Grace Jones singing. Upon Peyton's realizing it, Ina Godda the Diva seemed to have cloned herself. He stopped. It took him a moment, but he noticed it wasn't Ina Godda the Diva cloned. It was Cunny Corleone as the other half of the duo, also wearing a bright red caftan with shimmering sequins embroidered on it. Her hair was pulled up in a high ponytail. Cunny stared at him, pointing directly at him with her long fingernails while Ina Godda the Diva lipsynched the chorus of the song.

As a matter of fact, every time the song reached the chorus of "Walking in the Rain," Ina Godda the Diva seemed to split like a fertilized egg, cloning herself into another persona, until the tableau looked like The Supremes in concert, if The Supremes were statuesque drag queens singing underground avant-garde synthpop. Peyton noticed that the queen to Ina Godda's right, also clad in the same exact red-sequined caftan, was none other than Twatla Tharp. As far as Peyton knew, Twatla wasn't dead, so that alarmed him more than Ina Godda and Cunny on that stage. Twatla glared at him like he was transparent. He had the urge to shit his pants, only as hard as he tried, he could not actually drop the shit. It was like the world's worst constipation and not a laxative in sight. As the song continued, and the chorus of "Walking in the Rain" repeated, Twatla seemed to have split into two, only that time it was not a queen beside her. It was Duffy, clad in the same red-sequined caftan. The urge to shit his pants got stronger and stronger. They danced in unison, mocking him with every hypnotic lyric, every move of the hand, every swing of the hip. He noticed that they all had holsters on their hips, holsters that were loaded with guns.

They reached a point in the song where they all drew their guns in unison, only they weren't actually guns. They were dildos. Dildo-guns. And they were pointed directly at Peyton. And as they repeated the chorus of "Walking in the Rain," the sounds of actual raindrops falling against concrete filled the room. It was raining on Peyton, showering him with cold water, washing him clean. He could hear faint thunder. He saw flashes of lightning. As they continued to bellow in that vibrato-less monotone chorus, the lightning gave way to little sparkles. Glitter. Peyton thought it might be glitter. Is it glitter? Did somebody shit glitter? The glitter flashed like horny fireflies that were about ready to fuck each other in the bum. While he'd been momentarily distracted by the sparkles in the room, he snapped back to his senses and noticed that the queens were still staring at him, dildo-guns pointed squarely at his face, at his chest, at his crotch.

They smiled at him. He smiled back. His arms started to sway to the spellbinding melody. His hips started to sway. He felt warm. He felt hot. He felt scalding. His eyes rolled back into his head. He felt ready to cum. He was getting closer. And closer. And he was "Walking in the Rain." And he was… And he was… And he was about to…

"Fire!" A booming voice commanded.

And before Peyton could finish, before he could relieve the pressure, he opened his eyes, and Cunny, Twatla, and Ina Godda the Diva fired their dildo-guns at him, coating him in a sticky red substance. It looked like… It looked like… blood. It was *blood! He was covered in blood. He was like Sissy Spacek in* Carrie. *He felt the stickiness and the humiliation. He needed his telekinetic powers. But there were no doors to slam shut. Fire wasn't raging. He couldn't drag anybody across the floor by staring at them. He had no power. He was powerless. He was paralyzed. He couldn't move. He couldn't flee. He couldn't even scream for bloody help.*

Peyton noticed that Ina Godda the Diva started a contagious maniacal laugh, and Cunny and Twatla joined in. He darted his eyes back and forth, looking for Duffy. He couldn't move his head. Only his eyes. He couldn't find Duffy. Where was Duffy? Was Duffy behind him? Was she beside him? Where the fuck was Duffy?

A door appeared behind the trio on stage, a door that had not been there before. And that fucking song kept playing. It must've been on repeat. It was stuck on the chorus. It kept telling him he was "Walking in the Rain." Only, no more rain. No more rain to wash the blood. No more rain to wash the fucking blood. Please God, rain. Give Peyton rain. He needed rain. Peyton wanted to be walking. Walking in the Rain. He could feel tears well in his eyes, and those bitchy queens on stage laughing at him. They were laughing at him so hard he could feel an ache right down to the core of his soul.

Thunder crashed. Lightning flashed.

The door opened. Duffy appeared, riding a giant cannon like it was a large erect penis and she was a chick with a giant dick, only it wasn't a cannon. It was a giant dildo. It was a dildo cannon. What was with all those fucking dildos? Peyton was sick of dildos. He didn't want to see anymore bloody dildos. It was bad enough he was actually covered in blood from the dildos.

And that fucking chorus played "Walking in the Rain." Twatla raised her arm. She looked at him. She smiled. Duffy smiled. Cunny smiled. Ina Godda the Diva smiled. He couldn't speak. He wanted to speak. He wanted to apologize for what he did. But he couldn't. He couldn't move his mouth. He couldn't even blink. Twatla threw her hand down like she was waving a checkered flag at the Daytona 500.

"Fire!"

The cannon fired at him, and a giant comet of glitter hurled his way covering his soiled body with sparkly dew. Glitter everywhere. He was enveloped by a cloud of glitter. He couldn't breathe lest he would inhale glitter like it was gay cocaine. He felt it entering his orifices, his crevices.

He felt it enter his nose and his ears and his mouth and his bum. His bum had just booty-bumped gay cocaine. He was getting high. He felt like he wanted to burst from his skin, but he couldn't move. He couldn't smile. He couldn't say a word. The world's greatest torture was to feel the greatest pleasure and the most important urge to communicate and not be able to do anything about it.

In the haze of the glitter cloud, Peyton missed Ina Godda and Cunny and Twatla and Duffy forming a circle around him. Their hands were joined. They moved around him in a circle. He was getting dizzy. He wanted to fall over. He wanted to scream. He wanted to open his mouth.

They stopped. They laughed at him. They poked at him. They prodded at him with dildos and then threw them at his face like it was hurricane debris. They slathered the toxic goo of blood and glitter all over him, covering him in a red-sparkled paste that matched their red-sequined caftans. And after just a few moments, he realized that he was actually donning a red-sequined caftan—a fucked up, Walmart bargain-bin version of a red-sequined caftan.

And then, with every inch of gusto, every fibre of his being, with every wish he could muster, Peyton managed to scream, "Noooooooooooooooooooooooooooo!"

And he woke up, thrusting his body into the air in his own bed.

Peyton heard the telly on in the other room. Latrine must've still been out there sewing and preparing her competition gowns. His breath was belabored. With a leap out of bed, he ran to the bog for some water, turning on the faucet and splashing some water on his face. Hyperventilation. *Slow down the breathing.* He stood there with his hands covering his face, breathing, breathing, breathing. In. Out. In. Out. He took one more big breath and let it out. He stood up and—

JUMP! A soup of blood and glitter flashed all over his face.

He blinked repeatedly. *What the fuck was that?* Peyton thought it was all a dream—he thought it was all a nightmare. He started breathing hard again and—

A flash of light knocked him to the floor. His hands! His poor hands. His poor hands were covered with glitter. He clawed at the back of his palms with his fingernails, attempting in vain to scrub the red glitter that peppered his skin. He reached for a towel and wiped at them, hoping to make some form of clearing to see his pallor again. His hands were totally covered in spots of glitter. He scrubbed. Scrubbing spots of glitter. Away, spots. Away, glitter. Out, out spots. Out, spots. Out, out damned fucking spots.

He ran his hands under the faucet, but it did no good. He lathered them up with soap and scrubbed scrubbed scrubbed them until the glitter faded. He ran his hands under the faucet one more time, and it was finally working. The glitter was going. The glitter was going. The glitter the glitter the glitter was going. Out. Out. Out glitter. Out glitter. Out spot. Out, out damned spot.

Fuck you, spot. Fuck you, spot. You're gone now, you fucking cunt of a spot.

He took a deep breath, turning off the light and heading back to bed. With a thrust and a flop onto his stomach, he instantly felt ready to close his eyes. A few tosses and turns resulted in his lying on his back. A sudden flash illuminated the room, and a dildo hovered for a millisecond over his bed like it was going to fly at his face. He swallowed and broke into a sweat.

It's not really there. It's not really there. It's not really there.

"Latrine?" Peyton called out. "Latrine? Are you coming to bed?"

"I'm busy right now," she screamed back. "I will get my beauty sleep in a bit."

He turned out the light and lied in the stillness. A quick glance at his hands revealed they were clean, fresh, and pale.

And he was at peace.

Chapter 23

Peyton—with his tossing and turning all night—frustrated the shit out of Latrine, so she gave up and went out to sleep on the sofa. The glorious silence she'd anticipated was punctured by a cacophony coming from the loo. It sounded like he was an unruly child slamming things around. At one point, it sounded like he fell. She would've gotten up to check on him, but she was just too bloody tired and the walk unfathomably long.

She assumed once he left, she'd be able to climb back into bed. That was where she slept much better anyway. The couch was not a place for beauty sleep. Peyton emerged from their bedroom, tying his tie.

"Put your rucksack and your luggage by the door." She propped herself up on her elbows. "I want to just hop in the car when you come back to pick me up. No stops when you're coming home from work. I want to leave as soon as we can, and I don't want to get stuck in traffic on the way to Tampa."

"Okay. That's not a problem." His voice was raspy and bereft of any zeal for life.

"What's wrong with you?"

"Nothing. I just didn't sleep good last night."

"I know that, you fucker. You know how I feel about sleeping on this fucking couch." Latrine fluffed her pillow and plopped her head down as a cue for Peyton to get the hell out of there so she could sleep.

But he just stood there. "I didn't know you didn't like sleeping on the couch."

"How many times have I told you?"

"Never."

Latrine lifted her head. "Well, I'm saying it now."

"Okay." His voice was more than raspy and toneless. It was morose.

"Okay, something is wrong. What's wrong with you?" Latrine sat up completely.

"Me? Nothing."

She sensed his melancholy had morphed into anxiety. "Hold up your hands."

He held them up. They were shaking.

"Are you nervous?" Latrine asked.

"I'm cold. I'm just really cold." His hands sank into his pockets like lead weights as his shoulders lifted up around his ears.

"This is Florida. It's not cold here. Glasgow, I can understand, but Florida? No."

"I don't know why they're shaking, okay? I just don't fucking know." His voice crescendoed.

He was driving her fucking nutters. First of all, he was still there. Second of all, he was shaking like a lad who had to pish.

"What the fuck are you scratching at?"

"Nothing. I just itch. I think I'm getting eczema." He tried to smile.

"You keep scratching at it, it's going to get worse."

"I really don't fucking care. It itches. It itches a lot." He seemed on the verge of tears.

Latrine let out a sigh. "Peyton, I really can't handle a basketcase right now. We leave this afternoon, I have rehearsal tonight, and the competition is tomorrow. I have to keep my head straight. Don't fuck me up with your drama, okay? Get to work and be back by 17:00." She fluffed her pillow a bit.

He left, still itching at his hands and shaking effusively.

"Get some cream or ointment or something on the way to work. I don't want you with rashes in front of the other queens." Her head sank deep into the pillow.

• • •

Peyton stumbled out of his apartment, scratching at his hands. It was really a strange sight, and Duffy didn't really know what to make of it. Cokeheads scratched their noses, so was this meth? Who itched their hands like that? He walked like he was in some sort of manic, feverish state.

"Good morning, Peyton." Her voice jolted him and he stopped abruptly.

"Duffy. Hello. Good morning," he said in an exaggerated, whimsical tone as he plunged his hands into his pockets. He was definitely hiding something. "What are you doing here?"

"Is Latrine home?" Duffy's smile radiated ebullience.

"Latrine? Oh no. Sorry. She's not. She's pissed."

"Why is she mad?"

"She's not mad. She's pissed. Melted. Tanked."

"Drunk. So she is at home." Duffy tried not to make it painfully obvious she was trying to catch him in a lie.

"No. She's at her choreographer's flat," he said.

She nodded with facetious interest. "You okay?"

"I'm swell." Odd choice of words. The anxiety plaguing him was so apparent it was unnerving.

"You seem nervous."

"I had a terrible night's sleep."

"I'm sorry to hear that. Be sure to pick up some coffee on your way into work. I assume that's where you're headed."

"Aye. I'm running a wee bit late actually," he said.

"Don't let me keep you then."

Peyton finally removed his hands from his pockets and fiddled with his keys, his hands shaking. They actually looked red—like they'd been scuffed too hard. After fumbling for a moment, he opened the car door and sat down inside. She kept a keen eye on him before walking toward his apartment, wondering if he'd stop her.

Sure enough, he rolled down his window. "You know, waiting around might take all day."

"I thought I'd just take a little walk around the neighborhood while I wait."

"I said she's not home."

"I heard you," said Duffy, trying to hide any sign of condescension. "I believe you, but do you mind if I just wait by the door under the awning there? It's starting to warm up out here."

Peyton glared at her. "Are you stalking us?"

"It's not called 'stalking' when it's a detective doing it."

"You'll need a warrant if you want to start poking around."

"Why would I need to poke around?" she asked, feigning ignorance with so much sarcasm that she found it hard to believe he hadn't caught on yet.

"You don't. Cheers, Duffy."

She waved at him with a condescendingly animated smile on her face. He waved back and then looked at his hands, dropping them below window-view.

Duffy waited for him to drive away. He put his cell phone to his ear as he spun the steering wheel with one hand. That could only mean that he was calling to warn Latrine, whom Duffy assumed was at home and in bed—if indeed she was actually hungover.

She approached the door and rang the doorbell. No response. No frantic pitter-patter behind the door. After a few moments, she began to wonder if Latrine really wasn't at home. Or maybe she really was hungover and in bed. Or maybe Peyton really did warn her, and she jumped out the window and scurried away. Duffy turned and surveyed the neighborhood from where she was standing. No diva-ninjas were scaling walls or fleeing. Just birds chirping in an idyllic apartment complex.

After a couple of minutes, she opened the door, clad in a bathrobe with no wig, no makeup, and no boobs. Some queens were fortunate enough to be beautiful in and out of drag. Some queens only looked good in drag. It pissed her off that Latrine was the former.

"Don't you know not to interrupt a queen from her beauty rest?" Latrine's petulance was unnerving as she tightened the fabric belt around her waist. Duffy wanted to remind her that looks fade fast.

"I'm surprised to see you actually. Peyton said you were hungover at your choreographer's house," said Duffy.

"I was. I just got home," she said.

Duffy's nod seemed to feign surprise, but it was tinged with incredulity. "You know, he told me that right before he drove away. You might want to get your story straight before you open your mouth."

"Listen, Starsky and Butch. If you think for one second I don't know you need a warrant to enter this flat—"

"What's all this talk about a warrant?" It was an innocent question.

"Then why are you here?"

"Cunny's body was found and—"

"What?! Not Cunny." Latrine wailed, falling to the floor in the most ostentatious show of emotion she thought she had ever seen. She covered her mouth, writhing and rocking back and forth. Duffy always thought the Scottish were supposed to be a little more reserved, a little more dignified in moments of crisis and emotion. Not that bitch. She'd traded in her refined Scottish heritage for the flamboyant emotion of a hired mourner at the funeral of a Sicilian Mafioso. Duffy was pretty sure she rolled her eyes a few times—such was the case when talking to a suspect who attempted to hide guilt by assimilating into whatever emotion she thought was needed at the time.

"I'm sorry to be the one to break the news to you." Duffy folded her arms, her voice laced with indifference.

"She was just a princess." Latrine continued to rock back and forth and wipe away her crocodile tears. "Not yet a queen. She was a wee lass."

Okay, bitch. This is getting beyond ridiculous. Rein it in now.

"You were the last one seen with her," Duffy said.

And with that, she stopped rocking. She stopped clutching her robe. She stopped weeping.

"What are you saying?" Latrine rose without a single tear in her eyes, as if they'd evaporated under a blistering desert sun.

"I'm not saying anything other than that you were the last one seen with her." It was matter-of-fact.

Latrine's stare nearly bored through her eyes. "You're looking at me with judgment."

"My husband is a drag queen. Judgment is something I learned from you ladies." It was time for Duffy to get down to business. "Where were you two days ago?"

"I was at my choreographer's."

"And how late were you there?"

"Quite late."

"And Peyton? Where was he?"

"He was with me."

"Okay, then," said Duffy. "See? That was simple. Thank you for your time. And good luck. I know the competition is just forty-eight hours away."

Duffy noticed that she was glaring at her.

"Something wrong?" she asked

"Nothing," said Latrine, snapping out of it. "I'm just nervous. That's all."

"I'm sure you know how to get the job done," said Duffy. Sure, it sounded underhanded, but she fully meant it to sound that way. The bitch needed to know Duffy was on to her. It'd keep the rest of the contestants safe at the competition for her to know that she'd be watching her like a queen in line at Macy's on Black Friday.

Duffy could feel Latrine scowling at her as she walked away. She waited until she got into the car to call Twatla.

"That must've been quite the conversation," Twatla said as she answered.

"You called it," said Duffy. "What are you up to?"

"Making fresh squeezed orange juice for the trip down to Tampa. I'll let you have some before we go. You just need to head back this way, and we can get going," she said.

"I have just one more stop to make," said Duffy. "Who's her choreographer?"

• • •

Duffy was a wee bit too involved in the case at that moment for Latrine's taste. She didn't trust the bitch. She had her nose pressed against the window, waiting for Latrine to give any clue about Cunny and Ina Godda the Diva. What she didn't know was that Latrine wasn't budging. Not an inch. She took an acting class once in college. She knew what method acting was. She would method-act the shit out of the investigation and make herself believe that everything was perfect and everything was lovely and everything was normal. Those bitches died mysteriously. Those bitches messed with some bull-dyke bitch who had enough of their shit.

Since Latrine was channeling her inner Stella Adler, she figured the next step was to ensure her alibi was straight. That meant she should probably call Francisco Castro to verify her story and ensure that if Duffy poked her fucking nose into that studio, he'd know how to substantiate her story. It was probably too early in the morning to call, but she figured since she paid that little Colombian cunt, so he better pick up.

"Hola," he said in a faint voice.

"Hola, Francisco. It's Latrine."

"Why do you call so early, mija?"

"I need you to do me a favor." Latrine was trying to sound as pleasant as possible. "I need you to keep some things from this bitch that's been harassing me."

"Ay, mija. If it's a bitch who hates you, you know I am on your side. You're fabulosa."

"I am. Thank you," said Latrine. "Her name is Duffy MacDuff, and she's been going around town blaming me for things. You know queens and how they like to gossip about people when it's all lies."

"Sí. It's usually all lies, chica. Okay, I understand. I need to get back to bed now."

"No, wait." There was curt immediacy in her voice before she remembered not to scare him away. "I need to tell you what to say."

"Oh. I see. What's that?"

"If she asks you where I was two days ago, say I was with you," said Latrine. "And say that I was with you the whole night—late into the night."

"Ay mija," he said in that annoying accent. "I don't know why you need that. I don't like to lie."

"Remember how many clients I can bring to see you when I win this competition. Think about how many referrals. It could help prevent you from having to file for bankruptcy."

"I know, but this is hard. I don't know if I can do it."

"Just say you'll go along with it." Latrine tried to fake like she was choking back tears. "Please. This bitch is spreading rumors about me, and it's just wrong. You want to do what's right. I know you. You're a good man and a good friend."

Francisco let out a sigh. "Ay dios mio contigo. Okay. I lie for you, Latrine. But only this one time."

"Only this one time."

"I have to go. Someone is here." He hung up.

That somebody must've been Duffy. Who else would show up to a dance studio so early? Certainly not Twatla. Latrine could feel her hands starting to shake, even though it wasn't to the extent of Peyton's nervousness. It was just uneasiness. The circumstances of her investigation had been thrust into the hands of a Colombian immigrant whom she hoped would have the strength of conviction to stand up for her. It was the least he could do for a rising star.

• • •

The place looked like the dance studio from *Fame*, if *Fame* were shot at some rickety, tacky hole-in-the-wall dance studio. It hadn't been cleaned in months. Unframed posters of Broadway musicals lined the walls with no semblance of a pattern. Business cards and flyers were tacked en masse to a flimsy corkboard hanging behind a counter cluttered with towels and scuffed dance shoes. The place smelled like a cross between sweat and arroz con pollo. The old, dingy walls were painted with a cracking coat of canary yellow—the kind of pale yellow you'd see in a 1970s elementary school. A bell sat beside what looked like a dirty dance belt. She somehow evaded touching the questionable piece of clothing and rang it.

Out came a skinny Hispanic guy of about twenty-five or so. His head was shaven, and he was clad in pajamas, like he'd been sleeping in a bedroom somewhere in the back. As a matter of fact, the whole place was starting to look like some dancer's soiled apartment. Duffy suspected the place was actually not just commercial space for dancers to come and practice their art, but also a place for them to actually live.

"Hi. You must be Francisco. I'm Duffy MacDuff."

He smiled through a forced yawn. "Funny name."

"Francisco Castro. That's the pot calling the kettle black."

"I am not black. I am from Aracataca in Colombia," he said, rolling his 'r' with such an affectation it hardly seemed real.

"Right. My mistake," said Duffy with complete sarcasm she was sure he wouldn't pick up on. "You teach and choreograph for Latrine Dion, don't you?"

"Yes. Yes I do."

"Was she here two nights ago?" Her feigned pleasantness had returned.

"Here?"

"Yes."

"Yes. She was here," he said.

"I see." Duffy nodded in agreement, looking around the room. "I notice you have a security camera hanging from the ceiling. Would you mind if I look at the tapes?"

"Oh no. I can't do that."

"Why not?"

"Because." He paused a moment, like he was searching for something to say. "I film here."

Duffy was genuinely interested. "What do you film?"

"The pornography." He seemed like he was panicking.

"Porn?"

"Yes. I like the pornography."

"Do you have a license?" Duffy actually didn't know if a license was needed to film porn, but it sounded like she did. That was enough to ensnare him.

"No. I can't do that." He stumbled a bit with his words.

"So I can't see any of it," said Duffy.

"Yes. I mean no."

"And this studio. Do you live in this studio?"

"I spend so much time here it feels like I do." He tried to fake a laugh.

"I mean, do you sleep here?" said Duffy. "Because you know, that's a zoning violation."

"I do not sleep here," he said. She totally wasn't buying that.

"Then can I see the back room?"

"The back room?"

"Yes. The studio. I just want to see it."

"Ay no. I cannot let you do that because I am cleaning the floors," he said.

"I see. So then I can come back later with a warrant and see for myself."

"Ay. Sí." He nodded. His arms were shaking as he crossed them. "You will need a warrant for that."

"Fine by me." Duffy threw open the door and walked out. She could hear his muffled voice cry "Ay! Ay!" from inside as she walked to her car. Grabbing her phone from her pocket, she dialed Ross's number. The wind swept her hair around her face as she stood in the parking lot staring back at the building.

"Ross here."

"Hey. I'm leaving Latrine's choreographer's studio. I have definitely frazzled the boy. Latrine's story doesn't add up, and it's pretty clear to me that she contacted him to corroborate her alibi. I'll need a warrant to search and take a look at the security tapes if he doesn't destroy them first. I'm calling in a favor to Officer Siward to search while we're away. You're still down for riding with us in one car, right?

Ross hesitated. "I suppose. I'll meet you both at your place. Let me finish up here at the station and make sure I bring all the right files. Another weekend, another drag show. Never thought I'd say those words."

Chapter 24

Latrine was all set to leave: Bags were packed. Dresses were steamed. Shoes were lined up. Some beauty rest before Peyton got his arse home was still possible, in theory; however, the lingering anxiety of leaving coursed through her veins. She was about to transition from the relative safety of anonymity to responsibility of being a Duchess. Her pacing around the house to sedate some of her nervous energy was interrupted by a call.

"This had better be good, Francisco." She didn't waste time with a proper greeting.

"Ay, pero I don't know what to do." His energy was frenetic. "She came in here and she asked me questions and she wanted to see the security tapes, mija, and she wanted to see the back room where I sleep and she told me that I was breaking zoning laws and I don't have a place to live, mija, I have to sleep here and I think she's going to come back with a warrant and I think she might arrest me and I don't want to wear handcuffs, mija, because handcuffs make me hard and I don't want to get hard in front of a woman especially a woman like Duffy because she scares me, mija, and I—"

"Listen. I'm leaving for Tampa in a few hours and I need to get my head in the game. Now, you need to pull yourself together. She's bluffing."

"How do I know?" he asked.

"She has no proof of it. Of anything. It's all hearsay. Listen. I need to get going. Keep your mouth shut, Francisco." She hung up the phone.

Latrine poured herself a glass of Glenkinchie 18-year. The call from Francisco hadn't rattled her nerves, but it did make real the possibility that Duffy and Twatla would give her a hard time at the competition. Not everything was going to be easy. Thoughts about their rigging the system again plagued her, but they were quickly remedied by the realization that her routines were guaranteed to get the strongest applause from the audience. Any attempt to undermine the feelings of the crowd could be met with revolution—one that Latrine was not reticent to start if it needed to happen.

* * *

Peyton left work early, not because he couldn't wait to go home and leave for Tampa, but because his mind was swimming in a polluted pool of dysentery. He couldn't listen to people bitch and complain about tickets. He didn't care what his boss would say when she inevitably learned of his exit. Every time he looked down at his hands, they were covered with glitter. Shiny speckled tattoos dotted his hands and forearms, amidst reddish glistening birthmarks. He tried everything. Dousing his hands with sanitizer, soap, lotion, petroleum jelly. All day, he'd been putting his phone queue on hold and getting up to excuse himself to the bog. He'd run his hands under the tap. He'd lather up his hands and run them under the water again. He scrubbed his hands with the coarse paper towels, so much so he thought half of the rubbish was his. His pieces were distinguishable from all the rest. They shone like tinsel.

Peyton drove around for a couple of hours in the van, scrubbing at his hands, clawing at them like a frustrated cat scratching a carpet. He tried everything to stop thinking about Cunny and Ina Godda the Diva and Twatla and Duffy with their glitter cannons and their hypnotic songs. They were a fucked up version of *Dreamgirls* if *Dreamgirls* were on Quaaludes. He turned on the radio. He went to the park. He even stopped at a pub and ordered a Glenlivet. Nothing helped.

The nagging feeling he was responsible for it all dominated every step like a pebble in a runner's shoe. He had pushed Latrine too hard. She showed hints of being a wee bit nutters, completely transforming from the bash, quiet queen she used to be. She'd gotten bolder. Brasher. Fiercer. Maybe that was a good thing. Maybe she found that inner confidence she needed to win the competition that weekend. Maybe it was the new Latrine. A bright, sparkling, shiny new Latrine. It was also possible the new Latrine was tainted—like she had been shit on with cheating and bad decisions. Peyton could be the shitter. He could've tainted her entire career with his unrelenting ambition. One thing was for sure—Duffy and Twatla were riding their arses from that point on. They definitely thought the Scots were involved somehow, though Peyton didn't think they had any way to prove it. He hoped not.

But what if they did? What if they got a warrant? What if they searched his flat and saw the blood stains on the grout? He could just say he dropped olive oil on the floor when he was cooking pasta—that probably would stain. But what if they found Latrine's hair on the body? What if they found the bloody knife Latrine used? He didn't know where Latrine threw the knife. Peyton turned around and headed home, minding the speed limit so he wouldn't get pulled over but all the while trying desperately to get back as soon as he could. The whole way, he kept thinking how he didn't want to go the competition. He didn't want to draw any more suspicion their way or to have Latrine get herself in trouble. He didn't want to get himself in trouble either. He pondered how it might not be that bad to go back to Glasgow, how it might not be that tough. It might be at first, but it would get better. The urge to tell Latrine all of this grew stronger. She would probably get mad. She would probably explode at him. It was worth it though. He just kept thinking he should find a way to convince her. He was able to convince her to take out Ina Godda, even though that was a fucking accident. He was able to convince her to take out Cunny, even though that turned out way worse than they'd expected. All of the chaos swirling through his mind came to a screeching halt when the image of the knife and the heel floated just ahead of him. He closed his eyes and shook his head violently. When he opened them, they were gone.

His foot slammed on the brakes as he pulled up in front of their flat.

Peyton darted in through the door to see Latrine's bags and dresses and shoes ready to be packed in the van. She reclined on the sofa in elegant repose, a glass of whisky perched just below her lips.

"Good. You're back early. Let's get the van packed." She threw the remainder of the drink down her gullet.

Peyton stood in the doorway to the living room drenched with perspiration. "What did you do with the knife?"

"What knife?"

"The knife you used to kill Cunny."

Latrine didn't budge. "I didn't kill Cunny. I stood there, and she ran into my knife. She charged at me and ran into my knife."

"You still killed her."

"Apples and oranges." She stood up and stretched before walking over to the doorway, completely passing him by.

"You need to keep your story straight." His eyes followed her as he remained stationary. "You keep changing it."

"It's not important. Now, we've got to get going down to Tampa; I want to beat traffic on I-4. Are your bags in the car already? Because I don't see them out here."

All at once, every fear and uncertainty that had been flickering in his head erupted in one single unfettered sentence: "I think we should stay home."

She glared at him, her hazel eyes blazing. She drew nearer, quiet fury emanating from her pores. "Are you gone bats?"

"I'm not feeling up to it." Peyton's voice was a whimper.

Her patience was eerie. Her methodical footsteps drew near as she sized him up. He'd thought she might have exploded by that point. She looked like a cat who was just waiting for her prey to come walking by—like she was just resting there with her tail slowly flipping up and down and back and forth.

Unable to break free from her deathly stare, he retreated to the sofa, out of her line of fire. He glanced around the room for a bottle of whisky and a tumbler, but they were too far to reach over and grab. Latrine's predatory nature left him paralyzed. He looked down at his hands, the skin peeling and flaking off amongst the shining specks and rust-hued stains.

Latrine sat down beside him. "You know what? I may be the one who wears a dress, but you're the one with the vagina. What's happened to you?"

"I can't think straight."

"You'd better start."

And before he could stop her, before he could even realize what she was doing, she reached over to her sewing kit on the side table, picked up a needle with the thread still hanging out of its eye, and pricked him on the arm.

"Ouch! What the fuck?"

"Get your fucking bags packed." She pricked him again.

"Ow! You're drawing blood, you fucking loon. What's wrong with you?"

"Did that hurt? Huh, you fucking spastic?"

"Aye, it hurt."

"Good. Then there's plenty more where that came from," she said. "I've spent hours sewing sequins, stitching fabrics, choosing music, dancing my arse off. You will take me to Tampa now. You will watch me on that stage from the wings, and you will cheer and applaud when I win. We will take that prize money and buy a house after I get my new titties."

"Your new titties?"

"Pack your bags now," she yelled. "Or I'll prick you with something bigger."

Peyton didn't know what that meant—if she meant with her prick or with a knife. She'd used both before. There was a precedent. He was helpless. He felt like his Love had jumped off the fucking cliff and fallen into the mist below. She was cloudy, that one. She was unpredictable. He didn't know who she even was anymore.

He packed his bags as fast as he could and rolled them out to her. She stood by the door, her arms crossed and her face etched with a scowl.

"Pack the van."

Peyton obeyed.

Chapter 25

Thirty miles left. That was all that was left on their road trip. Halfway there. Thankfully the drive from Ocoee to Tampa wasn't that bad. It wasn't like Twatla really would have minded under normal circumstances, but her girl had decided it would be good for her to bond with Rossie-poo. Despite providing ample time for him to talk to her, he hadn't spent more than two seconds looking away from his phone. *Bitch.* Bitch was addicted to his phone. Bitch was rude. Bitch was too fucking man-pretty for his own good.

Duffy was half asleep, which Twatla appreciated. She'd rather her be asleep than listen to her try to make a conversation happen between her and Ross-paragus. Twatla was actually a little surprised he agreed to join them. It wasn't terribly convenient for him to work in Tampa. If he needed to do some investigating during the rehearsals or competition, then he needed to ask Twatla for the keys. That would be pretty bothersome. She guessed Duffy really wanted to make sure they were getting along.

Twatla wondered if it was her fault. Maybe she *should* try to talk to the guy. A glance up at him in the rear-view mirror, revealed he was still lost in whatever he was doing with his phone. What would she say to him? What do you talk about with a guy who'd probably never had a problem his whole life? He had that chiseled face. Those bright blue eyes. Abs to die for. Pecs with more bounce than an Olympic trampolinist. An ass with a shelf to rest your beverage on. People that good-looking didn't have problems. If he were gay, he'd rule the gay world.

They drove by a billboard with an aborted fetus on it, telling the passers-by that it had a heartbeat after just a few days, or some such shit. Nothing like driving between western Orlando and Trampa to show the world how red the space between is. Twatla just loved how the next billboard was an ad for some truckside stop ahead called Adult Party Land. The irony was not lost on her, and she was tempted to spark up a conversation with Rossie just to talk about it. But he kept looking at his phone, oblivious to the invisible gal who drove the car. Twatla looked in the mirror again and cursed him out with her eyes. *Fuck you, Ra-Ra-Ross. I'm so sick of you pretty boys. I'm so sick of you stealing my thunder and providing unreasonable expectations for the gay world.*

Twatla knew how the gay world worked—she'd been around it long enough. She witnessed it firsthand, and even though she was straight, she knew consciously what every gay guy knew subconsciously. Abs in the gay world were currency, and that made bitches like Rolly-Rolly-Rossen-Free control the central bank. In the gay world, your own self-worth was directly proportional to the number of abs you had showing. As a matter of fact, even if you had a busted-ass face, your status was still higher if you had a great body. Gays only respected a beautiful body. *Right, Rosseroni?* Now, if you had the perfect body and the perfect face, you were in the upper echelon of super-stardom in the gay hierarchy. What was even more of a deeper, darker trait was that every gay man measured his own self-worth not just by how many abs he had, but how close he got to be to one who had abs. People like Ross-Donis. People like him took the attention away from people like Twatla. Now, granted, she was a straight man dressing in women's clothes, and she wasn't looking for gay ass at the clubs. She was just there to express her feminine side, and she loved that the gay world let her do it. But it just bothered her that people like Ross-zilla were valued more for no reason. No reason at all. The only reason was because every gay guy wanted to be seen talking to the hot guy who was shirtless at the club—it made him look cooler, more appealing, more important. The guy could be dumb as fuck and have no personality, like the bitch behind Twatla in that car, and every gay guy would still claw at him like vultures.

That was why Twatla couldn't stand pretty men like Princess Diana Ross back there—because they knew all that. The pretty men knew their level on the hierarchy. They exploited it. *You do, bitch. Don't think I don't know you like to strut your shit around shirtless.* Those plastic people didn't want to talk to people like her because they didn't want to talk to anyone they thought was inferior to them physically. The only exceptions to the rule would be those who were fabulously wealthy (and who flaunted it) and those who were famous. And even then, the fame thing needed to be *really* famous, not YouTube famous. YouTube fame was fleeting. Twatla was thinking Brad Pitt famous, though that was probably a bad example because he was a pretty boy. George Clooney famous. Nevermind, another bad example. Damn. Hollywood was full of pretty boys. But if there was an ugly boy who was famous, that would be what she meant. The gays would just want to associate themselves with the ugly famous guy because then they could name drop—and then, they'd be perceived to be more important. Twatla knew the only reason she got any attention at the Parliament House was because she had the microphone and she could bring in guys with hot bodies to stand beside her and look pretty. Without that mic and without the entourage on stage, Twatla was just some dude who liked to dress in women's clothes.

And then it hit her. She was not on stage, and she didn't have a microphone. And even though Ross-tina was straight, Twatla was not one of his studly "bros" that understood the pain of being a pretty boy. They had nothing to talk about. She was not pretty. She wasn't even white. Twatla kept looking in the mirror at him. With each glance, she felt the grip tightening on the steering wheel until she was like Hercules about ready to rip it from the dashboard. *Keep looking that that phone, bitch. Keep being anti-social. Keep thinking you're the shit. Sweet Lord Almighty, I've so fucking had it with these pretty boys thinking they rule the world. I've had it with the gays letting the pretty boys rule the world. I am not a freak for dressing in women's clothes. I'm not a freak, Ross-tard. You got that?*

"You got that?" Twatla blurted out.

"Got what?"

"You didn't even hear what I said," said Twatla, covering for her unrestrained verbal diarrhea.

"You didn't say anything."

"Yes I did." She remained convinced he was lost in his own world.

"No, you didn't. You were too busy staring at me in the mirror."

Twatla choked on some of her own spit. "No, I wasn't."

"Yeah, you were."

"Well, you have something on your cheek. I think it's an eyelash."

"No, I don't. Seriously, why do you keep staring at me?" His tone was pointed.

She physically turned her head and looked at him. "Bitch, if you don't shut the fuck up, I'm gonna stop this car and bust you in the nuts." She looked back at the road.

"I just want to know why you don't like me. Jesus."

"Oh, Jesus don't got nothing to do with this. Don't you be praying to no Jesus, bitch."

"Will you two knock it off?" Duffy asked, waking. "I thought you two would get along better by being forced to sit through a car ride together. But nothing—not even a smidge of conversation. You skipped over the pleasantries and went right to the name-calling."

"Listen Ross-tentatious. This is my girl. She likes this dick, okay?" Her voice dropped into a lower register. "This mother-fucking dick. She don't want your dick. She wants my dick, m'kay?"

"M'kay. Calm down, m'kay."

"Oh, hell no." Her voice sunk another register, booming through the car like the amped-up bass of a dance song at the Parliament House. "This bitch is making fun of me now? I'm gonna pull over this car."

Twatla veered to the shoulder.

"No. Stop. What are you doing? Stop it right now, and get this car to Tampa already," Duffy said. "We don't have time for this shit. Stop acting like queenie bitches who take everything personally. Neither of you are queenie bitches."

"Some of us aren't even queens," he said.

Twatla gripped the steering wheel with such a vice her chocolate knuckles were turning vanilla. She tried to breathe through it, like she was a teen mom practicing lamaze.

"Look, I only want to be friends with the guy," said Ross.

"You don't want to be friends with me. You've been on that fucking phone for the past half hour checking your mother-fucking text messages and shit like you all important."

"I am important. And these mother-fucking text messages aren't text messages," Ross said. "They're emails, and they've got information about this case. You know, the one I'm investigating with *your* wife about your friends who were supposed to be in the competition that *you're* hosting?"

Twatla's grip eased up on the steering wheel. She took a deep breath and let her mind wander freely from whatever disdain she'd been hanging on to. "What was in the email?"

"Forensics team found Latrine's fingerprints in Cunny's apartment."

Duffy craned her neck around the side of her seat. "Those could've been from any other time she was over there. This could be tougher to prove than we thought. Do you think one of us should have stayed back?"

"Not at all. If Peyton Dingwall and Latrine Dion really are the guilty party, then our eyes need to be on them. We're doing the right thing," he said.

Twatla relented. "I think you guys are doing the right thing too. I really appreciate you two looking out for our girls." It was her peace offering. That's how she apologized. She hoped Ross understood. He nodded her way. That was straight guy lingo for *I feel you.*

Chapter 26

Latrine was happy to see the hotel as they pulled into the parking lot. Peyton had kittens the whole fucking way down. He didn't just birth them. He shit them too. He was all shaky and jittery and itchy and trying to talk to her about morality and some such bullshit, which was ironic coming from the swindler of Glasgow.

Peyton put the van in park, sitting there for a moment. "I don't want to go in."

"Of course, you don't want to fucking go in. Of course, you don't. But you're going, if I have to drag your bum all the way to our room. Now pull this car up to the front door so the bloke can get our bags."

He just sat there.

"Or would you like to take all of my things up to our room?" asked Latrine.

"What if these queens all suspect we had something to do with the deaths?"

Latrine threw up her arms. "We had nothing to do with the deaths."

"Latrine." He searched her eyes as if examining a hint of corneal damage.

"I'm here to compete. Remember? Money? Duchess?"

He stared at her for a few moments before scratching his hands again.

Latrine shook her head and looked out her window. "Now pull this van around to the front."

He complied and drove up to the front door, parking the car. She looked at him, waiting for him to get out and open her door. He was lucky; the bellhop beat him to the punch. Before they entered the lobby of the Hilton, Latrine primped a wee bit. She knew queens would be gallivanting about the space. The importance of projecting an aura of confidence and freshness could not be overestimated. Looking like she'd been cooped up in a van for the past hour and a half wasn't an option.

"How do I look?"

"Like you always do," he said. She glared at him, waiting for him to correct himself. "Bloody beautiful."

The automatic doors opened, and a slight gust of wind hit her in the face, thrusting her hair back like she was Beyoncé on a world tour. Standing with her hands on her hips, she flicked her regal head back to herald her arrival. She gazed around the lobby, searching for queens she might intimidate with her presence. The lobby bustled with its normal lobby-type activities, and nobody turned to look at her. Peyton joined her by her side like her very own Sancho Panza, except for Latrine, the windmills were real.

At the concierge, Latrine spotted a familiar face. She recognized a queen from Cunny's Facebook standing at the concierge. She was the bitch that used to post on Cunny's page, and they used to comment on each other's status updates. It almost seemed like it was a race to be the first person to comment; they were each other's own biggest fans, it seemed. The desire to introduce herself dominated Latrine's itinerary, but she'd forgotten her name.

She sashayed toward the concierge, Peyton walking a few steps behind as her retinue. Standing beside the mysterious queen, she placed her hands on the desk as if to pose a question to the gentlemen on duty. The queen was sizing her up. She could feel it. The bitch was a wee bit unkempt for being in a room so full of judgmental bitches. Her wig was pulled back into a frumpy ponytail. She wore a red and white striped sundress, like she cut off the stars from the American flag and decided the rest would compensate for her lack of taste. Latrine's eyes darted up and down, side to side, searching in vain for something to compliment. She had a nice ring on, which Latrine figured for cubic zirconia, but she wouldn't let that deter her attempts at conversation.

"Fabulous ring." Latrine cast a smile at her.

"Thank you." The queen searched her with the I-have-no-idea-who-you-are eyes.

"You're here for the competition?"

"Yes, of course," she said, with a wee bit of attitude.

"Brilliant." Latrine flicked her hair. "Me too."

"You're here from Ireland?" she said, still searching Latrine's eyes.

Latrine's smile melted into the floor like a flow of lava oozing down the side of a slowly erupting volcano. It took every fiber of her being, but she did resist the urge to backhand the fucking cunt so hard her wig would take a Trans-Atlantic flight. "Scotland."

"I see. I'm Blanche BuDois." She extended her dainty hand in Latrine's direction.

"Latrine Dion." Latrine grabbed her hand firmly.

Blanche's hand went limp. Her already faint smile dropped into a grimace—one that she tried in vain to hide. "Pleasure to meet you." Her voice trailed. "I really… I really must be going. I have such a… I have… I'm totally running late for tonight's meet and greet and the first rehearsal."

"That's not for a couple more hours." Latrine brushed it off on and turned on the charm. "We have time to get a cocktail and get to know each other better."

"Oh I would love to. Really. I just have so much freshening up to do."

"You do." It was a statement Latrine instantly realized must have come across as rude.

"You're right. I really do. I just… I must get going."

"I'll see you later tonight. We can sit by each other," said Latrine as Blanche darted toward the lift. She looked over at Peyton, who was seated in a chair nearby, watching her with little puppy dog eyes. "She seemed nice."

"She seemed scared." He stood up and walked over to her. "They all seem scared."

"Everyone is just busy now." She noticed the bellhop load their luggage into the lift. "Go upstairs with the bellhop to our room. I'll meet you up there."

"What are you going to do down here?" asked Peyton.

"I'm just going to have a look around. Take a look over at the pool. Try to meet some of the other contestants and try to get them to spill the beans about what they're all doing for their routines."

"Can I join you?"

"The bellhop is waiting."

Latrine waved him away and noticed a glamour queen walking off of another lift. The queen approached the concierge desk with a strut that belonged on a runway in Paris. Ten-centimeter black stilettos, killer calves in a black-leather pencil skirt. A magenta-crop top with perfectly hiked titties. From the neck down, Latrine thought it was Cunny herself, but from the neck up, it was a poor-man's imitation, though it seemed the bitch might give her some competition. Latrine just had to know what she was doing.

"Pardon me. Your skirt is bloody bonny. I'm Latrine." As Latrine extended her hand to her, the queen stiffened. "Is something the matter?"

"I know you. I know about you. Stay away from me," she said, gritting her teeth. Latrine found it almost comical, like the kind of acting you'd see on "The Young and the Restless." For a moment, Latrine felt like she'd just shagged her brother and the girl was going to get her revenge. The crazy queen didn't dart more than three meters away before tripping over her stilettos, falling flat on her face—her wig flying across the floor. A wee bit of blood dripped from her mouth as she lifted her head. Given the audience in the lobby, Latrine realized she should show some concern. She rushed over to her side.

"Get away from me." Blood sprayed from the queen's mouth. "Don't touch me."

The bitch looked totally off her head. A pair of dapper gentlemen in suits hurried toward them. "Chutney? Ms. Spears?"

Chutney Spears?

The handsome gentlemen knocked Latrine out of the way. She figured she probably should bemoan the perceived injury Ms. Chutney Spears acquired while trying to flee, but it really just looked like Latrine came out on top. Chutney would be so shaken from their encounter that she'd have to take the whole weekend to regroup if she wanted to have any fighting chance against Latrine in that competition. Best case scenario: she needed stitches.

Latrine strutted over to the lift and pressed the "up" button. Just a wee bit of freshening up, and she was off to the meet and greet to see what other queens she could befriend.

Chapter 27

Twatla's head was all over the place. She had choreography to teach, egos to tame, and a show to host. Nagging thoughts about never wanting to direct again persisted. The murder spree on top of it all was just too much drama all at once, and that was saying a lot—Twatla worked at gay nightclubs.

She headed over to the Birnam Auditorium as soon as she got to Tampa to get herself situated before all the contestants and extra dancers showed up. She stopped by the Dunkin' Donuts to buy a few dozen, not for the queens, but for the crew. Her mantra as a director: *Always bribe the crew with food.* They would do anything for a pastry and coffee. If Twatla were to ask them to lick her asshole clean, they'd do it as long as she offered them a chocolate-covered glazed donut with a cup of Joe.

Once Twatla got the team happy, she hung her dresses in her dressing room (she was the star) and prepared her notes for the night's meet and greet and rehearsal. Her timing couldn't be any more perfect. No sooner was she finished backstage than her male dancers showed up. They were all good-looking and blah blah blah. They were the required eye-candy portion of the show, and they'd only be featured in the opening number. She'd pick one of them to be the presenter, unless Ross wanted to reprise his performance from the local competition, which was not likely given the gravity of the investigation.

"Take off your shirts, gentlemen," said Twatla, which almost didn't need to be articulated since many of them had already taken the liberty of doing so upon entering the auditorium. Men in the entertainment industry were attention whores. It drove her nuts actually. Every actor, dancer, singer, model—straight or gay—knew that if you had abs, you showed them off so that the gays would flock to you. Abs were the new casting couch, and with a glance across the stage, it looked like everyone was okay with that.

Little by little, many of the contestants made their way inside also, pairing up with the dancers and giggling like fifth grade girls on a field trip. Naturally, at a meet and greet of that nature, the queens were all there to size each other up and to scope out the competition. They should've been dressed to the nines and looking fabulous. They should've been, but they weren't. Twatla wouldn't allow it. That night was a meet and greet, yes. But it was also a rehearsal, and they were rehearsing the opening number of the show. Therefore, Twatla required comfortable movement attire. For many of the contestants, that meant leotards, dance belts, wigs, hair extensions, full-makeup, and whatever extra paraphernalia they could think to layer over their basics. Twatla saw one in a dance skirt and Capezios, and another in a 1980s Jane Fonda Workout leotard. Quite a few resembled the original cast of *A Chorus Line.*

Twatla partnered each contestant with a male dance partner, over whom they gushed like twinks to a daddy. Blocking would commence once they got over their infatuation. She did notice she had one leftover male dancer, and she looked around for her last remaining queen. Latrine was nowhere to be found. Twatla didn't have a problem with that, until the thought that she might be lurking somewhere around them stalking her next victim crossed her mind.

She shook it off and smiled at the leftover dancer. "Congratulations, Mr. Pecs. You get to be the model that awards the sashes, the flowers, and eventually the crown. That means you can be seated for this portion of the rehearsal."

Twatla approached the center of the stage.

"Ladies and gentleman, I know this was supposed to be a meet and greet as well as a rehearsal, but let's face it, ya'll. It's getting late, and the rehearsal is really the important part. So, rather than going through and introducing you all one by one, we're going to get through the choreography and blocking. Then you can all adjourn to the hotel bar for a cocktail and get to know each other better. As you move around backstage, please don't touch the scenery; there's a touring company of *Miss Saigon* playing here tomorrow night, which is why you queens all have to compete in the daytime. No groans. You'll live. Anyway, the stud with whom you've been paired is your partner for this opening number. Take a moment to introduce yourself to him."

Twatla heard a murmur of introductions and a few giggles.

"Okay. Now that that's out of the way, it's time to start the combination. I'd like to introduce you all to my lovely assistant, my wife Duffy. Duffy will act as the male partner here for demonstration. Duffy? You here, girl?"

Duffy emerged from the wings of the stage in a pair of stretch pants and a faded t-shirt that looked like she dug it out of a Goodwill bin. Her hair was up in a bun, and she was ready to move. Duffy placed her hand in Twatla's, and Twatla held it up elegantly.

"Now, you're going to enter hand-in-hand, and then—"

Twatla had barely gotten started before she heard the slam of a door. A silhouette strutted down the center aisle of the auditorium. The outline of a flowing skirt whipped behind the figure like Scarlet O'Hara after she vowed never to go hungry again. Twatla knew Latrine Dion had come to play. Sure enough, stepping into the light was a sparkling Latrine—donning a blue dance skirt over a pair of pink leggings, and a blue-sequined halter top.

"Well, if it isn't Little Miss Sunshine." Knowing the gazes of all the queens had alighted on the bitch, Twatla tried in earnest to make the best of a tense situation.

"Hello, Ladies." Latrine's effervescence was unnerving. "I apologize for my tardiness."

Twatla really wanted to count to ten amidst a series of meditative breathing exercises, but she feared that would eat up valuable time. "Take your place at the end of this line. Mr. Pectacular, please join Miss Latrine Dion."

"Countess Latrine," she said, correcting her.

"Please join *Miss* Latrine Dion."

"Do I still get to be the flower and sash guy?" the poor, innocent, clueless model said.

"Yeah, yeah, yeah," said Twatla, blowing him off. "Now I'm going to go through the choreography first with Duffy, and then we'll run it a few times."

Twatla noticed Latrine taking her position and her fellow contestants trying to inch away from her like she had been stricken with tuberculosis. She seemed largely oblivious to the stares and judgment being cast in her direction.

Twatla demonstrated the series of lifts, grapevines, twirls, and jetés. It was just a simple routine, really. She ran through it a few times with Duffy, casting a few glances back at Latrine, who was trying to focus on the combination with a few beads of sweat forming on her brow.

"Okay. Let's take it from the top." She smiled to herself as Latrine fumbled to her starting position. "Wait for my cue. And a five, six, seven, eight."

The music blared, and Duffy and Twatla watched the combination come together. Twatla's fan kicks looked fantastic when executed by the queens, and the partnering was wonderful. She'd outdone herself with the choreography. The only blip on the well-synchronized radar was Latrine, whose two left feet and Scottish heritage had apparently not prepared her for a number of that nature. The bitch must've taken years to learn the choreography for her own routines. Twatla found it amusing watching her trip over herself and Mr. Pec-torial. The poor guy was being massacred by Hurricane Latrine. He was so confused that he'd basically given up trying to follow the choreography since he realized she was watching everyone else's feet instead of engaging with him like she should. It was an indication of the bitch's personality. No ability to connect with people.

"Stop," Twatla shouted, giving some reprieve to Latrine and Pec Boy over there. "Latrine, is this combination too difficult for you?"

"I just need a moment. I'm a little winded, that's all." Her breathing was heavy and exaggerated.

"I did not choreograph *Swan Lake* as the opening number."

"I think I just need my choreographer's help. My personal choreographer."

"Bitch, you need a lot more than your choreographer," Twatla said under her breath. "Alright, you know what? Let's take five." Twatla looked at Duffy. "I need to figure out how to re-choreograph this so it doesn't look like the Latrine emptied her shit all over this stage."

• • •

Latrine actually thought she was doing well with the choreography, in spite of what Twatla said. It was very smooth and flowing, and she was certain she'd look fantastic dancing it. Her dance partner was a hot bloke too. His body was bloody ripped and muscular. Fantastic abs. Huge pecs—the biggest on the stage. And why not? Latrine deserved the biggest.

Excitement flowed through Latrine's veins; she was amongst the presence of so many talented queens. The thought that she would beat them all made the endorphins circulate throughout her body, radiating the pride that came from imagining herself as Duchess. Even Grand Dame. She looked over at Peyton, who sat in the audience watching. A smile widened on her face. She thought she saw him smiling back. It was dark. It looked like he was itching again.

"Ladies, as you take five, I posted the order of competition backstage. You might as well go ahead and take a look," said Twatla.

Latrine darted for the wings, but a stampede of wild queens flooded the backstage area before she could get to the schedule. She turned around to see if she could just ask Twatla her placement instead of jumping over the bitches.

"I want her gone. She's going to ruin this opening number, and she's going to ruin this competition. She already has," Twatla said to Duffy.

Duffy stood before her, arms crossed. "Try it again. If she doesn't get it, cut her from the opening number."

"That doesn't stop her from competing."

"We're working on it. We're getting there."

They must have had some big problems with Chutney Spears since she tripped in the lobby of the Hilton. It must've completely thrown Twatla off. Latrine thought it best to leave her for a wee bit. She looked stressed.

The queens backstage looked like a brood of hens after a pile of seeds had been placed just outside the coop. Latrine tried to see over their clamoring to view the single sheet of paper with names handwritten in sharpie posted to the back wall but was unsuccessful. She took a deep breath and forced herself through the crowd to get a better look. They scurried at the contact with her body. Latrine noticed that according to the schedule, she was second—after Blanche BuDois. What perfection. What a gift. She was a hot mess. Maybe Twatla didn't hate Latrine after all. She smiled with satisfaction and backed away from the paper, allowing some of the lesser bitches to get their chance to see the schedule and get their chance to lament their having to follow her.

Lost in the haze of contentment, Latrine turned her head to see none other than Cunny Corleone standing right beside her, grinning from ear to ear with a maniacal look in her eyes. Latrine jumped, and not in the Pointer Sisters-kind-of-way. In the scared-shitless kind of way.

What are you doing here? You're dead. You're fucking dead, bitch.

Cunny's eyes widened as she raised a knife up over her head with the clear intention of thrusting it down upon her. Cunny's smile grew even bigger as she took a deep breath. Latrine could've sworn she saw the knife coming down at her. She flinched and let out an involuntary squeal of fright.

"You bitch!" Chutney Spears said. Latrine realized why she jumped like the Pointer Sisters might have told her to. It was just Chutney—in all her gapped-tooth glory—standing beside her, trying to get a look at the paper. "I told you to stay the hell away from me."

"Fuck off, you cunt," said Latrine, only it didn't come out nicely.

"Can I have everyone back to the stage please?" Twatla called from the front of the house.

Latrine made her way back to the front. Her hot dance partner took her hand in his. She looked at him and smiled before looking out into the audience to see Peyton watching on, itching his hand. She held up two fingers to let him know she was second. His head moved up and down in the darkness.

Twatla clapped her hands. "Let's take it from the top. A five, six, seven, eight."

The music started. Twatla danced. Her partner turned her, dipped her, spun her, lifted her. And after her second pirouette, she spotted the wall only to find Cunny standing at the front of the formation, turned and looking square at her. She was in a 1940s femme-fatale skirt and jacket, kind of like Barbara Stanwyck in *Double Indemnity* with that horrible blond wig. However, instead of holding a gun like Barbara Stanwyck would be, Cunny grasped that knife again. She raised it slowly, pointing it in Latrine's direction, confusing and scaring her a wee bit. Latrine closed her eyes and shook her head. She wasn't even going to grace a thought on that. When she opened them, Cunny was gone.

"Are you okay?" her dance partner asked.

"Aye. I'm totally fine." Latrine looked over at Twatla, who glared with her arms folded. She got right back into the combination, the music blaring and thumping, forcing her hips to accent each beat. She felt herself getting lost in a trance, feeling the music, living it, as Francisco told her to do. Her partner lifted her and then spun her out. When Latrine found her spot, she noticed that Cunny had reappeared—closer to her that time, her knife still pointed at her, only that time, she laughed like the Wicked Witch of the West. Latrine stopped in her tracks. The other queens continued dancing in her periphery.

She stood in breathless anticipation of what Cunny would do. Her dance partner tapped on her shoulder to get her to mind the dance, but she couldn't move. Her paralytic state kept her from fleeing. Cunny stood directly under a ghostly overhead light, her presence a phantasmagoric reminder of Latrine's transgressions—any transgressions she'd ever committed. But Latrine knew she wasn't there. She was all in her head. *You can taunt me all you want to, bitch. You can walk toward me like you are. You're not scaring me, you fucking cunt.*

Latrine's eyes narrowed as she drew closer. Her sphincter clenched so tight it could suck every dancer on the stage into its inescapable gravitational pull. She still couldn't move. She was still completely under the spell of her gaze, of her maniacal laugh, of her knife. And before she knew it, the whole room was dancing to the chorus of Duran Duran's "A View to a Kill." They orbited Latrine, swaying and thrusting their bodies into amorphous shapes and patterns that only synched in unison when the chorus sang the word "fire." When it echoed through the auditorium, a massive ring of fire did indeed form around them. Cunny naturally had to be so literal with her phantom appearances. A ring of fire. A ring of queens. A ring of shirtless men. They all danced around them as Cunny circled Latrine with her knife, joining in with the chorus and telling Latrine what they saw was a view… to a kill. The music got louder. The circles got closer. And closer. And closer. And—

"Stop!"

Latrine jumped, her heart practically leaping out of her chest.

"Latrine, what the fuck was that?"

"I just got a little distracted is all. I will mind the choreography. Let's get started again." Latrine lifted her hand and snapped her fingers. "Cue music."

"No, bitch. I cue the music," Twatla said.

Cunny reappeared beside her, raising her knife again, ready to resume her phantasmagoric rendition of the song. "She cues the music."

"Fuck off, Cunny!" Latrine nearly scarred her trachea from the force of her scream. The stage drew silent. She looked around. All of the bitches on stage stood with their mouths agape. Cunny was gone.

Twatla shook her head. "Sweet Baby Jesus, you are completely off your rocker."

Duffy walked over to Twatla and stood with her arms folded. Detective Ross appeared from the shadows of the audience, his hands on his hips.

Latrine smiled and blew them off. "I was just a little distracted."

Twatla put her hands on her hips. "I just can't have this in my opening number."

"I am a Countess. I will compete."

"You can compete all you want to. You can dance the dance of the seven tampons for all I care. I don't give a shit. You're not going to ruin this opening number," Twatla said.

"Just wait until I blow the roof off this place. You bitches will see glitter like you've never seen before."

Duffy took a step toward Latrine. "Is that a threat?"

"Fuck you, Duffy!"

"It's time for you to leave," said Twatla.

Cunny reappeared beside Twatla once more, echoing her statement. "It's time for you to leave."

Latrine wanted to run after Cunny and punch the shit out of her, but she took a deep breath and made for the edge of the stage. She climbed off and turned around, facing the whole barrage of queens and dancers. "Fuck all of you! I will win. You'll see."

"We won't see," Twatla said. "Bye, bitch."

"Whores!" Latrine stormed toward the exit with Peyton following in tow like a scorned medieval troubadour.

"That displaced the mirth," Duffy said to the girls on stage. Latrine heard giggles, and that was all it took for her to fire one last "CUNT!" at them all. *Fucking cunts. All of them.*

Chapter 28

Peyton didn't know what he'd just witnessed on stage, but his heart beat out of his chest. Surely surely surely Latrine was seeing things. She had to be seeing the things he saw. She'd lost her fucking head too. He couldn't believe it was all happening. He couldn't believe he couldn't get rid of the glitter. He couldn't couldn't couldn't believe it.

And fuck!

Peyton couldn't get rid of that glitter. He hated glitter. He hated hated hated glitter. *Get out glitter. Get out Get out Get out glitter. Get off of my hands.*

Latrine stormed toward the van before him. "Those fucking bitches. They can eat my fucking glitter."

"Glitter? You have glitter too?" Peyton continued to itch his hands as they shook. "You have glitter too on your hands?"

Latrine stopped and turned to him, grabbing his right hand in hers, examining it. "You don't have any glitter."

"Glitter. Right here." Tears clouded Peyton's gaze as she inspected his hands again.

"No. No glitter."

"A lot of glitter. Let me see your hands." Tears slid down his face. "No glitter. Why do you not have glitter on your hands?"

She stared at him. The need for a hug crept forth from his shoulders. He wanted her to tell him it was all going to get better and that the glitter would go away. *Please hug me, Latrine. Please please please hug me. I need to feel my Latrine.*

Latrine opened the van door. "Get in. I need to practice for tomorrow. They cut me out of the opening number? Then they won't know what's going to hit them. My routines will be so fierce they'll think a hurricane came from the British Isles and pished all over the state of Florida. And that Duffy. That fucking bitch Duffy. Something needs to happen to her. She needs an accident."

"I think we should chat about this. Can we please chat about this?" said Peyton. But she wasn't listening to him. She was lost in her own world.

She climbed in the passenger side, her door still open. "Get in the van." Peyton heeded her command, climbing in and starting the motor.

"Drive."

The car sat idle. "I want to talk about this."

"Drive, you fucking slow coach."

"But Love—"

"Drive."

"Where?"

"Back to the Hilton."

"Why can't we stay here and chat?"

"What is this? A fucking quiz show? Get my arse back to that hotel now!"

"I can't." Peyton turned off the motor.

"Drive!" Latrine punched him in the shoulder.

Ouch. As he massaged the spot where her fist made contact, she threw open the passenger door and hopped out. After a few seconds, Latrine reappeared on his side of the van, opening the door, unbuckling his safety belt and pulling him out of the van, tossing him on the asphalt of the car park. She slammed the car door, started the motor, and drove away. Peyton lay on the ground, pools of tears forming in his eyes and dripping down his face like little winding rivers before they met the firths.

• • •

Accidents happen. Latrine knew Duffy was whispering in Twatla's ear. She had to have been telling Twatla that Latrine was behind Cunny's and Ina Godda's accidents. Latrine had nothing to do with them. They were accidents fair and square. It was very possible Duffy might find a way to blame Latrine for it all and prevent her from participating in the competition. After parking the van in the Hilton car park, she grabbed her phone from the center console. It took her a moment to get out as she pondered the ways an accident could happen to Duffy.

Google was her friend. She searched "Chloroform" to see how it worked. It would prove useful in knocking Duffy out if she were to approach her from behind when nobody was around. Then, she could drag her body down over to the wall and dunt her face into it a few times. That'd fuck up her face worse than it already was from heredity.

If it worked on Duffy, she could use it on Detective Ross and then dunt their heads together a few times. She might be able to stage a little rendezvous between their unconscious bodies to spite Twatla. Duffy's nude legs wrapped around the exposed waist of Detective Ross, his dong hanging around her nether region. Their mouths would be open and placed beside each other, as if they'd been in the act of flicking their tongues around the interior of each other's mouths.

The possibility of using chloroform on them both and planting a gun in Ross's hand and firing it at Duffy crossed Latrine's mind. Ross's prints would be on the gun, and it would look like a murder. But where would she get a gun? A silencer would be important to get too, but she didn't know where she could buy a silencer. She wasn't a U.S. citizen yet, so she didn't think she could buy one. But then again, they were in Florida. She probably could have been born on Al-Qaeda Island in the Republic of Al-Qaedastan, and they'd just hand her the gun for the low low price of it's-your-right-to-own-one. America's freedom was her biggest asset.

Latrine needed something fast. Even heading to a gun shop would take up some time. Adrenaline coursed through her veins, sending her heartbeat into double-time. She got out of the van and strolled toward the main entrance of the hotel. Perhaps she could substitute a knife for the gun. There had to be a knife somewhere in the hotel—or perhaps in Peyton's bags. Maybe she could use another method. Maybe if she drenched Duffy's tampons with witch hazel. But then again, it might disinfect her perpetual yeast infection. Any way it happened, she needed to take care of that woman—and soon.

The lobby was barren as Latrine headed for the lifts, her head held high. Her stride slowed to a coy march. The steady beat of her heels on the polished tile echoed. The frenetic and desperate need for an accident scheme had calmed to a more organized thought process. Latrine pushed the button on the lift and smiled to herself as she waited for it to arrive. She'd think of something, one way or another.

Chapter 29

It ended up being a long rehearsal. Duffy was tired, and she wasn't even directing the show. Twatla, on the other hand, was completely on edge. Duffy suspected she bribed a contestant for a Xanax to calm her temper, but it didn't seem to be helping. Twatla spent the duration of the car ride back to the hotel bitching about Latrine. The anger seemed misdirected, indirectly thrust on Ross, although it wasn't helping that he was trying to take matters into his own hands to calm her down. Duffy realized she probably should have jumped in and calmed them both down, but she really was just tuning them out. She heard voices, not actual words.

They got up to their floor in the hotel. Duffy bid Ross a good night. He was just two rooms away so they could keep an eye on Latrine and Peyton. Their rooms actually surrounded the suspects' room—Ross on one side, Duffy and Twatla on the other. Twatla was still unaware, and there seemed to be no opportune time to tell her up to that point.

Twatla plopped on the bed. "That bitch always had a little glint of cunt in her eyes."

"I know, sweetie." Duffy hung on her shoulders and rubbed her neck. "She won't start any trouble with you."

"I ain't afraid of her. You think I'm afraid of her?"

"No. Of course not. But keep your voice down. She might hear us." Duffy dug her fingers deep into Twatla's shoulders.

Twatla grabbed her wrists to stop. "What do you mean 'she might hear us?'"

Duffy pointed at the wall.

"You didn't."

"We had to. Detective Ross is on the other side. We need to keep an eye and ear on her at all times."

"We're having loud sex tomorrow after the competition, just so you know." Twatla tapped her hands to continue kneading her shoulders.

A faint smile crossed Duffy's face. Twatla was relaxing—she took the news better than was expected. After the massage, they both changed into their pajamas and tried to get in some much-needed sleep.

A hush came over the room. Twatla snored, lost in the deep recesses of her mind. But Duffy couldn't seem to sleep. She tossed and turned for a few moments before sitting up. There, right before her was Latrine, standing at the foot of their bed. Duffy jumped.

"What are you doing here?" Duffy pulled up the blankets tight around her. "Twatla! Wake up!"

But she just kept snoring. Latrine didn't say anything. She just pointed at Duffy and curled her finger, beckoning her to come toward her. Duffy grabbed her gun from the nightstand and pointed it straight at her. The bitch was not going to try anything. She didn't know who she was messing with. Most girls were just gossipy and only cut people with words. Duffy would actually physically cut a bitch. Better yet, she'd shoot a bitch. She followed Latrine toward the door, the barrel of her gun still pointed squarely at her and the hideous red-sequined pageant gown she was wearing.

Duffy heard the faint sounds of Celine Dion's "Misled" echoing from outside the door. She opened it, and a mist blanketed the floor of the hallway outside, billowing into the room like a ghostly tsunami. The mist surrounded Duffy, yet Latrine still glowed like a beacon, beckoning her to the treacherous shores of her mysterious queendom. She followed, her gun gripped tightly. Latrine exited the room out into the hallway. Duffy approached the door with the caution of a lynx approaching a helpless baby deer when a protective doe was nearby.

As Duffy rounded the corner, she noticed that at the end of the hallway, a throne was perched where the elevators were that morning. There was no throne there before. What was that horseshit? And why was that fucking Celine Dion song still playing? The ambience made Duffy felt like she was in an early 1980s music video.

Latrine ascended the stairs to the throne and turned to look at Duffy. She raised her arms in some Eva Peron–inspired gesture, glaring at her. Duffy drew closer to her, her gun cocked and finger on the trigger. She reached behind her, grabbing something from the actual throne.

"Hands in the air!" Duffy shouted

She held up a piece of paper and what looked to be a crayon of some kind. She started etching something into the paper, and before Duffy knew it, the whole hallway became a charcoal drawing, like in the video for A-ha's "Take on Me." She was in black and white, only the bitch had made Duffy's skin tone much darker than it actually was. Fucking racist bitch. She wanted shoot her, but her gun had become nothing more than a paper cut-out. She started to run toward her, but she scribbled away at the drawing, and a herd of shirtless charcoal-drawn male models ran after her, grabbing her and holding her back. Duffy screamed at her, but Latrine scribbled some more, and a piece of gray duct tape appeared on her mouth. More duct tape appeared on her legs and on her feet, and she ended up bound and left alone on the floor, mist engulfing her. The models were gone. She looked down the hall, and the throne was gone. It was just Duffy. Duffy in the mist.

And above Duffy was a scythe. A swinging scythe, ready to slice her into bits. She was bound and gagged like some blonde white bitch in a B-movie. She noticed that it was Latrine standing over her, swinging it back and forth like a pendulum. Duffy blinked, and she was no longer a charcoal drawing. She was real. The hallway was real. Latrine was real. And the blade drew closer.

And closer.

And closer.

And closer.

And—

Duffy shook from her sleep. Daylight from the space between the curtains streamed in.

Twatla wrapped a floral sarong around her one-piece. "You looked like you were having some kind of a weird dream. I didn't want to wake you. You know how they say that's bad for you. Or is that what they say about sleepwalkers?"

Duffy sat up. "What are you doing?"

Twatla opened the curtains completely. The sun poured into the room. "I don't have to be at the auditorium for another two hours, and that really pretty pool down there is calling my name. Care to join?"

"I need to keep an ear out." Duffy nodded toward the wall that separated Latrine's room from theirs.

"Call Ross-tafarian and tell him to listen."

"He's either asleep or masturbating. You don't disturb a detective when he's doing either."

Twatla picked up her tote bag and walked. "Great. So then he's got a loaded gun and an itchy trigger finger. We're in the clear. Put on your swimsuit and let's get going. We can order breakfast by the pool."

Duffy relented and got out of bed. She needed a moment to relax and regain her grip on reality.

Chapter 30

Peyton didn't know what to do. He'd been walking the streets of Tampa all night, trying to figure out what to say to her. The intention was to walk for only a wee bit, but then he got lost and ended up spending all night trying to find his way back. A call for help much earlier was the logical step, but his phone was in the van, along with his wallet with his credit cards. Fucking digital age. He would've flagged a taxi or approached a policeman or something like that too, but the thought of someone seeing the red glitter on his hands petrified him. They'd see it and surely know he was connected to the accident. And the murder. Then they'd ask him about Latrine. He'd have to lie and say she didn't have anything to do with it. He would go to jail. She would still be free—free enough to forget about him, especially after winning all the money.

But what if they confessed? Latrine could admit she killed Cunny, and Peyton could admit he drove her to poison Ina Godda the Diva's dildo. They'd both go to jail. She wouldn't forget about him then. They could go to jail together. They could be in the same jail and live happily ever after. With a marriage and everything. They could have conjugal visits. Jail would make staying in the U.S. that much easier. And if they confessed, maybe he could finally wipe the glitter off his hands.

Peyton recognized the Starbucks on the corner. He wasn't too far from the hotel.

• • •

Latrine didn't think she'd actually get any sleep, but with the knowledge of her destiny to win, she ended up getting some real quality beauty sleep. She awoke invigorated, ready to take the competition by the wig and beat the shit out of it. Then her mind jumped to the jealous bawbags who ran the fucking thing. They were not going to stand in the way of her winning again. That was for sure. She researched chloroform again, only that time, she was keen on finding a place to actually buy some.

She opened the curtains and marveled at the cityscape. The hotel had awarded her a room with what she believed to be the most exquisite view in the whole building—a view of the pool, where some hot jocks were doing their morning swim. Two smudges on the concrete below caught her attention. Twatla in a one-piece and a sarong with a huge, ugly, floppy straw hat, sat poolside. Beside her was Duffy in a bikini. Latrine dry-heaved. No queen should be forced to see the accumulation of such cellulite first thing in the morning, even from that high an angle. She sat back down and resumed her chloroform research.

Wait a minute.

Their room was unattended. She could do something—ambush them maybe. She remained sans firearm, and that posed a problem. What to do? She tried to reach a trance-like state. Her mind went blank. She took a deep breath. And another. Inhale. Exhale. Inhale. Exhale.

She could strangle them, but she could only do it one at a time. That meant she needed one of them to come up to the room—only one. That would be tricky. She paced about the room for a bit, trying to think of a game plan when she spotted the phone cord from the landline. With one swift tug, it ripped out of the wall. She threw it into a tote bag. That would take care of the strangling.

She sat on the edge of the unmade bed. What if it didn't work? Shit. A back up plan was needed.

A glance around the room revealed her toiletries arranged on a small table. Among the myriad of powders and lipsticks, lotions and curlers, she spotted her steel nail file. She threw that into her tote bag and headed over to the door before being stopped short by its opening.

It was Peyton.

"We need to talk, Love." His eyes were red and glassy. "Where are you going?"

"To the auditorium."

Peyton glanced over her shoulder at the alarm clock. "Now?"

"Aye, now."

"Listen, I don't want you to compete. I want us to turn ourselves in." He reached for her hand and held it in his.

Latrine paused, staring down at him. "I never realized how short you are."

His jaw dropped. He seemed breathless. "I mean it. This has to end. Now, Duffy's going to know either way, so either you choose the right thing and come with me, or you can choose the lights and the wigs and the dresses—"

"And the crown." Latrine tugged her hand out of his. "And the money. And the title. And my new boobs."

"Boobs? You said that before." Peyton crossed his arms over his chest. "Whatever happened to the house?"

"I'm not turning myself in. I did nothing wrong. Accidents happen."

"Come on, Love. It's not worth it."

"Of course, it's worth it. It's what we're here for. It's what we worked hard for. Me, actually. It's what *I fucking* worked hard for. Now get the fuck out of my way."

Latrine pushed him. He tripped over a rucksack, falling square on his arse. She grabbed his van keys and the room key off the dresser before opening the door and slamming it behind her.

Once in the hallway, the realization she needed to get into their room left her paralyzed. She took a deep, meditative breath. Latrine looked up, and there she was. A maid. A red-headed goddess-of-a-maid stood at a cleaning cart with her back to her. A Scottish sister. Probably a poor Glaswegian woman like her parents employed back in Edinburgh. She'd come to the United States to climb the steep mountain of success looming before all immigrants. Latrine did too, but she started at a higher base camp. Scrubbing toilets were for the untalented common folk, not for would-be royalty like her.

She strutted right over and smiled, batting her false eyelashes.

"Excuse me. I just locked myself out of my room. I was wondering if you could open it for me so I can grab my key."

"Pardon? I don't know if I'm allowed to do that." An Irish lilt in her voice rang like a series of church bells atop Shandon Steeple. "You can go to the front desk for a new key."

That was not an option. She'd have to get the Irish banshee to unlock the door.

"You're from Ireland! Which county?"

"Cork."

"Cork is the Irish Riviera." It really wasn't. She once dated a guy from Cork who, no matter how much he showered, always reeked of Murphy's Stout and seagull shite. It was a stench embedded into the skin of every poor man from the county she'd ever met. Cork was the Glasgow of Ireland. "Lassie, you're going to love it here in the U.S., but I know how much it must hurt to be so far from home. The green hills. The meadows filled with the cutest sheep."

"Yes, I do miss it so much."

Latrine looked down at the maid's hands.

"Your nails!" They alternated colors of orange and green, as if she were pushing a float in the St. Patrick's Day parade. "This polish is fabulous."

"Thank you." The maid flashed a shy smile.

She didn't seem to be budging on the key issue. Latrine had to think of something fast. Her head lowered in mock-solemnity. "I really do think all of Ireland should be free. Northern Ireland should break from the UK."

The maid gasped. "You're the first person from there I've ever heard say that. We're sick of those Loyalist feckers!"

"An Ireland free and united. Isn't that why Bobby Sands and Michael Collins sacrificed their lives?"

"Michael Collins was a heart of gold and a pocket of rainbows." Tears welled in the maid's eyes.

Latrine stifled a laugh and threw her arms around the diminutive woman. "Lassie, it would really be a big help if you could open that door so I don't have to go all the way back down to the lobby."

"Of course!" The maid reached into her pocket and pulled out a key. With a turn of the knob, Latrine was in.

"Thank you, Lassie. Let's chat more later!"

Latrine walked into their room. The stench of cheap perfume nearly knocked her unconscious. She dropped her tote bag down on their bed and took out the cord and the nail file. All that was needed was a place to hide herself. As she scanned, she saw it there. If Latrine were in the middle of the desert, she'd swear it was a mirage.

Duffy had left her gun.

It was an unspoken prayer from the Baby Jesus being answered. Ever since she got to Tampa—scratch that—ever since Cunny's accident, fortune had been smiling upon Latrine. What Rhiannon said was true. There were big things. Big things for her in Tampa. The title of Duchess and even Grand Dame were going to be hers. The universe agreed.

Latrine picked up Duffy's gun. She'd never actually held a gun in her hand. Firing a test round was her immediate thought, but she feared that would just give away her stealthy plan. Killing just one of the bitches wasn't the only option anymore. With a gun, she could kill them both. She could shoot and then run before anyone realized what'd happened. It would be cosmic revenge for the injustice perpetrated by them against her. The universe had given her the chance. It favored Latrine.

The room was close enough to the emergency staircase. She just needed to get them up there. A simple excuse to lure them back would suffice.

And again, fortune smiled. A cell phone rested on the dresser, nestled discretely among a storefront of cocoa butter and Dark n' Lovely hair products. She picked it up, and like a digital Godsend, she didn't have it password protected. It must've been Twatla's phone, because Duffy wouldn't be that stupid—the fucking security cunt that she was.

Latrine scrolled down her numbers and found Duffy's. It would make sense as a detective that she'd have the phone with her at all times. If Latrine called and said that she'd found Twatla's phone somewhere, she'd come meet her where it was found. She wouldn't come to the room. It'd be best that Latrine call from the landline. She just needed something to tell her.

She dialed her number from the room's phone.

"Duffy here."

"Duffy? Latrine muffled the receiver with her hand. "This is Blanche BuDois. I'm up in your room. I really need your help and Twatla's help with some alterations. Can you please come up?"

"Hello? I can barely hear you."

"It's Blanche." Latrine moved her hand away from the receiver ever-so-slightly so as to clarify the articulation a wee bit. "I need your help and Twatla's. Come up to your room."

"Blanche, I can barely hear you. You want me to what?"

"Come up to your room."

"You know what? I'm just going to come up. Where are you?"

"In your room."

"Our room?"

"Yes."

"How did you—? Okay, you know what? We'll be up in a minute."

And just like that. Just like that, Latrine had them in the bag. Now what could she do? Could she sit and wait in the chair like she was a mobster? Did she stand behind the door? Hide in the bathroom and ambush them?

Latrine crept over to the window to peer down at them and verify that they were coming up. She stood back slightly in case they looked up. Duffy walked toward the building, but Twatla was still seated with that ugly floppy hat on her head. It didn't look like Twatla was moving. The bitch must've fallen asleep.

Latrine decided to wait in the closet. The surprise attack was a better tactic. Peyton would approve, and if he grew some bollocks, he'd have been there to help her.

• • •

Duffy turned and darted away, dialing Ross's number on her phone. It rang a few times and went straight to voicemail. She hopped in the elevator alongside some queens who each carried a mimosa in their hands. They smiled at her. Duffy issued a smile in return to mask her anxiety. When the elevator let her off at her floor, she stopped by Ross's room and knocked on the door. Actually, pound was more like it. No answer. She tried his cell phone one more time. No answer. He must've been in the shower.

Duffy attempted to call Blanche on her phone, even though she said she called from their room. No answer. Straight to voicemail. Duffy approached their room and inserted the key.

A gust of cold, air-conditioned air hit her as she slowly pried the door open.

• • •

The doorknob turned.

It didn't take the bitch long.

The door slowly opened.

Duffy crept past the closet door.

Latrine snuck out behind her and raised the gun before she could—

"Bitch!" Duffy back-kicked her, knocking the gun out of her hand and the wig off her head. Latrine fell to the ground. Duffy pounced on top of her. They wrestled around like they were in some straight man's lesbian mud-wrestling fantasy, except Duffy was the more masculine one. She tried to pin Latrine down, but her tall and lanky frame was too much to handle for Duffy's diminutive stature. Latrine was a little surprised at herself—she didn't realize she had so much strength. It must've been the variety of whisky she'd been drinking the past week. That shit was Scottish protein.

Her efforts to overtake her were futile, so she attempted to break free to head in the direction of the gun. She was a nimble one, that Duffy. Latrine grabbed her ankle and slid her back across the carpet, but Duffy kicked her square in the mouth.

"Fucking cunt." Latrine punched her in the face. Duffy's head fell to the ground, her mouth dripping with blood. Latrine seized the opportunity to grab the gun, but Duffy kicked her right square in her bollocks. Because she hadn't yet put in her tuckage since she woke up, it hurt like a motherfucker. Latrine doubled over in pain. Duffy made some headway in trying to slither past her for the gun.

No, bitch. Not a chance in fucking hell.

Latrine grabbed her by the hair and yanked as hard as she could. Duffy let out an involuntary cunt-grunt, which is basically when a cunt like her grunts. Latrine dragged her to her feet before hurling her in the other direction. She made a mad dash for the gun, grabbing it from the floor and spinning it around to point at Duffy. Before Latrine could take aim to shoot, Duffy threw herself onto Latrine and wrestled her to the bed. They struggled over the cold, lethal weapon like they were fighting for penile attention in a jealous three-way.

Duffy's grip on the gun was vice-like. She wasn't letting go. She wasn't even letting Latrine tug at it. She was on top of her.

"Am I a better ride than Twatla?"

"You find this funny?"

"I find Twatla funny."

"Leave my wife out of this."

They struggled a wee bit more. Duffy seemed to be winning. The barrel drew closer to Latrine's chest. Latrine's chicken-cutlet breast inserts weren't going to be enough to protect her if that shit went off, but she ran the risk of losing the struggle if she let one hand go to push her out of the way.

Latrine took that chance. In a split second move, she freed her left hand and grabbed Duffy's hair as hard as she could, shocking her enough to slacken her grip on the gun. With all her force, Latrine yanked it from her hands. As Duffy dove toward her, Latrine hurled the gun at her face, smacking her over the side of the bed. Duffy's body hit the floor. A dull thud echoed in the room. Latrine looked at her for a moment to see if she was moving. She didn't seem to be, but she couldn't be sure. So Latrine took the pistol and let her head bash into it again. And again. And again.

She deserved it. She deserved for her head to bash into the gun. Latrine threw the piece into her tote bag, grabbed her wig, and ran out the door. Fortunately, the hallways were empty; the Irish banshee was in a room at the other end of the hall. She managed to sneak down the emergency stairs unnoticed, flying down them until she reached the bottom. Though she was breathing more intensely than the last time she climbed Arthur's Seat back in Edinburgh, Latrine managed to slow herself down enough so as not to look suspicious. She glided through the lobby with the grace and elegance befitting a Duchess before strolling across the car park to Peyton's van. She hopped in and placed her tote bag in the passenger's seat.

Latrine drove away and turned on the radio. To her delight, Celine's "It's All Coming Back to Me Now" started playing as she pealed away. As the goddess sang, her hands flew into the air in exultation. Tears rose in her eyes, tears of joy—for she was finally able to achieve what fate had promised to her. Her transformation into a superstar could begin, morphing from Latrine Dion to the newly boobified, newly re-branded *Saline Dion.*

A bridge came into view up ahead. The van veered into the far right lane of traffic. She rolled down the passenger window, reaching into her tote bag as she decelerated. With a flick of the wrist, she chucked the gun out the window and into the river below. As she picked up her speed, she could feel the crown being placed on her head, the sash on her fabulous body, her breasts growing from mere pectorals to mammary masses. She was doing the victory walk, waving to her new subjects as she would represent them in the Grand Dame Nationals, taking the title. For if a weak queen like Ina Godda the Diva could do it for consecutive years and come back empty-handed, she would take all.

The Birnam Auditorium wasn't too far away. It was early still. She could use the space and extra time to stretch and run through her routines.

Chapter 31

Twatla woke up from her nap, only to find Duffy gone. She scanned the pool to see if she was swimming or just lounging around somewhere. Chutney Spears sunbathed nearby.

"Chutney, girl."

"Twatla, love."

"Girl, have you seen Duffy? Did she go to the ladies' room?"

"Girl, she left like half an hour ago. She was on the phone and then went back into the hotel. She's probably up in your room."

Twatla grabbed her bag and headed upstairs. She didn't intend to be down there that long, but her morning mimosa knocked her out. It should've been predictable. She didn't get a lot of sleep because of Duffy's restlessness. Anyway, getting into hair and makeup and heading over to the auditorium was a top priority. Fortunately, her gowns were already there, so she didn't need to worry about changing until right before the show.

Twatla approached their room and reached into her bag. The maid was at the end of the hall, and she wondered if the beds were made. It was possible Duffy decided to come up for a nap. Twatla pulled out the key, inserted it into the slot, and walked in. The room was messier than they left it. She rested her bag on the bed.

And then she saw her.

"Duffy!" Twatla dashed to her side, shaking her, but her body was cold and limp. "Duffy, please!"

Twatla put her head against Duffy's chest. She felt for a pulse. Nothing. She felt nothing.

"Oh no! Oh no! Oh no! Nooooo!"

She grabbed the phone and dialed 9-1-1.

"9-1-1. What's your emergency?"

"I need an ambulance to the Hilton in Downtown Tampa. Room 2204. My wife isn't breathing."

"Ambulance is on its way. Do you know CPR?"

"I think I do."

Twatla put the phone down and applied rhythmic pressure to her chest, breathing into her mouth. She pulsed on her chest over and over and over again. More breath. More pressure. But she wasn't moving. She lay limp. Twatla collapsed on top of her, crying and groaning in agony. The air in the room felt heavy. The world moved in slow motion for a few seconds. A dry-heave issued from her loins. Her insides felt like they were being torn from her body.

She took a few deep breaths, managing to compose herself enough to remember that Ross was only a couple of doors down. She grabbed the key and dashed out of the room, pounding on Ross's door.

Ross opened up. "What's going on, Twatla?"

"Duffy. She's not breathing."

Twatla led him to their room and he threw himself on top of her, performing CPR and trying to breathe into her mouth. Normally she'd beat a guy's ass for doing that to her wife, but under the circumstances, she really didn't have a choice. He tried. He tried very hard to get her to breathe, as the time passed, the harsh realization set in. Twatla could feel her heart shatter, its shards stabbing through her veins and arteries. A lump rose in her throat as she let out a whimper. She pushed him out of the way and pressed her mouth to Duffy's. The last lips she ever knew couldn't be Ross's. They had to be hers. She could feel Ross's hand on her back, trying to comfort her.

After a moment, she got up and wiped away her tears. "That bitch did this to her. I know it."

Ross was on his phone. "Detective Ross here. I need backup. Downtown Tampa Hilton, Room 2205."

He hung up and looked at her. "I'm going in."

Twatla followed him to his room, where he grabbed his gun and his badge.

"I want you to stay in here. It's safer to be out of the way. We don't know what she's got in there."

"How about I stand in the hallway out of the line of fire?"

"How about you stay here?"

"Ross, she killed my wife. I will wring her fucking neck before she even has the chance to draw a weapon." Twatla wiped another tear from her cheek.

He relented. "Just stay out of the way." They headed out to the hallway.

Twatla leaned against the wall just outside the door to Latrine's room. "I want to talk to her."

"You're going to have to let me do that."

"I know it was her." Twatla's voice rose slightly.

"Shh. Keep your voice down. We've been looking for evidence so we can produce a warrant."

"Duffy isn't enough evidence?"

He glared at her a moment before knocking on the door, his gun drawn and pointed square at it.

The door opened. Twatla heard "Holy fucking shit!" in a Scottish accent.

"Hands in the air! Hands in the air!" Ross shouted. He forced his way into the room, his gun leading the charge. Latrine peeked in and saw Peyton with his hands up, his mouth open in shock.

"Where the fuck is Latrine?" Twatla looked all around the room.

"She's not here." Peyton's voice was tight.

"Where is she?" Ross's gun was still pointed at him.

"I don't know. I haven't seen her since last night when she tossed me out of my van and left me in the car park at the auditorium."

"I suggest you don't make this difficult," said Ross.

"I'm telling the truth." There were tears forming in Peyton's eyes.

Twatla drew perilously close to Peyton, pointing at him. "This is your guy. He's part of it. You want answers? You start by questioning him and his fucking Napoleon Complex."

"I'm looking for her too." Peyton's voice was pathetic. Sweat stains formed under his armpits, growing quickly in diameter.

"How are we supposed to believe that?" asked Ross.

"Because I don't know anything. I don't know anything anymore." Peyton began to sob. He dropped his hands by his side before collapsing onto his knees. "I want my life back. This thing. It's like an oil spill, and I'm a fucking oil-stained pelican. With glitter. I fucking hate glitter!"

Twatla glared at him, completely unimpressed with his histrionics. She grabbed him by the collar. "She killed my wife. Now where the fuck is she?"

"Twatla, let go of him. Please," Ross said. She let go. "She must've said something to you."

"Nothing. I swear."

"We are going to proceed with this investigation, and you're going to cooperate. Do you understand?" Ross said.

"Aye."

"That means helping us find Latrine. Do you understand that?"

"I want to help. I want her to turn herself in."

"I don't want you leaving this room," Ross said.

"I understand. I won't."

Ross nodded with his head for Twatla to move out to the hallway. She obeyed that time. Though her heart yearned to mourn, her mind was flooded with the potential to catch the murderer. A call to her backup emcee for the afternoon was needed.

"Vagilina Jolie? I need your help. I have an emergency, and I might not be able to make it to the theatre on time. If I can't, can you get the competition started for me? We'll just be down one judge."

"I can do that," Vagilina said. "What happened?"

"I'll fill you in later." Twatla hung up.

Ross backed out of the room, his gun still pointed at Peyton. He closed the door behind him. "He's clean."

"What?"

"He didn't know about Duffy."

"Well, that's Duffy. What about all the others?"

"That remains to be seen."

Twatla threw up her arms. "It's so obvious he's defending Latrine. Lord knows he's addicted to her ass."

"Just so we're clear. Should I refer to Latrine as a he or a she? I mean, it's an official investigation, and I want to be culturally sensitive."

"How do you refer to me?" Twatla crossed her arms.

"Uhhh."

• • •

Fucking glitter. Fucking spots all over me.

Peyton's phone rang. He hurried over to it, picking it up so fast it nearly fell from his sweaty hands. It was Latrine.

"Latrine. Where are you?"

"I'm at the auditorium. I'm in my dressing room rehearsing my first number. The competition starts in an hour. The crowd is already gathering outside. I have everything I need here." Her voice was calm with a slight musicality to it.

"Everything?"

"Everything except you. I'm going to win this, and I want for you to be here to see it."

"You want me there?" Peyton tried to hold back his sobs, a smile creeping over his face. It was like the light from a post-thunderstorm solar appearance was shining on him.

"Aye. I want you here. I want you to see them put the crown on my head."

"I wanted to hear you say that. I really did." Tears of joy trickled down his face. He wanted to take in the moment, relish the warmth that was growing in his heart. With a sniffle, he sobered up from haze of happiness to which he'd briefly succumbed. "But I really need you here. Can you come back to the hotel?"

"Why would I come back to the hotel?" Her tone had flattened.

"Because I need you here. I need you to hold me." When he uttered the words, he could feel her arms around him, her height towering over him. The warmth and comfort of her embrace made all their worries disappear.

"Why do you want me to go back to the hotel, Peyton?" She felt distant.

"I told you. I need you to hold me." Peyton tried to reach her with his sense of romance.

There was a pause. "You're baiting me."

"I'm not baiting you," said Peyton.

"You're baiting me with baited breath."

"I want you to come back. Please. I'm going mental. I'm a fucking mad rocket." Despair had made the room start to spin. He ran his fingers through his hair, tugging at it in frustration.

"I knew I couldn't trust you, Peyton."

"Of course, you can trust me."

"You never believed in me."

"I never believed in you? I fucking helped you kill people. You've turned me into a fuck-up. And not just any old fuck up. A fuckety fuck fuck-up." He started smacking his head.

"You're blaming *me*?"

"Just come back to the hotel, and we can chat about it." Peyton tried to soften his voice to change tactics.

"I need to finish getting ready for the competition."

"The competition is not going to happen for you." Peyton realized what he'd just blurted out.

"Yeah?" she asked, completely oblivious to his disclosure. "You and all the rest of the fuckers in that auditorium are going to be wiping glitter out of your arses because I'm about to rape this shit with my fabulosity. And you know what else? We're finished. I don't want to see you ever again."

Peyton's heart had just been ripped from his body and kicked in a rugby match between ugly, smelly, gap-toothed players. He fell to the floor and punched it repeatedly, dropping the phone on the floor.

An agonizing moan grew from his gut and grinded through his throat. It was the most horrific sound he'd ever made. He burst from the room, tearing down the hallway to the emergency stairs. He just couldn't do it anymore. He couldn't live.

Chapter 32

Twatla was a mixed bag of emotions. She could feel sheer rage inside of her, wanting to clobber Latrine when they arrested her ass. But at the same time, she had worries about the show's needing to go on. It had to be successful. Duffy would want the competition to continue. They had already been through so much with it. And there was Twatla, having civil-ish conversations with Ross. Duffy had gotten her way. They actually *could* respect each other.

Ross got word backup and paramedics had arrived. They hurried toward the elevator to meet them. They were about to round the corner to the elevator banks when Peyton dashed out of his room, darting over to the emergency stairs as fast as a Scottish Pygmy Road Runner.

"You take the elevator," Ross called out while running after him.

Twatla turned around and ran in the opposite direction back toward the elevator bank. Of course, it had to stop at every fucking floor. People getting on. People getting off. People laughing. People talking on their phones. *Fuck all ya'll.* She finally got down to the lobby and barely caught Peyton running out the front of the hotel. The chase continued. She took off her flip-flops for a better stride. Running down the street in her sarong probably wasn't helping, but she wasn't about to take that off to reveal her tuckage to all of Downtown Tampa. Ross scrambled into the lobby and joined her as they continued the pursuit. They followed him down a few blocks before Twatla stopped to huff a little and catch her breath. Ross glanced back at her.

"You okay?" he shouted.

"Keep going." She resumed running at her tortoise pace, glancing down every so often to be sure she wasn't treading over broken glass. "I'll catch up. That fucking miniature Loch Ness Monster is gonna give me a heart attack."

After alternating a run-walk combo for what felt like half a mile, Twatla saw Peyton stop in the distance on what looked to be an overpass bridge with the interstate beneath. He got up on the railing. Ross stopped before him, shouting, as she ran in her bare feet to catch them.

"Get down. Please." Ross's shouts had calmed to a simple negotiation as Twatla approached, huffing.

"It never goes away." Peyton examined his trembling hands with his back toward them.

"What are you talking about?" asked Ross.

"It's always there. I'm tattooed with it," said Peyton, despair caught in his voice. When Twatla finally arrived, she doubled over to catch her breath.

Ross glanced over at Twatla before looking back at Peyton. "Where is Latrine?"

"She doesn't want me anymore."

"Where is she?" Twatla repeated, more sternly than Ross. Peyton continued to stare at his hands for a moment longer before staring down at the traffic below.

"She chose the title over me. She's drag royalty now."

Twatla finally got it. She knew exactly where Latrine was. Bitch was going to compete. Bitch was totally going to ignore everything that just happened and compete.

Twatla put her hand on Ross's shoulder. "Birnam Auditorium. We've gotta hurry."

Ross reached into his pocket and pulled out his keys, handing them to her without taking his eyes off of Peyton. "Go get my car."

Ross looked to have the situation under control. He concentrated hard on Peyton. His gaze revealed he was about to try something. Even though Twatla knew time was of the essence in finding Latrine, she couldn't take her eyes off of them. Peyton's hair flopped in the wind, the whooshing of the highway below magnifying the danger.

"Peyton, come down." Ross's voice seemed to soften to the decibel level of a dulcet hummingbird. "We don't want to hurt Latrine. We want to help her. She's in trouble."

Twatla inched closer to them, completely enraptured in the tactic being employed.

"She's in trouble?" Peyton asked, his voice a mousy shadow of his former Scottish tough-guy brogue. It was like he was eight years old again and he was asking his asking his mother for more porridge or whatever the fuck they ate over there.

"Yes. She's in double trouble. Like double, double, toil, and trouble." Ross's confidante approach seemed to be working.

"She needs me?" Peyton turned his head toward Ross and looked him in the eye for the first time.

"Yes. She needs you. We need you." A gentle smile crossed Ross's face.

That did it. *Too soft, Ross.* Peyton's eyes narrowed. He turned back around, looking to the traffic below. In the distance, Twatla heard police sirens approaching.

"You don't need me," Peyton mumbled.

Twatla had to intervene or the shithead might jump. "No, Peyton. We don't need you. But Latrine does. I just came from the auditorium. She's asking for you. She forgot her music. It's on a flash drive. She said you know where it is."

"Her music?" He perked up.

"I think it was Celine Dion," said Twatla.

"Celine means a lot to her." Ross held up his arm to help Peyton. "Come on. You can help her."

"She needs me." It was a declaration. A smile formed across Peyton's mouth. He turned completely around to face them, slowly leaning over to grab Ross's hand. But he couldn't clasp it. Something must've flown by because he started swatting at the air around his face.

"The dildos! The fucking dildos!" It was like he was trying to fend off a swarm of killer bees. "Get them away from me!"

He swiped some more—violently. Ross shouted something at him, reaching to grab him, but Peyton lost his balance and fell off the side of the bridge, plunging into the traffic below. Twatla's hands flew up to her mouth as she gasped. Her heart seemed to stop beating for a moment. She should've been satisfied at such a horrific end to someone who was so clearly guilty, but the shock and the horror of it all was overpowering. Peyton could've been an asset to throwing the book at Latrine. Some sort of plea deal could've been struck. He seemed to be that gullible. It felt like a missed opportunity.

Ross peered over the railing and looked Twatla, nodding his head to confirm the death. He took out his phone and placed a call.

"We have to get to the auditorium," said Twatla. He held up his finger while he finished up his conversation. She glimpsed over the railing to see a swarm of police cars pulling up beside Peyton's lifeless body, which was sprawled out on the road below. Traffic was being diverted.

Ross finally hung up. "We've got a warrant."

Seemingly from nowhere, a police car pulled up and they hopped in. The siren blared, and they sped toward the auditorium.

• • •

Latrine would've just gone ahead and performed in the opening number, but Twatla cut her from that, so she didn't expect her dance partner would be there for it. Anyway, that gave her enough time to perfect her look for her first routine. Fortunately, all of her gowns were in Peyton's van, along with her make-up and wigs. And since she'd be keeping the van in their split, it was all very apropos anyway.

She squeezed her taut, soon-to-be-tittie-accentuated body into her shimmering emerald-green gown. It had a sequined bodice on which she labored for hours, a neckline that resembled a boomerang, and a fabulous skirt of layered green tulle that flared at the waist. That, combined with her ten-centimeter green platform faux Manolo Blahniks would earn her high marks for the first number.

The sound of the opening number was beginning just as she put on her strawberry blonde wig, which had been meticulously curled into ringlets. She donned fabulous emerald drop earrings with a genuine cubic zirconia outline. She shimmered. That was the important feature.

She took a long look in the mirror as Lady Gaga's "Applause" echoed backstage. It may have been a good song choice for an opening number, but without Latrine in the mix, she doubted it could be anything more than mediocre. Twatla's choreography was bland as it was. As the opening number came to an end, Latrine left the communal dressing room. She knew those bitches would tear in there like a feeding frenzy—especially that Blanche BuDois, since she was going first. Latrine rather liked that she had the time to prepare and not have to be bogged down with the stress of a quick change. The stars were in her favor.

Latrine strode confidently out to the wings after the opening number and noticed that it wasn't Twatla doing the hosting—it was Vagilina Jolie. Vagilina was one of the judges originally, so Latrine gazed out into the audience to see if she'd been replaced. She hadn't. Twatla was nowhere to be found. Latrine wondered if her absence had anything to do with Duffy's accident. Vagilina was much funnier than Twatla anyway. She had the audience laughing harder than Twatla ever did, figuring the audience finally understood the level of unfunny cunt-itude Twatla had reached in recent days. Her jokes were just flat out mean. People didn't like that. Snark was one thing. Meanness was another. They could tell when someone wasn't talented, and Twatla fit that bill. They also recognized when someone was jealous.

Blanche BuDois appeared in the wings beside Latrine, doing her final primping as Vagilina's monologue drew to an end. Latrine did a double take at the tragic southern American high school cheerleader outfit Blanche was wearing. It looked like *Bring It On* on crack. She was wearing her wig in pigtails tied up with what looked to be shoelaces. Her green and yellow cheerleader sweater had green leather fringe hanging from it that did nothing to hide her lopsided titties. Over her breast was a school logo that read "Cuntry High," which Latrine imagined had a graduation rate of 15%. Her green cheerleader skirt revealed her hideous spray-tanned tooth-pick legs, made longer by the most bizarre platform Converse shoes she had ever seen.

"And now, ladies and ladies, I invite to the stage our first competitor in her first number for the night. Please give it up for Miss Blanche BuDois!"

Blanche strutted out on stage, pom poms in hand. She struck her opening pose—not surprisingly—with the pom poms in the air. The music began. It was some obscure Dolly Parton song. Something about a "Potential New Boyfriend." She marched around the stage to the heavy bassline, doing some embarrassing jailbait choreography that would probably incarcerate the judges should they over-reward the performance.

Latrine stretched out her legs a wee bit more as the song continued to tell her she should keep her hands off of the bitch's potential new boyfriend, which must've been something of Blanche's life story. No man could ever have risen above the status of being merely "potential" in her dating history—not with those knobby knees.

She took a few breaths to center herself. In a few moments, the spotlight would be on The Great Latrine.

● ● ●

The car pulled up to the auditorium. The cop who drove slammed his breaks. A few other squad cars pulled in behind them. They surrounded the building like they were in a full-on raid. Actually, it *was* a full-on raid. It was a first for Twatla.

Ross and Twatla scrambled in through the stage door just as they heard: "Ladies and gentlemen, Countess Latrine Dion." Twatla's heart started racing. They ran to the stage right wing and watched her take the stage. Her opening pose was shit. What was she wearing? She looked like what would happen if a Solid Gold dancer stole a costume from a *Wicked* cast member. The music started, and predictably, it was a Celine Dion song. *How in the hell did that bitch think she'd ever win doing a Celine ballad? "A New Day Has Come?" Really?* The audience and the judges wanted a song, a dress, and a routine that made a statement. That was how you became Duchess. You didn't win Grand Dame with a trite song that made no kind of—

Wait a minute.

She *was* making a statement. It was a new day for the bitch… in prison. A new day had cum—on her face.

Twatla watched her twirl in her layers of green tulle, her wig flowing like she was in a Clairol commercial. Latrine honestly felt no remorse. She was genuinely enjoying herself. A pang of spite struck deep in Twatla's gut. Her liver processed the bile to spew at her when she got off the stage. She felt her arms trembling as Latrine rejoiced in the "positivity" of the lyrics. Twatla was positive too—positive she wanted to pummel her and claw at her face.

Twatla's hands trembled. Any sense of control vanished from her body. Rage like she'd never felt before manifested in sweat beads around her brow. Her head darted around, trying to avoid staring at the bitch for too long, fearing her eyes would shoot some laser beam of animosity at her. Then something caught Twatla's attention. A series of pulleys hung right beside her. She looked up and noticed they were attached to the flies over the stage. Those were the strings that controlled the curtains and all the set pieces that dropped from the ceiling. She looked to see what was up there. A series of velvet fabrics, some muslin, and what looked to be a wood-paneled backdrop with some kind of metal bar at the bottom. It might have been iron. Twatla couldn't figure out what it was for—but it looked heavy. A quick examination of the pulleys quickly led her to deduce which rope controlled the one with the iron. She was no stagecraft expert, but she had directed enough drag shows to know how those flies and curtains operated. Latrine was still on stage, swaying and twirling to the ethereal ballad.

Ross put a hand on her shoulder. "Are you okay?"

"I'm fine."

"Now is your chance to humiliate her by arresting her in front of everyone. We've got the place surrounded."

Twatla held up a hand. "No, wait. I want her to finish. Let her come off stage. I don't want the competition interrupted. It means too much to Duffy. Actually, can you get to the other side just so you can get her in case she exits that way?"

"Sure. Yeah." Ross walked away.

Twatla waited for Latrine to pass beneath the fly at just the right moment, when she bent over backward with her neck extended in its elegant splendor. With a quick thrust of her forearm, Twatla knocked into a lever, releasing an overhead fly to the floor. It released so fast that not even a full second later, she heard a booming thud, followed by shrieks from the audience. Twatla glanced at the stage. Latrine lay on the ground decapitated, her torso and legs facing the audience. Twatla shrugged. She just thought she'd mess up her routine and trap her in so the cops could make the arrest. The fly must've been broken. For a moment, she fantasized about taking off Latrine's shoes and allowing her legs to curl up like the Wicked Witch of the East after that white bitch Dorothy dropped the house on her.

Ross darted on stage. Twatla suddenly realized she'd better make herself look shocked, so she rushed onto the stage to help in spite of her inappropriate attire for the occasion.

"What the hell happened?" Ross asked as he squatted down beside Latrine's headless torso. A couple of other officers hurried onto the stage also, their mouths agape.

Twatla turned and faced the audience. "Ladies and gentlemen, I'm going to have to postpone the rest of the competition until further notice." Twatla noticed the crowd completely ignoring her, pointing and chattering about the corpse on stage. A few spectators even took video and pictures of the fatality.

Ross stood up. "Alright, people. This is a crime scene. I'm going to need you all to exit the premises."

Several cops appeared at the various doors, motioning for the crowd to leave. Ross walked over to Twatla and leaned in. "Did you see anything?"

"Nothing. I don't even know how something like this could happen." Twatla clutched her hands to her chest.

He glared at her. "Not with all of the times you've held the competition on this stage, right?"

"I really don't." Twatla's eyes stayed on his.

A faint smile appeared on his face. "I didn't think you would. It was just a freak accident, wasn't it?"

"A freak accident."

"That's what's going on the police report." He put his hand on her shoulder before their attention was diverted to a couple of officers cuffing Latrine's headless body.

"Seriously, guys?" said Ross.

Twatla took a deep breath and walked off the stage to talk to the contestants. They needed reassurance that it wasn't over. The show would go on. A Duchess would still be named.

Chapter 33

Who knew that when Duffy was made Ross's partner, he'd end up learning more about drag queens than he ever hoped? He definitely missed Duffy. Twatla made it so her funeral was the most "fabulous" event ever to take place in the United States of Anywhere.

They talked regularly, Twatla and he.

He'd been calling her every day just to check in. She was adamant about making sure the Regionals continued and the Duchess was named, despite a Grand Dame being officially crowned at Nationals. Not long after the funeral, she called all of the contestants back for a free weekend at the Parliament House. The competition was less fierce than it was before—fierce in that it wasn't as hotly contested.

And there he was. Watching all the fierceness and fabulousness—in a pair of square-cut boxer briefs, with a police hat on his head. Twatla insisted. He just couldn't say no to the bitch (bitch in a good way). She designated him "eye candy" for the night. He could live with that. He had come to enjoy it. It kind of didn't feel normal to walk into a crowded room without someone whistling at him anymore. Ross was even thinking about volunteering to provide security at the club on Sunday nights for their T-Dance. Somebody had to keep the queens safe, even if it was from each other. As it turned out, other queens were the ones drag queens needed to fear the most.

Twatla invited all of the contestants on stage. They stood in a line that stretched from end to end across the stage. Costumes, dresses, wigs, all of their over-the-top craziness. Ross even developed opinions on their dresses. A few weeks prior he couldn't give two shits, but on that stage, he feared one queen's choice to wear mauve chiffon would become her Achilles' heel.

"And now, ladies and gentlemen, the moment you've all been waiting for. Ross, can I have the envelope please?"

Ross strutted on to the stage.

"Give it up for this sexy piece of man-gina, ya'll. He was Duffy's partner, and now he's mine. In a platonic way, of course."

Ross smiled at her and kissed her on the cheek, eliciting "awws" from the audience.

"And the second runner up is." Twatla took a dramatic pause. "Countess LaQueefa Divine."

Ross placed a sash around LaQueefa and handed her a bouquet of carnations.

"The first runner up, who, if anything should happen to our Duchess—which it fucking won't—but if anything should happen, will graciously take her place is… Miss Salma Nella." Twatla placed a sash around Salma Nella—which wasn't easy given the height of her hair—and Ross handed her a bouquet of sunflowers.

"And ladies and gentlemen, the moment we have all been waiting for is here. This year's Regional Duchess and the winner of $25,000 is… Countess Blanche BuDois!"

Blanche sobbed. Some of her makeup trickled down her face like little polluted streams you'd never want to fish in. Ross placed the crown on her head and handed her a bouquet of red roses. She walked the runway, waving to her new subjects.

Ross looked over at Twatla who had tears in her eyes as Alexis Jordan's "Happiness" played. She told him it would be the song playing as the Duchess made her coronation walk. It was a song that Duffy requested on nights when she worked security. She and Duffy even had their own little choreographed dance to it. For a second, Ross pictured them on the dance floor—the two of them alone—dancing some cheesy moves to the cheesy song and tears welled up before an abrupt eye rub.

Ross watched the guys in the room and was inspired.

He watched Twatla.

He watched the queens on stage.
The whole competition.
The celebration of life it represented.
Latrine tried to undermine it.
It was never about winning or being rich.
It was about being able to say "I beat The Scottish Bitch."

About the Author

Jameson Tabard is a novelist and playwright from Orlando, FL. He holds a BA and MA in English and is currently a professor in the Creative Writing Master of Fine Arts program at Full Sail University. He studied and performed Shakespeare at Shakespeare's Globe Theater in London, where he learned that Renaissance theater was just an excuse for queens to dress like queens.

Jameson has an unhealthy appreciation of the male physique, antiquated pop culture, and architectural relics. While he is a charming guy, he pales in comparison to fabulous queens he has birthed on paper.